Laura could not look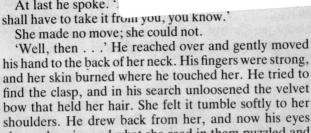
claimed her very sou
him with invisible c
helpless.

At last he spoke. '
shall have to take it from you, you know.'

She made no move; she could not.

'Well, then . . .' He reached over and gently moved his hand to the back of her neck. His fingers were strong, and her skin burned where he touched her. He tried to find the clasp, and in his search unloosened the velvet bow that held her hair. She felt it tumble softly to her shoulders. He drew back from her, and now his eyes changed again, and what she read in them puzzled and frightened her, for his gaze awakened something inside her which she had not known existed. For a long moment his eyes held her ruthlessly captive, and there existed no world outside their intense exchange . . .

Kate Janney is not one, but two Americans living outside Baltimore, Maryland. A mother-daughter team, this is their first joint venture into the realm of historical romance. Kate is the author of fiction, non-fiction, plays and short stories over the years; Janney brings to this, her first try at fiction, editorial know-how and a fresh young perspective.

THE PIRATE'S LADY

Kate Janney

MILLS & BOON LIMITED
ETON HOUSE 18–24 PARADISE ROAD
RICHMOND SURREY TW9 1SR

All the characters in this book have no existence outside the imagination of the Author, and have no relation whatsoever to anyone bearing the same name or names. They are not even distantly inspired by any individual known or unknown to the Author, and all the incidents are pure invention.

The text of this publication or any part thereof may not be reproduced or transmitted in any form or by any means, electronic or mechanical, including photocopying, recording, storage in an information retrieval system, or otherwise, without the written permission of the publisher.

This book is sold subject to the condition that it shall not, by way of trade or otherwise, be lent resold, hired out or otherwise circulated without the prior consent of the publisher in any form of binding or cover other than that in which it is published and without a similar condition including this condition being imposed on the subsequent purchaser.

*First published in Great Britain 1988
by Mills & Boon Limited*

© Kate Janney 1988

*Australian copyright 1988
Philippine copyright 1988
This edition 1988*

ISBN 0 263 76040 5

*Set in 10 on 11 pt Linotron Times
04–0488–76,180*

*Photoset by Rowland Phototypesetting Limited
Bury St Edmunds, Suffolk
Made and printed in Great Britain by
Cox & Wyman Limited, Reading*

CHAPTER ONE

WITH HER hands clasped tightly around the small reticule in her lap, Laura Trevor's eyes followed the path of late afternoon sunlight as it swept the inside of the carriage. It did not settle long in one place, as the carriage lurched and swayed behind the pair of spirited horses ahead. For a moment the bright patch illuminated a worn section of cracked leather interior next to her head, then skittered along the roof to fall in shifting patterns on the face of the sleeping child on the seat opposite her.

She is big for her age, Laura thought. 'I'm seven years old!' the little girl had boasted earlier, and had told her, 'I had two sisters, but one of them died at five and the other one lived only three years.'

The child's father had nodded. 'Yellow fever,' he had said. 'So you see how blessed we are to have this one still with us.' The young man slept now too, lulled by the motion of the carriage, his cheek against the soft fall of his daughter's long black hair.

Laura turned to look out at the flat Texas landscape that stretched treeless and parched as far as the eye could see. They would reach the Port Bolivar ferry landing at dusk, the coachman had informed them at the last stop, and could expect to be in Galveston by nightfall.

'My mother will meet us there,' the girl had said to Laura, her eyes bright with anticipation. 'Is your mother going to meet you too?'

Laura had felt for the cross that hung around her neck on a slender silver chain. 'No,' she had replied, smiling across at her. 'My mother died nineteen years ago when I was born.' Perhaps I should not have told her that, she thought now; for the girl had said no more but nestled closer against her father and watched her sadly until her small head began to nod in the dry dusty heat of the carriage. Laura closed her eyes to rest them. Her throat felt as parched as the yellow dust that settled thick on everything in the small passenger compartment. It will be a long time, she thought, before I travel south on this road again. There was an eerie finality in the thought, but no longer any hesitancy about the decision she had made just last week, sitting in Father Jiminez' small cell of an office.

She had announced then to the priest that, when this visit to her father was over—her first trip home to Crosswinds in two years—she would return to the convent to begin her novitiate.

'Are you certain, my child, that you wish to confine yourself to a life behind cloistered walls?' the priest had asked her, leaning across the cluttered table which served as his desk, his kind eyes watching her.

Laura had looked away, knowing that he was remembering the free-spirited girl whose most recent escapade had been to bathe naked in the small stream at the other side of the wooded copse behind the chapel. She had been quick to reassure him. 'After eleven years here, Father, I believe my defiant nature has at last been tempered. You'll see,' she told him with a smile, 'I'll be a model of propriety—and piety!'

Nevertheless, the priest's final words to her as he bid her goodbye before she left Santa Clara yesterday revealed his lingering reservations about her commitment to a life of Christian service. 'This visit to your father's home will give you time to search your heart, my child,' he had advised her. 'But whatever you decide to do, I will understand.'

Laura smiled as she recalled the priest's moist handshake, the tender, awkward moment when he started to reach out and give her a fatherly hug, then pulled back, grinning shyly at her. She would be content at the mission, Laura thought now; content and useful. She had grown accustomed to the life there, to the sturdy adobe buildings baking in the sun, the stark white walls of her tiny cell, the echoing footfalls of the nuns as they walked, two by two, along the shadowed cloister. She had made friends among the dedicated women who had been her teachers, and many of the Mexicans and Indians who filled the beds at the mission hospital where she had spent so many of her waking hours these past two years since her formal schooling ended were dear to her. The mission at Santa Clara was her home, as Crosswinds could never be.

The little girl on the seat opposite stirred in her sleep, and Laura opened her eyes to watch her. Small drops of perspiration beaded the smooth forehead. One hand lay open on her lap, the wrist as fragile as a wren's wing. Sunlight danced across the child's face and lingered a moment on thick black lashes that lay against her cheek. She reminds me of myself at that age, with her long legs and serious face, Laura thought. She wondered if this child too was a wild gypsy, as Aunt Stark had often called Laura. Perhaps she too loves to run out along the sand dunes, free as a gull, the wind whipping her hair behind her, with only a cloudless sky above, and the serene waters of the Gulf stretching away to the horizon. Maybe, too, when she reaches an isolated beach at the far end of the island, she discards her constricting clothing, as I used to do, and wades into the sparkling green water, delighting in the gentle surge of the tide against her body, hugging its coolness to her.

But no, Laura thought as she watched the sleeping child nestle closer in the circle of her father's arms, this girl's needs are not like mine. She has a mother who cherishes her and knows the warmth of a father's love. She reached again now for the silver cross at her breast, and her fingers traced the letters crudely etched on the back of it by the woman who had died giving her birth—'Defend, O Lord, this child'. She whispered the words to herself as she had done so many times before, and, as always, they comforted her.

CHAPTER TWO

LUCAS TREVOR'S house on the north shore of Galveston was, as was much of the architecture and many of its townspeople, a casual mixture of French, Spanish and frontier American. Of French colonial design, the mansion was graced by wide Spanish balconies stretching across the front of it, upstairs and down. Their lacy iron grilles supported twisted ropes of wistaria vines, bright with fat clusters of deep lavender blossoms. As a precaution against frequent flooding from the capricious waters of the Gulf, Crosswinds was set high on its foundations with a steep set of stairs to the path below. From there it was only a few short steps to Galveston's main street, the Strand, on whose opposite side a sturdy sea wall snaked along the smooth waters of the ship's channel.

Earlier on this March evening of 1836 the air had been deceptively calm. Light from a hundred candles washed from the open doors of Crosswinds on to Galveston's main cobbled street and extended gold fingers out across the calm waters of the channel. Music and laughter could be heard all up and down the Strand. But just one hour after Lucas Trevor's guests arrived, a sudden squall blew in off the Gulf and shook the big house. Servants hurried to close shutters at each balcony door against the wind and rain that now lashed at the small island.

'It isn't fair!' his sister complained to anyone within hearing distance in the crowded salon. 'I do think this storm might have had the decency to hold off until after the party!' The many guests had been summoned hastily to Crosswinds by brief handwritten notes in Ernesta Stark's best script to 'join us in celebration of Texas's independence from the Republic of Mexico, and to honour Mr David Burnet, president of our new regional government.' Those delegates—of which Lucas Trevor was one—had returned the previous day from the assembly at Washington-on-the-Brazos, and were by now rested and eager to talk of the historic meeting.

But at that moment Ernesta Stark was not as concerned with the making of history as she was with her niece's whereabouts. She had someone special she wanted the girl to meet. 'Have you seen Laura?' she asked one of her niece's old friends from the days when they had both attended Miss Porch's school on the Strand.

'Yes, and isn't it awful?' the girl replied airily. 'What's happened to her? She used to be so pretty!'

'That's not what I . . . Oh, never mind!' Aunt Stark had never liked the frivolous girl anyway, and tonight she looked like a shuttlecock with the absurd display of white feathers in her hair. She gave the girl a withering look, one which she had developed to a fine art, and made her way cautiously across the floor, searching for her niece. Twice she was caught up in the frenzied dancers as they flew past her in a rowdy mazurka, but at last she spied her brother standing at one side of the salon, engaged in a spirited argument with their guest of honour. 'Lucas!' she cried. 'Where is Laura?'

Lucas Trevor was taller than his sister by a good ten inches, and had kept his slender figure, while Aunt Stark had not. He was an imposing man, with a splendidly erect posture and luxuriant greying side-whiskers. 'How am I supposed to know where she is?' His big voice had no trouble competing with the chatter and music about them. He turned back to Mr Burnet, ignoring his sister as best he could, for Aunt Stark kept one mittened hand on his sleeve as her eyes anxiously searched the room.

'I'd say he's incompetent, at best.' Mr Burnet continued the discussion with his host, ignoring the interruption. 'At worst he may be a damned coward! How many times do you think Sam Houston's going to get the chance to square off with the hothead Santa Anna anyway? The enemy's laughing us to scorn, Mr Trevor.'

Lucas Trevor scowled at him. 'I'll bet they're not laughing at those men of ours who are holding the Spanish mission up there!'

'They haven't a chance,' Mr Burnet said mournfully. 'You realise how many armed Mexicans surround 'em? I'm not so sure you couldn't say Sam Houston was crazy, going off to organise new forces and leaving a hundred and sixty-three men fighting for their lives in a grove of alamo trees! If you ask me, we made our biggest mistake when we named Sam Houston commander of our army!'

Aunt Stark grasped her brother's arm again. 'Lucas, you must help me! I can't find Laura anywhere!' She fluttered a feathered fan in front of her rosy face, trying to create a breath of air in the stifling heat of the room.

Before he could speak, he had to pull back to avoid being knocked off his feet by the sweep of a crimson taffeta skirt. Angrily he pulled out a linen handkerchief and began to wipe his face. He had already had several brandies, and blinked now as if to shield his eyes from the blaze of candlelight in the crystal chandelier above him.

His sister tugged a third time at the sleeve of his coat. 'You must help me to find her, Lucas! She's not yet met our distinguished English guest, Lord Skelton.'

'I told you, Ernesta . . .' Trevor began, irritated beyond endurance, but he did not finish. He failed to see the towering ostrich plume of a lady's fanciful headdress as she whirled by, so neither he nor Mr Burnet had a chance to duck. It hit them squarely across the face. Each man swore, but their colourful expletives were drowned by a burst of laughter that erupted near them. One couple had fallen to the floor, and sprawled now in a heap of ballooning skirts and flying crinolines.

Aunt Stark could not suppress a cry of indignation.

She had so hoped that their guests would conduct themselves with restraint on this important evening with so many notables present. She moved away from her brother's side and went out to the broad hall, where she saw her niece's maid, and called to her. 'Maria!' She rustled over to her side. 'Where is Miss Laura? That naughty girl—she hasn't gone upstairs to bed, has she?'

'No, Señora,' Maria said. 'Maybe she's still in the dining-room. I can get her for you.'

'No, never mind. I'll do it.' Aunt Stark made her way to the door of the dining-room and looked in. At first, in the dim light of silver candelabra that graced the centre table, she was unable to locate her niece among the couples who moved past the array of food which had been set out in a lavish display. She noticed with satisfaction that the servants were keeping the trays of delicacies filled as fast as the guests depleted them. There were scallop-shells filled with creamed crab, and curls of brown bread wrapped round buttered asparagus tips. Crisp hot pastries, fat with succulent lobster meat, still piping hot from the ovens, sent up small spirals of steam. A tray of dainty crystal glasses filled with fresh strawberries and wine were still misted with frost, and the bowl of grapes, crusted with sugar, sparkled like amethysts in the light of the many candles. Somewhat mollified to see that the large army of caterers were doing their job, Aunt Stark peered back into the shadows, where empty chairs had been pushed against the wall. At last she saw Laura engaged in conversation with her brother's old friend, John Messersmith. She circled the table and stood before them, impatiently waving her fan. Her clipped words were directed at him.

'You are no help at all, John,' she said. 'You are monopolising Laura and keeping her from meeting our titled guest from England!'

John Messersmith, his face flushed with good brandy, pulled himself to his feet. 'Skelton? My dear Ernesta,

I've met him, and I don't think Laurie would be much impressed!' He laughed, and threw an arm playfully around Aunt Stark's shoulder, but she instantly shrugged it off.

He was a giant of a man, with the pioneer blood still hot in his veins. Like Laura's father, he had come to Galveston before it had achieved fame as the busiest seaport in the Southwest. Each man bore the stamp of the rugged West in manner and speech. Loud—often too loud—rough-hewn and profane, each had made a name for himself in the small town; Lucas Trevor in banking and John Messersmith in shipping. It was well known that Messersmith had been courting Ernesta Stark for several years, to no avail. Now, with an exaggerated show of courtly airs, he bowed, extended one hand to Laura, and drew her to her feet.

'I had to get the poor girl away from that circus in the next room. By God, you can't even hear yourself think in there!'

'All the same,' Aunt Stark said, eyeing her niece critically, 'I want Laura to meet everyone here tonight, and not sit here in a dark corner with you!'

Her bright button eyes ran up and down her niece's amber-coloured gown, a simply cut silk which did little to set off her slender figure. I should have taken her straight to Madame Georges's shop despite her protests, she thought. Laura had not allowed Maria even to do her hair, but wore it swept loosely back from her face and fastened behind by a brown velvet bow. The stubborn girl had refused every suggestion to improve her appearance for this splendid night. Really, she had been tiresome! There was so much that could be done for her, Aunt Stark thought, if only Lucas would let me. Why, with the proper assistance to enhance her eyes (they were extraordinary eyes even so, she admitted—the blue of a midnight sky), and the proper emollients and powders, the right clothes and coiffure, what a beauty she could be! Still, as she felt the girl's arm go affectionately around her waist, she softened.

'Thank heavens you didn't forget how to smile at that dreary mission school,' she said. 'Smile more, love. It becomes you so.' She took Laura's arm. 'Now you're coming with me. Pinch your cheeks, dear. Men love girls with rosy cheeks!'

'Leave her alone, Ernesta,' Messersmith told her good-naturedly. 'She looks a good deal better than those painted Jezebels out there!'

Laura smiled at him, and threw him a kiss. 'Thanks, Uncle John,' she said as they took their leave of him.

'Thank him for what?' Aunt Stark demanded when they were out of earshot. 'He didn't encourage you in this idea of yours to become a nun, did he?'

'No.' Laura took her arm. 'But he didn't try to discourage me, either!'

They made their way through the hall to the salon, where the orchestra had begun to play the accompaniment for a stately quadrille. Many of the women stood fanning themselves, flushed and out of breath from the exuberant rhythm of the mazurka. While some tried valiantly to pat back into place the bows, brilliants and plumes that had come loose in their false curls, others patted at perspiration on bare shoulders that glowed under sparkling jewels. The big room was almost suffocating with the balcony doors closed against the storm outside.

'Come,' said Aunt Stark, tugging at Laura's arm, for the girl stood transfixed, again dazzled by the vivid colours of rich silks and brocades of the ladies' gowns. 'There he is now!'

She led her to a stranger standing alone near the small orchestra, watching the assemblage with a bemused expression. 'Lord Skelton!' she called out over the music. 'At last you meet my niece, Laura!'

If the gentleman has been impatient to meet me,

Laura thought, he has concealed it well! He looked coolly at her, and the wintry smile he bestowed never touched his pale eyes.

'Delighted,' he said as he bowed over her extended hand.

Laura noticed that his sandy hair had been generously lacquered until it shone in the candlelight. Even in this gathering, where the pungent aroma of a hundred perfumes hung heavy in the air, she detected a strong odour of rose-water. When he straightened, Laura saw that Lord Skelton was not as young as she had first thought him to be. There was a world-weariness in the fine lines about his eyes, and a tightness at each corner of his thin lips which his handsome moustache did not conceal. There was nothing displeasing about his features, but a certain wariness in his eyes seemed to belie his suave manner.

Aunt Stark prattled at Laura's side. 'The dear child has been home only a week, and still persists in saying that she wants to become a nun! Can you imagine, Lord Skelton, that anyone would actually want to spend her life behind convent walls?' She pouted prettily. 'Well, I shall talk her out of it, you may be sure. I must show you the portrait of Laura's mother in the parlour. Amanda was the daughter of Victor duFlon, you know, from New Orleans. Very well connected, extremely wealthy. Amanda, in her few short years here, was a leader in society, of course. Such a beauty. Poor lamb . . .' her voice faltered, 'to die so young of childbed fever! I raised Laura, you know, and am determined to do for her what her mother would have done, despite my brother's wishes that she should return to the convent.' She raised her painted brows high as though to impart a family secret. 'Lucas and I seldom disagree,' she confided, 'but on the subject of Laura's future, why, we may very well come to blows!'

'Ah, surely not,' Lord Skelton protested mildly.

Laura shook her head, smiling. 'Most assuredly not.'

'All the same . . .' Aunt Stark began again, but when she saw that Lord Skelton's attention had wandered, she decided to pursue the subject no longer. 'Now, love,' she turned to Laura, 'do let Lord Skelton put his name down for a dance. Oh!' She stopped, seeing that there was no dance card attached to the girl's wrist. 'Why didn't you get a card?'

Laura smiled apologetically down at her aunt. 'Because I don't dance.'

'Nonsense!' Aunt Stark protested. 'You had dancing lessons only . . .'

'Eleven years ago, Aunt! I've forgotten the steps.'

'No matter.' Lord Skelton patted at his silky moustache with a well-manicured hand. 'I myself am not a dancer, Miss Trevor. Perhaps later we might have a chat?'

'I shall look forward to it,' Laura told him, relieved.

'Until then,' he said, and bowed stiffly.

Aunt Stark, seeing that the conversation was over, reluctantly turned and, with Laura at her side, moved back across the room. 'I do think, love,' she complained loudly, 'that you might have shown a bit more spirit. After all, Lord Skelton is a nobleman, dear, enormously eligible. He and his secretary only arrived yesterday, and will be here for such a short visit.' Her words were lost in a sudden burst of music from the violins behind them. Since none of the guests had shown any interest in forming the intricate figures for a quadrille, the orchestra had wisely determined that a lively polka would be more popular. Laura and her aunt had only barely reached the hall before the frenzied dancing began again.

'Mercy!' Aunt Stark panted, patting her carrot-coloured curls in place. 'What a bunch of ruffians! One could be trampled to death in there. Now, Laura,' she said sternly, 'when once you get that foolish religious notion out of your head, we can arrange dancing lessons with Monsieur Bruce. He is the best dancing instructor here. I want you to circulate tonight, love, while I find Mr Burnet. I've been almost totally ignoring him, and I do so want this to be a night he won't soon forget.' She bustled off to find the guest of honour.

Laura moved to stand at one side of the arched doorway where she could watch the kaleidoscope of shifting colours on the dance floor without being seen. At a light touch on her shoulder, she turned to see her maid standing behind her. 'Oh, Maria,' she said, 'have you ever seen reds quite so red, or blues quite so blue?' She spoke in her maid's native language, as she often did. She pulled her closer to the doorway. 'Look, see how the women's skirts fan out like the petals of a flower!'

Maria nodded dubiously, a frown forming on her dark face. '*Que me perdone Dios, niña*, but I have never seen the petals of a flower open to reveal so much petticoat!'

'You haven't changed,' Laura laughed, studying the face of the woman who had been at Crosswinds since Lucas Trevor built the big house for his bride, 'and I'm glad you haven't!'

Maria moved away from the door and motioned to her mistress to follow her to where a gilded mirror hung above the hall pier table. 'Your hair,' she said. 'One of the locks has come loose. Let me fix it, *niña*.'

'Oh, bother!' Laura teased, but went with Maria all the same. She faced her own image with a wry smile. 'It's quite useless, you know,' she said, 'trying to make a silk purse out of a sow's ear.'

'*Madre mía!*' the maid exclaimed indignantly as she patted Laura's hair in place. 'Yours is the most honest beauty here tonight. See how your eyes sparkle, and there is not a single woman here who would not pay a fortune for your complexion!'

Laura laughed delightedly. 'Thank you! Oh, what am

I going to do without you when I return to the convent? I only wish there were a way I might bring you with me.'

Maria's black eyes met her mistress's in the mirror. 'Let me come?' she cried. 'I have missed you so, *niña*! I have taken care of you since you were an infant, don't forget. I can see to your bath, attend to all your needs . . . There are so many ways I could be useful!'

Laura turned, and took her rough hands. 'I'm afraid Father Jiminez would hardly allow . . .' She stopped at the sound of a sharp noise in the salon behind them. Both women tensed. 'It's probably one of the shutters,' Laura said. 'The wind must have blown it open.'

'I'll go and get someone in the kitchen to help secure it, *niña*,' Maria said and, holding up the full skirts of her black dress, disappeared into the service door at the foot of the stairs. Laura walked over to the door of the salon and looked in, but instantly drew back in dismay at the scene before her.

Both balcony doors stood open, it was true. But it was not the wind that had forced them wide. Eight, perhaps ten, rain-soaked men stood poised on the sill, running insolent eyes over the dancers. As the violins at the far end of the salon whined to silence, one of the intruders jumped on to the newly-sanded floor. Like the others, he wore a faded bandana over the lower half of his face, and all but he brandished a sword. He was a tall man, a striking figure. His coarse white shirt, drenched with rain, clung to his broad chest like a second skin.

As Laura watched, the young man struck an arrogant pose, hands on hips. 'Good evening!' His voice was strong over the roar of the wind behind him. 'We apologise for bursting in on you like this. But since it is not in the nature of pirates to seek entry in a more gentlemanly fashion . . .'

'Pirates!' A lady's shrill voice screamed the single

word before she fainted into the arms of the man at her side.

'You have nothing to fear,' he assured the stunned group. 'We wish only to relieve you of your valuables. My men will pass among you, and you can save us all time, gentlemen, if you will empty your pockets. Just form a straight line, if you will.' He watched, amused, as the confused gathering tried to focus champagne-reddened eyes on the intruders, and added, 'Or a crooked line, no matter.'

Laura held her breath, watching the tall pirate as he strode swift and sure as a panther up and down the line that was slowly forming. As he came closer to where she stood, she heard him repeat assurances to the ladies that their lives were in no danger. By now, most of the candles had been extinguished by the wind, and only the white of the pirates' shirts showed clearly as they moved quickly through the half-light collecting their bounty. The leader was now only a few feet from her. She moved back behind the arched doorway, but too late, for he saw her standing there.

'Don't be frightened,' he said as he moved in front of her. 'We mean you no harm.'

It was a moment before Laura could find her voice. 'You mean no *harm*?' she asked him, pretending a courage she did not feel. 'You force your way in here, strip our guests of their valuables, and you say you mean no *harm*?'

'*Our* guests?' he asked, his voice registering surprise. 'Do you mean that this is your home? These are your guests?' He ran his eyes roguishly over her figure. 'But I see no ostrich feathers in your hair, no curls, no brilliants, no diamonds. You wear only a plain silver cross at your neck.' He had moved so close to her now that Laura could smell the salt air of the sea on him, the freshness of the wind and rain in the dark hair that curled damply against his sun-bronzed forehead. She backed further away into the hall. He moved with her, and the light from flickering candles in the brass wall-sconces fell full on his face.

Laura felt her heart beat faster at the nearness of him, the powerful maleness of him. She dropped her eyes and found herself staring at his muddy boots planted firmly on her father's Oriental rug. 'You might at least have wiped your feet,' she said.

It was a moment before the pirate reacted to her words. Then he threw back his head, and his laughter filled the hall. 'Wipe my feet, indeed! You have a bit of spunk, I'll say that!'

'Please get on with your work and leave,' Laura told him, still not meeting his eyes.

'I shall,' he assured her. 'In a few minutes we'll be heading back to our ship in the channel, I promise you.' He reached over and fingered the cross that hung round her neck.

Instantly she moved to cover it. At the touch of his hand under hers, she felt her cheeks flame. 'This is of no value to anyone but me!'

'It's a poor thing, surely,' the young man agreed. 'But I will take it as a memento of the little lady who minded most our muddy boots. That is . . .' he added quietly, 'if you will first let go of my hand.'

She released it instantly.

'What's this?' He caught her hand and held it. 'This certainly isn't the hand of a lady of leisure. This has seen hard work, unless I'm mistaken.' He paused, and turned her hand slowly over in his. 'The poet Keats said it well: "This living hand, now warm and capable of earnest grasping." I like this hand very much.'

She pulled angrily away from him and at that moment their eyes met. Laura felt her breath catch in her throat, for she had never seen such eyes before. They were a luminous jade green, alive with small flecks of gold, and of an intensity that shook her. They were the eyes of a man to whom life constantly offered a challenge, with a confident gleam that told her he could accept a win or loss with equal grace. As she watched they softened and deepened, and she could not look away, for they seemed to have claimed her very soul. It was as if he had drawn her to him with invisible chains, and left her shackled and helpless.

At last he spoke. 'If you do not give me your cross, I shall have to take it from you, you know.'

She made no move; she could not.

'Well, then . . .' He reached over and gently moved his hand to the back of her neck. His fingers were strong, and her skin burned where he touched her. He tried to find the clasp, and in his search unloosened the velvet bow that held her hair. She felt it tumble softly to her shoulders. He drew back from her, and now his eyes changed again, and what she read in them puzzled and frightened her, for his gaze awakened something inside her which she had not known existed. For a long moment his eyes held her ruthlessly captive, and there existed no world outside their intense exchange.

Suddenly a harsh voice shattered the private world that had isolated her with this stranger, this pirate. 'All set, Captain!'

The call came from the salon. The pirate's eyes left hers at last as he grabbed the slender chain that held her cross. With one quick jerk it came away in his hand. He turned abruptly and ran back into the salon to join his men.

Laura heard his voice as he called out over the roar of the wind. 'Thank you for your patience and co-operation, ladies and gentlemen.' Then all was silent.

It was a moment before she was able to move hesitantly to the door of the darkened salon and look in. For an instant it seemed that each guest stood frozen where he had been placed in an eerie tableau. Each face appeared to be carved out of stone and was turned towards the open balcony doors through which the men had disappeared. Suddenly, as if on a signal, the tableau began to break apart. Some of the men ran to close the ceiling-high shutters. Others went in search of tapers to relight the candles. A few pushed past Laura to get their cloaks, intent on setting off down the Strand to alert the authorities. Maids were quickly summoned to wipe away rain and mud that had been trodden into the dance floor.

As if slowly waking from a dream, Laura drew back into the shadows. She was only dimly aware of her aunt's voice crying, 'Mercy, mercy!' over the hysterical cries of the women as they tearfully counted their losses. The fresh sea smell of the pirate still lingered with her. His voice still echoed in her ears, his eyes still looked deep into hers. And his touch . . . She still burned at the searing warmth of his touch. She lifted one hand to her flaming cheeks and moved it slowly back to where his hand had been under the heavy fold of her hair as he searched for the clasp of her cross. Her cross! Only now did she realise that it was gone, that he had indeed taken it with him.

He shall not have it! she thought wildly. I must get it back! He had mentioned his ship lying out in the channel, and without a thought for her own safety, she lifted her skirts and ran down the hall to the front door. She threw it open and stepped out on to the balcony. The wind caught her, and she held tight to the iron railing to steady herself. She shielded her eyes from the driving rain, and felt her way down the steps to the path and out through the gate. She crossed the uneven paving-stones until at last she felt the familiar handrail that followed the sea wall to the quay. She edged carefully along it until she gripped the sturdy post that marked its end, then fought her way on to the quay, quickening her steps on the slippery planking. She heard men's voices over the howl of the wind, but could see nothing through the impenetrable curtain of rain. She sensed rather than saw dark forms taking shape ahead of her at the end of the pier and saw below, just a little in front of her, a small boat pitching against the piling. Suddenly two strong arms encircled her waist, and a man's voice cried close to her ear, 'Ho! What have we here?'

She struggled to free herself, but the man's arms tightened round her. 'Let me go!' she cried. She turned her face towards him and saw that one of his eyes was white, covered with an opaque film that glowed in the darkness. She screamed, and flailed at him with her fists. He released her suddenly, and she would have fallen into the churning water below had not another pair of arms caught her from behind and held her fast. 'Let me go!' she cried again, and fought her new captor like a tiger.

'What do you think you're doing?' It was the pirate leader's voice, fragmented by the wind. He managed to catch her wrists. 'You don't belong here, you little fool!'

'My cross,' Laura sobbed. 'Give me back my cross!'

Without another word, he picked her up in his arms and strode quickly down the quay to the street.

'It's only a small thing,' Laura cried, 'but it belonged to my mother, and it means everything to me!'

'It means more than your life, does it?' He set her roughly on her feet. 'Now go home!'

'Please, please!' she begged, but he had turned away and was peering through the rain towards the upper end of the Strand. Her eyes followed his, and she saw a procession of yellow flares coming towards them. Over the roar of the wind came angry shouts from the men who carried them.

The pirate leaned closer to her. 'If you have any sense at all, you'll go back where you came from, and quickly!' He turned her round and gave her a gentle push out on to the street.

She turned back to face him, but he was gone,

swallowed up in the blackness and fury of the storm. She put her hands to the wet wildness of her hair and pulled it back from her face. Then, gathering up her soaking skirts and trying to keep her balance against the force of the wind at her back, she battled her way blindly across the wide street. It was just inside the gate of her father's house that she fell into the waiting arms of her maid.

Later, Laura could recall being carried up to her room by her father, and the touch of Maria's strong hands as she undressed her, rubbed her down and put her to bed. She could not stop shivering, so Maria fetched a quilt from the linen-room and tucked it round her.

'Why did you go outside on such a night?' she scolded.

Laura felt the cool, callused hands on her burning forehead. 'The storm?'

'It is over, *niña*,' she assured her.

'And the men, the pirates . . . Did they get away?' Her own voice sounded dim and far away.

'*Sí*, they did not catch them. Now you must close your eyes and try to sleep.'

Once, during the night, Laura opened her eyes to see her father standing beside her bed in the candlelight. Lucas Trevor leaned over his daughter, lifted her head from the pillow and put a tumbler of brandy to her lips. She could hear the murmur of Maria's voice, deep in the shadows, telling the beads of her rosary. Then her father's voice, faint yet angry. 'Why in God's name did you let her leave the house, Maria?' Then her own, muffled and tremulous. 'Do not blame Maria, Father. It was my own doing.'

It was perhaps towards dawn when she wakened, startled from her semi-consciousness. She did not know what had woken her. She only knew that she was trembling and clutching the covers to her, staring into the darkness. She slid her feet on to the floor and made her way unsteadily to the small prie-dieu where she had prayed since she was a child. She dropped to her knees on the worn velvet cushion and lifted her eyes to the gold crucifix above it. Instinctively she reached for the cross she had always worn at her breast and, realising it was gone, she found it impossible to pray. Her thoughts turned again to the stranger who had taken it. Perhaps even now, she thought, he turns it over in his hands and reads the letters etched roughly across its back. What will he make of it? Will he throw it away because it will bring no money? She could almost see his fine, dark head bent over it in the light of a dark ship's cabin, studying it, laughing, then tossing it aside.

Laura's head fell forward on to the wooden lectern, and it was thus Maria found her later. She was scolded soundly by her maid, who helped her back into bed, where she fell into a light and feverish sleep.

Time lost all dimension for her in the days that followed. She drifted in and out of a deep, resonant emptiness, shaking with chills one minute, racked with fever the next. Often, when she would rouse for a moment from the stupor that deadened the world to her, there was a new face at her bedside. She was aware of the doctor's anxious frown as he bent over her and administered bitter medicines. Sometimes her father's face swam into view. Another time Laura thought she saw Father Jiminez, his dear familiar face etched with sadness, and she wondered why the priest from the mission school at Santa Clara had been called to her bedside.

Sometimes she stirred in her canopied bed to see bright sunlight running knife-slits of gold down each side of the portières at the balcony door. At other times a single candle burned on her night table. But the days and nights melted into each other, a slow progression of hazy images and periods of blackness. Street noises outside were muffled and had no reality. And often she heard the soft voice of Maria as she prayed at the side of the bed.

Once she was woken by a shaft of bright moonlight reflected in the full-length oval mirror by the open door. She heard Maria's voice: 'Señor, please, *por Dios*, you must tell her now!' And her father's reply, in a whisper: 'Never, Maria. And you have pledged your word before God. Do not forget it.'

Another time—how much later she did not know—she had been startled fully awake in the shadowed room to find that the curtains had been drawn back from her door on to the balcony. Furtive rays of a timid moon moved in shifting patterns across the high ceiling. The wide lace canopy over her bed seemed for an instant to be fragile wings that somehow became her wings, and she felt herself drift to the heavens as light as an evening breeze. She felt at one with the new-washed sky, adrift with the moon, smelling the good salt air of the sea and feeling the fresh wind caress her face. Perhaps, she thought, I am dying. Was it only today she had felt the sign of the cross imprinted on her burning forehead by Father Jiminez?

She sat up, her eyes wide with terror. Slowly, she was able to make out familiar objects in the room: her chest of drawers, her wardrobe, her prie-dieu, the armchair where Maria usually sat through the night with her. It was empty now. The thought came to her that, had she indeed been dying, she would not have been left alone.

She lay back exhausted, and drifted to a place of darkness. She might have slept; she did not know. When she opened her eyes again, she turned her head towards the night sky and watched as a soft breeze moved the white silk curtains at the door as though a hand had picked them up and spun them slowly, slowly, then let them drop until the next breeze caught them. A shadow fell across her bed. It would be Father, she thought, come to see that all is well. The room darkened as the tall figure blocked the moon's rays. Laura closed her eyes and waited for her father's heavy hand on her forehead. But, curiously, it was not the familiar brandy and tobacco scent of him that she was conscious of, but a different aroma . . . new and exciting, yet known to her. It was the good salt smell of the sea.

A brief rain-shower shortly before noon had done little to freshen the hot afternoon air. It was not even April, but already summer heat hung heavily over Galveston. Street cobbles sweated and sent up curling tongues of steam. Those who valued their health stayed indoors, shutters closed against the sun.

Father Jiminez perched tentatively on one of the benches in the open courtyard of Lucas Trevor's home. His small feet, in worn and dusty shoes, were set primly under him. The smell of mildew was strong on his scruffy clericals, and perspiration glistened on his leathery cheeks. A fountain murmured lazily in the cool shadows only a few feet from where he sat. All around him, giant plants loomed high over his head, sending out waxy feelers as if to catch and hold anyone who came too close. The flowers that grew in this climate made the priest uncomfortable. They were too bright; their colours almost obscene. He knew the name of only one, oleander, and had heard that its garish bloom was poisonous. He could believe it. Accustomed as he was to the drier climate of the mission, he was certain that in the three weeks he had been in Galveston his lungs had begun to grow moss in the humid air.

He had been sitting in the courtyard for what seemed hours, his small breviary open on his lap. He had been conscious of angry voices in the parlour at the front of the house and, although he could not make out the words that flew between Lucas Trevor and his widowed sister, he knew that the argument concerned whether or not young Laura would return with him to Santa Clara to begin her novitiate.

His host and hostess had been kind to him since his arrival. They had given him a large bedroom facing south towards the Gulf, and had so lavished him with local seafood and rich sauces that the sash of his soutane stretched uncomfortably over his stomach. But he wanted to go home. The girl was better. Her fever had broken just this morning. In a week or so she should be sufficiently recovered to return with the priest—if indeed that decision was ever agreed upon by Lucas Trevor and his flinty sister.

He drew a crumpled kerchief from a pocket deep in the folds of his cassock and wiped his bald head. A door slammed from somewhere in the house, and he dropped his eyes quickly to the open breviary.

'Ah, Father,' Trevor's big voice filled the courtyard. 'Sorry to have kept you waiting so long.'

The priest looked up and managed a faint smile for the figure in the doorway. Trevor, always a commanding presence, seemed to stand ten feet tall. With his hands clenched at his side, his linen stock askew and sweat beading his strong forehead, he was a formidable sight. His sister, Mrs Stark, stood slightly behind him, fanning her scarlet face with a large palmetto fan. Father Jiminez's smile slid slowly from his face as Trevor strode purposefully to the iron bench across from where he sat and dropped heavily on to it. Mrs Stark, her bosom heaving under the lace bertha that crossed it, did not move.

'Sit, Ernesta! Sit!' commanded her brother, slapping the bench beside him. With a toss of her head that sent the pink ribbons on her house bonnet flying, Aunt Stark nudged in beside him.

Father Jiminez's smiled reappeared. 'Your garden, Señor Trevor,' he said quietly, 'must be the coolest spot in all of Galveston.'

Trevor laid his large immaculate hands flat on his knees, and the priest quickly concealed his own rough ones under a fold of his cassock. 'Now,' he began, 'you are aware, Father, of Mrs Stark's opposition to my daughter's entering the monastic life, of course.'

'Yes,' he replied. 'I understand that she . . .'

'However,' the big man cut in, 'my sister has nothing whatever to do with matters concerning my daughter's future. I am Laura's father, and I, of course, will have the final say.' He patted both knees emphatically. 'It has been settled.'

Aunt Stark rattled her fan more briskly. 'The matter has *not* been settled, Lucas.' She turned towards the priest. 'Father, it is my duty to carry out my late sister-in-law's wishes for her child. Why, if Amanda could look down on us from heaven . . .' she crossed herself absently behind the fluttering fan, 'she would insist that Laura have all the social opportunities that she herself enjoyed here all too briefly.'

'That will do, Ernesta!' Trevor shot a glance at the patch of white sky above them in exasperation, but now he addressed himself to Father Jiminez. 'My sister thinks of nothing but parties and Paris gowns and frivolous ways to spend my money!'

'But you are not a poor man, Lucas!' Aunt Stark said angrily. 'And in only two years Laura will have her own money!' She leaned closer to the priest, and told him in a burst of confidence, 'Lucas has never told Laura of her inheritance, for he somehow feels it might spoil her. But Laura's maternal grandfather left her a large sum of money in trust, and she will be a wealthy young woman on her twenty-first birthday, so you see . . .'

Trevor jumped to his feet and scowled down at his sister. 'Will you never learn to hold your tongue, woman? Our family business is of no concern to Father Jiminez! What *is* his concern, and mine, is the girl's immortal soul. On that we agree, don't we, Father?'

The priest fidgeted nervously. 'Most certainly. But,' he hesitated, 'since Laura is nineteen, should she not be allowed to make her own decision?'

Trevor eyed the priest contemptuously. 'You surprise me, Father!' His voice was heavy with sarcasm. 'I am sure you are not unmindful of the generous contributions I have made to Santa Clara over the years.'

'Good gracious, no,' he replied. 'I am indeed aware of your generosity, and we are exceedingly grateful!'

'And,' Trevor continued, 'you also know that, despite the vow of poverty my daughter will be obliged to take, my contributions to your mission will continue.' He fastened the priest with steely eyes. 'If, and only if, she becomes a nun!'

During her brother's outburst, Aunt Stark had risen from the bench and moved over to the fountain, where she dipped her handkerchief into the water and dabbed with it at a corner of her mouth. Suddenly she spun around to face her brother. 'I can't let you do this, Lucas,' she cried. 'You know nothing of a woman's wants, her needs! I cannot think why you want to do this to her. Why, the very idea of shutting her away . . .'

'There will be no more discussion, Ernesta!' Trevor's face turned crimson above his wilted stock. 'Laura will enter the convent as planned. And,' he hurled his words at the priest, 'the sooner the better!' Then without another word, he turned on his heel and stormed back into the house.

For a few moments there was an uncomfortable silence in the courtyard. Then the priest sighed and stood up. He looked bleakly at Ernesta Stark. 'It is God's will,' he said.

She stroked her chin thoughtfully with her fan and frowned at him. 'No, Father,' she said. 'It is not God's will. It is my brother's will. But,' she went on, a slow smile spreading across her pink face, 'I have a will of my own, as he will see!'

Laura's future was not being discussed up in her bedroom as it had been just moments ago in the courtyard. Maria hummed a tune as she bustled about the room, plumping up pillows and setting them out to air on the sun-drenched balcony. Her mistress lay in the canopied bed, weak still, but her eyes had regained some of their lustre and colour was slowly coming back to her cheeks.

Laura fingered the silk coverlet that Maria had just put back on the bed. In her quick movements around the room, the maid had twice leaned over the convalescing girl and put her hand to her forehead. 'Cool!' she exclaimed happily. 'I never thought to feel it cool again, *niña*. Surely the Holy Mother was with you!'

'You must help me to dress, Maria. I shall never get strong again, lying here like an invalid.' Laura closed her eyes against the sun's glare.

Maria's black eyes flashed at her. 'No,' she said firmly. 'Perhaps tomorrow or the day after, but not today. Father Jiminez can wait. He enjoys himself here if one can judge by his empty plate after each meal. He takes long walks on the beach and keeps himself occupied. After all, he does not want to take back with him a small wisp of a girl. He wants you to be strong,' her smile revealed excellent white teeth, 'so that you may do good works when you become the Bride of Christ.'

Laura wiggled her toes under the coverlet. 'I am restless, Maria.'

'That is a good sign. But you are not eating enough,' the maid scolded her lightly. 'We will wait until your appetite returns and then we will talk of getting you on your feet again.' She gathered up the linen she had laid by the door. 'Now I will take these things away, *niña*, and you must rest. Sleep, if you will, but let the strength return.'

But Laura would not let her leave. 'I don't want to sleep,' she said. 'I had such a disturbing dream, and every time I close my eyes I'm afraid I'll dream it again.'

'A dream?' Maria peered anxiously at her. 'What sort of a dream?'

Laura sighed. 'It's no matter,' she said dismissively. 'Dreams mean nothing.' She did not want to describe it, for it was difficult to make sense of it. She had been able so far to keep it hidden, blocked away, refusing to take it out to analyse it. She had almost convinced herself that, as she had told her maid, dreams mean nothing.

'I know what is needed to comfort you, *niña*,' Maria said, as she dropped the linen on the floor and went to the wardrobe on the other side of the room. She pulled open a drawer, took something from it and returned to the side of the bed. She held out her hand, and in her open palm lay Laura's silver cross.

'Where did you get it?' Laura cried, unable to believe her eyes. 'It was stolen from me the night the pirates came. That's why I went after them in the storm, to get it back!'

'No, *niña*, they didn't take it. The next morning, when William found the bag the pirates dropped at the end of the pier, Señora Stark went through everything, and nothing was missing. But your cross was not with the other things, *niña*. I know, because I helped her to sort everything out.' Maria watched her mistress with concern. 'I found it round your neck one morning during your illness. You got up in the night to put it on, no? It must have comforted you to feel it close to you.' She smiled down at Laura. 'When your mother gave this cross to me to keep for you, she said it was her dearest wish that you always have it with you. Put it on, and perhaps then you will have no more disturbing dreams.' She turned and walked briskly to pick up the bundle of linen. 'Sleep now,' she said, and left the room, closing the door softly.

Laura stared after her, her fingers closed tight round the silver cross. The metal was cold, solid, substantial. There was nothing imagined or illusory about its familiar contours. She ran a finger across the back of it and felt the letters etched there. Real, she thought. It's *real*! But the pirate had certainly taken it, as surely as she had failed in her effort to get it back. She slowly slipped her legs over the side of the bed and stood up. The texture of the carpet under her feet—this was real! Voices out on the street, the rumble of cart-wheels further up the Strand—these were real! And—she looked down at the cross in her hand—this too was real!

At a sudden wave of light-headedness she reached out and clung to the bedpost, closing her eyes until it passed. When she was able, she made her way slowly across the room to the open balcony door. Pushing aside the soft folds of silk curtain, she looked out at the sparkling waters of the channel. She tried again to suppress the memory of that night during her illness, but now she could no longer keep it away. She remembered being woken by a man's shadow blocking the moonlight that lay in silver sheets across her bed. She had thought it was her father, but as the figure came nearer she was conscious of a new aroma, different, exciting, *familiar*.

This much had happened. She remembered it well. But the rest—the part she had tried to forget—rushed in on her now as if a dammed-up flood had suddenly broken free and threatened to overwhelm her. It was not her father who had come to her that night! It was the pirate! She had felt her head lifted gently from the pillow as something was slipped round her neck. It felt cold against her feverish skin, and she had put one hand up to find that her cross lay on her breast. As her fingers closed over it, she felt the brush of his lips against her forehead, and remembered the incredible warmth that flowed through her. She had reached out to him eagerly and drawn him closer, closer, until at last he lay beside her.

His arms went about her, gathering her to him, and she had trembled against him, cradling his head in the hollow of her shoulder. His hands were gentle as they pushed aside the thin cotton of her nightdress and began to caress the swell of her breasts. She recalled the surge of passion that washed over her like a crimson flame as his hands moved across her hips and to the secret places of her body that she yearned for him to claim as his own. She had arched against him, echoing the urgency of his need for her as though she would melt into his very substance.

He said her name—only her name—over and over again, 'Laura, Laura', until she stopped his mouth with a kiss. She remembered exulting in the fire each ignited in the other, and while she said nothing, it was her own voice she heard, low and soft, like the sound of a night wind moaning out over the sea. She did not remember seeing him leave. She only knew that she had reached across to where he lay, to find him gone.

Laura leaned now against the door frame for support. It was *not* a dream, then? It had really happened? Her eyes fell on the thick wistaria that twisted up the wall. The pirate had climbed it, and vaulted over the iron railing into her room! A sudden wave of anger brought fire to her cheeks. How dared he, a stranger, a *pirate*, break into her bedchamber and force himself on a girl too ill, too weak, to resist him? Yet, even as she asked it, she knew that it was *she* who had reached up to pull him closer, her arms that held him fast, her lips that had searched for his. She had not once called for help. Her father's room was just across the hall, and he would surely have heard. Instead, she had rejoiced in the pirate's strength, the gentle insistence of his hands on her body, the sound of his voice as he said her name—only her name.

She turned away from the blinding sunlight. As she walked back towards the shadows of her room, she caught a glimpse of her own reflection in the oval mirror, and stared at the radiant image, transfixed. The figure reflected there was outlined in an aura of incandescent gold, the clear wash of sunlight behind it defining its soft contours under the thin nightdress. She found herself exulting in the slender hips, the graceful arms, the lift of the young breasts, the radiant beauty of the body she had so rigorously been taught by the nuns to deny. She did not know how long she stood there, bewitched by her own shimmering loveliness.

At last, as she watched, she saw one hand move to the neck of her nightdress and slowly push it aside. The sheer fabric slid easily from her shoulders on to her bare breasts, down the soft curve of her hips and on to the floor. At that moment a gentle breeze lifted the silk curtain behind her and blew it lightly against her naked body. She reached back to draw it round her, not to hide her nakedness, but to enhance it. At the gentle caress of silk next to her skin, her body came alive with yearning —a yearning she had known only in the pirate's embrace and seen clearly echoed in his response.

She leaned back against the wall, all strength gone. When she looked away from the mirror, in that instant she saw her prie-dieu with the gold crucifix hanging above it, and the worn velvet kneeling-pad where she had spent so many hours in prayer. She closed her eyes to shut it away, for gone in that moment was any remnant of the girl fresh from mission school who had been prepared to give her life to the church. Her hand loosened around her silver cross and she felt the chain slip through her fingers slowly—slowly—on to the floor.

CHAPTER THREE

LAURA WHIRLED gracefully before the gilded mirror at one side of Madame Thérèse Georges's shop, watching the full sweep of her skirt as it swung wide to reveal a cloud of starched crinolines beneath it. 'It's beautiful!' she exclaimed. 'See how the light dances in it and plays tricks with the silk.'

The French dressmaker stood back and smiled at her customer's enthusiastic approval of her handiwork. Galveston's leading couturière was a handsome woman in her middle years who still retained the translucent complexion and clear eyes of a much younger woman. She wore her hair swept back from her face and gathered into a trim knot at the nape of her neck. Madame Georges numbered among her clientèle most of Galveston's fashionable ladies, for nowhere else on the island could they get fabrics and designs straight from Paris, and her exquisite hand-stitching was without equal. The little shop was so arranged that not a single inch of wall space was without its carefully tended shelves full of lace, gold and silver trimmings, brocades, feathers and velvet ribbons. The sparkling bow window that faced on the Strand was full of the latest bonnets and hand-made gloves, all imported and all a delight to the feminine eye. 'Would Mademoiselle consider a rose here at the *décolleté*?' the dressmaker suggested hesitantly. 'Perhaps the neckline is too revealing?'

'Certainly not, Madame!' Aunt Stark cried from the tufted pink damask chair she had perched on when they arrived. 'When my niece has the most beautiful bosom in the Southwest, she should certainly show it off!' She fanned herself with the latest issue of *Godey's Ladies'*

Book, and began to tap one tiny foot to the rhythm of her niece's movements. 'Poor dear Edgar,' she said mischievously. 'When he dances with you tonight, love, he will be beside himself!'

'I'd rather he be beside himself than dancing with me,' Laura exclaimed with a light laugh.

'You naughty girl,' her aunt remonstrated, 'you know you don't mean that!' Then, again addressing Madame Georges, she said firmly, 'No, Madame, no rose at the bosom!'

Aunt Stark smiled contentedly. It was six months now since her niece had come to her senses and decided not to return to the convent with Father Jiminez. The months had sped by quickly, and during that time she had taken the girl firmly in hand. There had been dancing lessons with Monsieur Bruce, music instruction at the richly-carved rosewood piano in the salon, French lessons, endless fittings at Madame Georges's shop, and concerts, boat outings, beach picnics, oyster roasts—a continuous round of parties. Laura had been exceedingly popular with all the eligible young men on the island. Now, if everything proceeded as Aunt Stark planned, the girl would be advantageously married off before the year was up. She brushed at a bright curl that had fallen from beneath her close-fitting poke bonnet, and winked broadly at her niece. 'Your father will not altogether approve of that gown, you know, love.'

'Father will not even notice,' Laura observed. 'He is far too busy with politics to care what I wear—or indeed if I wear anything at all!' Conscious of her aunt's giggles at her irreverent statement, she stood still now before the mirror, studying the image before her and admiring the tiny waist and the milky-white slope of her shoulders against the soft jade green silk that encircled them. 'Oh, Madame, you *are* a genius! This is the loveliest gown I've ever seen!'

'It is indeed,' Aunt Stark agreed. 'And one of which

your mother would certainly have approved. Mercy, if only Amanda had lived to see you so grown up!'

'*Alors* . . .' Madame Georges knelt to arrange the green velvet roses that cascaded down the billowing folds of Laura's skirt, 'I hope you will not regret choosing the green silk over the blue, Mademoiselle.'

'The blue silk would have matched her eyes exactly,' Aunt Stark exclaimed, 'but sometimes we must submit to the whims of the young, mustn't we, Madame? Now . . .' she turned her full attention on the dressmaker, 'I must see that new pattern you ordered for me. I hope you've shown it to no one else on the island, as you promised.'

'No, no,' she replied, getting quickly to her feet. 'It is yours, Madame Stark. I'll get it for you.'

Laura, relieved that her aunt's attention was diverted, moved away from the mirror and walked over to the multi-paned bow window at the front of the shop.

When Ernesta Stark was sure that her niece could not hear her, she whispered to the dressmaker. 'Did you know, Madame, that Laura is being courted by the most eligible man in Galveston?'

Madame Georges was instantly attentive. 'Oh? And does Monsieur Trevor approve of the young man?'

'Oh, yes,' the little lady said happily. 'Although the gentleman in question is not young, exactly. But my brother could not be more pleased with the prospect of Lord Edgar Skelton as his son-in-law.' She darted a furtive glance in her niece's direction, and went on. 'Lord Skelton has already asked my brother for Laura's hand, and while she has so far refused his proposal,' she smiled slyly, 'I will see that she comes round. Laura always listens to me, you know. And Lord Skelton has such excellent qualities. He is the sixth (or is it the seventh?) Earl of Skelton, and lives at his ancestral estate, Olney, near Wyckham, in England. He comes to Galveston quite regularly—on business, I understand.

But of course, he doesn't have to work, you know, being a nobleman. Laura would be Lady Skelton! Think of it!'

Madame Georges moved closer. 'He is *gentil*? That is to say—he is a good man, this Lord Skelton?'

'Good?' Aunt Stark looked at the dressmaker in surprise. 'Yes, of course he's good. But then he *is* British, after all. And quite handsome, too. In a British sort of way.'

A cloud passed over Madame's face. 'But should your niece marry this man, she would live in England then? Would it not be hard for you to have her living so far away?'

'It will be difficult for me, of course,' she said shortly. 'But I am quite willing to sacrifice myself for my niece's happiness.'

At the window, Laura was conscious neither of the whispers behind her not of the people passing up and down along the Strand. As she ran her fingers over the lustrous silk of her new gown's bodice, she remembered the day she had chosen this green fabric from among the many swatches Madame Georges had shown her. She had chosen it instantly, and only later had acknowledged to herself the reason why. It was the same lively green as the pirate's eyes! It had seemed foolish at the time, but still more foolish, and quite beyond her control, was the fact that she had not been able to forget him. Six months had passed since he had come to her bedchamber, and she still found herself searching for him in every crowd along the Strand. She would not know his face, for it was only his extraordinary eyes that could be seen above the bandana. Nor on that night he came to her—oh, it was the memory of that night that haunted her! She had met and danced with many men these past few months, and not one of them had awakened in her the same emotions she had felt with the pirate. Just the memory of him even now caused her cheeks to flame.

She reached down and touched one of the bonnets in the dressmaker's window. It was cabriolet-shaped, faced with yellow pleated silk and trimmed with a large bow at one side, with ribbons to tie under the chin. If she were to ask for it, Laura thought, her aunt would buy it for her without question. She had been absurdly generous with her 'good little pupil', as she called her niece. And the term fitted, for Laura had complied with her every wish. She wore the fashionable gowns and elaborate coiffures that fashion dictated, and was careful always to shield her petal-soft complexion under wide hats and lacy parasols. She had ordered the prie-dieu to be removed from her bedchamber and replaced it with a dressing-stand filled with vials of softening creams and French perfumes. She had packed her silver cross away and had chosen instead to wear her mother's fine jewellery. She had become, and the term was again Aunt Stark's, the 'belle of Galveston', and in only six months.

Six months, Laura thought, and another six months still to go. She had promised her aunt a whole year. 'Your mother would be so pleased, love,' Aunt Stark had said when informed of her niece's decision not to return to Santa Clara. 'But of course it's what I've wanted for you all along. And, you'll see, you'll have such a good time that you'll wonder how you ever imagined that a nunnery was the place for you!' Laura had consented to the plans for her, grateful for the whirlwind of activity that had instantly swept her up, for it gave her no time to reflect on the single event that had changed her life—the night she had so eagerly welcomed the pirate's embraces.

And in truth she did enjoy the French, music and dancing lessons. But all too often now she wearied of the role she was playing: the foolish games, the meaningless flirtations, the endless gossip that seemed to come so easily to other women. If it were not for the fact that she had promised a full year and could not yet envision an immediate alternative to Aunt Stark's programme for her, she would have abandoned it long since.

'Come, love!' Aunt Stark's voice invaded her reverie. 'Madame has gone to fetch the ostrich fan you will carry tonight. Oh, think of all the hearts you will break! Come, twirl again for me, you pretty thing!'

But Laura only smiled as she walked past her aunt and slipped behind the folding silk screen. 'I'd better change now, Aunt,' she called out. She heard the rustle of Madame Georges' full skirts as she came through the curtained doorway that separated her rear apartment from the shop.

'Magnificent, Madame!' Laura's aunt exclaimed. 'Now, if Laura would just learn to use her fan in the proper way. The small talk, the flirting, the art of walking . . . Ah, you know well, Madame, being of French extraction. You know the lengths we women must go to, to attract and hold a man, don't you? Now, don't forget, our coachman will pick up our parcels early this afternoon. I want my niece to have plenty of time to primp for my brother's party tonight.'

Madame Georges joined Laura behind the screen to help her out of the billowing yards of silk. As she gathered up the folds and arranged the gown on a satin hanger, she searched the young girl's face. 'Something troubles you, Mademoiselle? Are you happy?'

Laura was quick to protest. 'Why, Madame, what could trouble me?' She stepped carefully into her pastel-striped street dress. 'I am very lucky!'

'*Oui*,' the dressmaker agreed, tying the ribbons of Laura's Tuscan straw under the girl's chin. 'But I did not ask you if you were lucky,' she said in her native tongue. 'I only wanted to know if you were happy.'

Laura shrugged and laughed lightly. 'But they are the same, *n'est-ce pas*, Madame?' At the dressmaker's questioning look, Laura reached over and took her hand. 'Forgive me, Madame, for I am *not* so much of a fool that I believe happiness and luck are the same thing!'

Madame Georges squeezed the girl's hand. 'You are not a fool at all, Mademoiselle.'

Laura sighed. 'Well, sometimes I think there are times when . . .'

'Come, love, come!' her aunt called shrilly. 'William should be here any moment, and we mustn't keep him waiting.' Already she had opened the door on to the street, setting the little bell above it ringing brightly.

Laura kissed the dressmaker on the cheek. 'Thank you, Madame,' she said warmly. 'Thank you for everything.' Then she quickly moved to join her aunt. Once outside in the clear sunlight, with a soft morning breeze coming in off the channel, Laura breathed the invigorating air deeply. 'May we not walk home, Aunt? Crosswinds is only three short blocks away and the day is so beautiful!'

But Aunt Stark would hear of no such thing. 'Walk? Mercy, no! You don't want your pretty feet to spread, do you? And we have so many more things to attend to. Come.' She pulled her niece to her side when once they were on the pavement. 'We must stay close to Madame's door, for we do not want to be dirtied by a passing carriage, do we? Now, keep your eyes out for William.' She put a gloved hand to the tight orange curls that bobbed freely about her forehead in the breeze. 'I want you to wear your mother's diamond necklace tonight, to show off that pretty . . .' She suddenly stiffened at Laura's side. 'Oh, mercy!' She put a restraining hand on her niece's arm. 'Don't look! Turn away!'

But Laura had already seen the small group coming up the middle of the street towards them. Four black men moved slowly along, each fettered by leg-irons and shackled to the man in front of him. They were clothed in rags, and stumbled across the uneven cobbles on swollen feet. Following close behind was their white captor, who seemed to delight in flicking a whip at the bent shoulders of his prisoners.

'What has happened to those men?' Laura whispered.

'Now, love . . .' Aunt Stark tugged at her niece's sleeve. 'I warned you not to look. Just turn your head.'

But Laura could not. As she watched, one of the prisoners fell to his knees, his head down, his body low to the ground.

'On your feet, you!' the white man shouted. When the fallen man did not move, he raised his whip high and brought it down sharply on the black man's back.

Laura pulled instantly from her aunt's grasp and ran out to the middle of the street just as the whip was lifted for another lash. 'No!' she cried. 'Don't, don't!' She grabbed the man's arm. 'Can't you see he's hurt? How could you?'

Her words appeared to amuse him, for he shrugged off her hand and smiled crookedly down at her. 'This ain't your business, lady.' Still, he lowered his whip and did not deliver a second blow.

A small group of curious onlookers had gathered, and Aunt Stark cried, 'Come back here this instant! Oh, mercy, mercy!'

Laura paid no heed to the commotion but moved to help the fallen man. She put out a hand to him, and he turned to look at her. For an instant their eyes met, and when she saw the pain and despair written there, her heart went out to him. 'Please,' she said quietly, 'let me help you.' But he looked away. She watched as he struggled painfully to pull himself up to his feet, and in a moment the slow march began again.

A man's voice spoke directly behind her in a languid Southern drawl. 'Your compassion shows a warm heart, ma'am, but they are runaway slaves who have broken the law and must pay for it. Now,' the stranger took her arm, 'let me escort you back to the pavement.'

Laura shook off his hand and walked quickly to where

her aunt stood, crimson with embarrassment and dabbing at her face with a lace handkerchief. 'Mercy, whatever possessed you?' Aunt Stark cried. 'Look at you, you're a fright!' She turned to the stranger who had followed just a few steps behind. 'Please forgive my niece, sir. I cannot think why she acted so impetuously!'

'No apology is necessary, ma'am,' the stranger said, doffing his tall hat, 'unless it is mine to the young lady for exposing her to such a distressing sight on a fine September morning. For, you see, these are my slaves, and the overseer is only obeying my orders in taking them back to my ship.'

'*Your* slaves?' Laura spun to face him. 'And you stood there and did nothing to help that wretched man?'

'Laura, please!' Aunt Stark looked apologetically up at the young man. 'I declare I don't know what has got into her today. She's usually quite reasonable.'

Laura, her anger far from spent, now took time to examine the stranger, who had leaned down to converse with her aunt. He was undeniably handsome, immaculately attired in a fawn-coloured morning coat, his creamy stock and black boots glistening in the bright morning sun. His clean-shaven face was burned brown, and his generous mouth (she had expected to find cruelty there) revealed perfect white teeth when he smiled down at Aunt Stark. As she studied him, he turned in mid-sentence to look over at her. Laura caught her breath, for in that fraction of a second when their eyes met, she felt sure that she was looking into the pirate's eyes! They were the same jade green with small flecks of gold, lively and full of humour.

But no, she thought, it can't be, for as he turned away he flicked affectedly at a speck of lint on his velvet lapel with the exaggerated mannerism of a young dandy. She watched him, hoping—no, fearing—that he might be the same man, for there was something familiar in his voice, the strong line of his forehead and his hair, which shone now like burnished copper in the sunlight. Even though her aunt and the stranger were engaged in conversation, she heard none of it as she tried to still the rapid beat of her heart.

'Laura, pay attention!' Her aunt's voice startled her. 'Why, I do believe the girl's in a trance. You've not been listening to a word, have you, love?' She bobbed her head at the gentleman beside her. 'This is Mr Sloan Benedict, and he has graciously consented to attend our party tonight. You will have no trouble finding my brother's house,' she told him. 'Crosswinds is just down the street, a large white house with balconies across the front in the New Orleans style. We face directly on to the ship channel.' She reached over to straighten her niece's bonnet. 'Oh, here is our coachman, just rounding the corner. We look forward to seeing you this evening then, Mr Benedict.' She put her hand lightly on the young man's arm and was escorted to the kerb, where William had already jumped down from the box to open the carriage door. 'Now don't forget!' she called as she arranged her full skirts around her on the seat. 'You won't disappoint us, will you? Come, Laura dear!'

Laura felt the young man's hand on her elbow as he helped her up the step. Just before she settled herself, he took her hand and squeezed it, just once, then let it go. She looked at him again, and her heart sank, for now there was no mistaking that he was indeed the pirate, for he acknowledged their previous meeting with secret amusement. With a courtly bow and a smile for them both, he backed away.

Laura sat rigid, her eyes straight ahead as the carriage moved off. 'I cannot think why you were so rude, love,' her aunt complained at her side. 'Such a handsome man, quite charming enough to drive poor Edgar mad with jealousy!' She patted Laura's knee with her beaded bag. 'Do be nice to Mr Benedict tonight, won't you? He seems to be very rich and most refined. A South

Carolina plantation-owner! Fancy!' She sighed happily. 'Mercy, life is full of surprises, isn't it?'

When the two ladies returned to Crosswinds late that afternoon after accomplishing a dozen more errands in the town, Laura went straight to her bedchamber to rest. She took off her outer garments and threw herself across the bed. After the shocking encounter with the pirate, she once again admitted to herself how persistent her thoughts and dreams had been of him. She closed her eyes, but even now she saw his face as he had looked down at her today. With her eyes open, she still saw it. At the sight of him today a part of her wanted to cry out with joy at seeing him again, while another recoiled with shame at the memory of her own passion as he had held her here—in this very room!

She found that she could not relax with the conflicting emotions he had stirred in her, so she jumped from her bed and ran to the balcony, where she stood far back from the railing so as not to be seen from the street. The gentle breeze that had afforded some relief earlier in the day had diminished, and the small town baked under a cloudless sky. Lucas Trevor used to boast that he built Crosswinds facing northeast so that there would always be air circulating through its big rooms during the hot months. But there was no air today; just the sultry heat that wilted everything it touched. The gardens at the front of the house blazed with a riot of oleander and bougainvillaea, and their vivid splashes of pink, coral and crimson leapt from the parched soil like tongues of flame.

Going over to her washstand, she poured cold water into the basin. She dipped her face-cloth into it, squeezed it out and held it to her burning forehead. The water brought no relief. Why, oh why, she wondered desperately, did Aunt Stark invite him here tonight? What could I possibly say to him? How shall I act? How will *he* act? Will he taunt me with his knowledge of our night together? Will he laugh at me, make fun of me? And what was the reason for his disguise? Will I be the only one tonight to know that the pirate and Sloan Benedict are one and the same?

But enough of this, she told herself hotly, dropping her cloth into the basin. She must not—she *would* not—let him see how he affected her! Her eyes fell on the ostrich fan she would carry tonight. It hung by its loop on a drawer knob of her wardrobe, and as she pulled it off, opened it and watched it spread into luxuriant plumes of emerald green feathers, an idea came to her! If the pirate could masquerade as a Southern gentleman, then so might she play a role of her own!

Tonight she would be all the things Aunt Stark wanted her to be—a shameless flirt, a tease, bewitching, unattainable—not at all like the girl he first met here just six months ago! She would wear her mother's diamond necklace as her aunt had suggested. Maria would crown her madonna curls with a circlet of emeralds instead of the wreath of pale roses she had planned to wear. She walked to her mirror and fluttered the beautiful fan experimentally under her chin. She winked coyly at her reflection, and a slow smile spread across her face as she studied the effect.

When Sloan Benedict presented his card at Lucas Trevor's front door that evening, the party at Crosswinds was well under way. He could hear music and laughter from the salon, but instead of going directly there, he was drawn to the parlour at the other side of the wide hall. It was a formal room, decorated in the vibrant reds, blues and golds of the Empire period. His eyes focused immediately on a large portrait that hung over the stately black marble mantelpiece. The subject, a young woman, reclined languidly on a small love seat. Her gown, a deep sapphire velvet adorned with tiny seed-pearls, dipped gracefully around her gently sloping shoulders and plunged daringly to reveal her high bosom. A glittering diamond necklace encircled her slender throat. Her blonde hair, parted in the middle, cascaded in golden ringlets to her shoulders and framed a face as delicate and fragile as a piece of rare porcelain.

But there was something in her face that sent a chill through him. It was her eyes, Benedict decided. They were ice-blue and, though strikingly lovely, they stared out at him with a cruelty and indifference as cold as a winter moon.

'Why, there you are!' He recognised the voice at once, and turned to greet the little lady who had invited him here. Mrs Stark's plump figure was draped in pale rose lace, and vivid colour stood high on her cheeks. 'Our man said you had arrived, Mr Benedict, but I could not for the life of me find you!' She smiled up at him, offering her gloved hand.

'My dear lady!' Benedict brought it gracefully to his lips. 'We meet again!'

Aunt Stark nodded happily. 'We do indeed. But I see that you are admiring the portrait of Amanda Trevor. Wasn't she beautiful? Laura's mother died in childbirth, poor darling. Such a tragedy. She was Amanda duFlon from New Orleans before she married Lucas. The duFlons were exceedingly wealthy; cotton money, you know, and a great deal of it!' She punctuated her words with a lift of her eyebrows. 'They ranked very high on the social ladder there. My brother suffered so at his wife's death . . . Such a loss! I myself had recently been widowed, and I came here to live shortly after it happened, to take care of Laura. No sacrifice is too great when one's family needs help!' She sighed lightly. 'Do you think Laura favours her mother?'

A frown crossed Benedict's face as he reached into his breast pocket and pulled out a gold monocle to examine the portrait more closely. 'It's difficult to say, my dear lady. Surely both mother and daughter are beautiful, but the mouth, the colouring are different. And the eyes—I see no resemblance in the eyes at all. A Bernadotti portrait, isn't it, ma'am?'

Aunt Stark bit her lip thoughtfully. 'Mercy, I have no idea! But I believe it was an Italian painter. They're all so good at that, though, aren't they? But you can see that a fashionable, socially aware beauty like Amanda would never have consented to Laura's wasting her life away in a dreary convent, can't you? Which is what Lucas wanted for her. And, poor darling, she came very close to it!'

Benedict's brows raised in surprise. 'A convent? Your niece considered being a nun, then?'

'Oh, yes. My niece has always had a soft spot in her heart for those less fortunate than ourselves. Would you believe, she said she actually enjoyed being cooped up in that awful hospital there at Santa Clara, but I knew in my heart that it was not for her. Looking at her mother, Mr Benedict, can't you agree with me?'

'Indeed yes,' he said, putting away his monocle.

'Now,' she put her hand on the sleeve of his burgundy evening coat, 'you must meet our guests and dance with my niece. I should like you to know her as she really is! You saw her in such a bad light this morning on the Strand. She's really a love, you know.' Her fingers tightened on his elbow as she led him out into the hall. When she saw her brother standing at one side of the salon near the door, she called him. 'Lucas, come meet Mr Benedict, the young man I told you about!'

Lucas Trevor looked over at his sister with some irritation, but all the same he made his way slowly to her side. During the introductions, as the two men shook hands, he studied his guest's flamboyant attire disdainfully.

Aunt Stark said quickly, taking note of her brother's disapproving look, 'Mr Benedict is from South Carolina,

Lucas. His plantation is not very far from President Jackson's.'

At her words, Trevor's interest was aroused. 'A neighbour of Old Hickory, eh?' he said. 'I'm a great admirer of his. Texas would follow Arkansas into the Union tomorrow if Andrew Jackson was well enough to run for a third term.'

'I understand that you yourself have an interest in politics, sir,' said Benedict. 'Mrs Stark told me this morning that you're thinking of running against Sam Houston in '38 for president of your independent government.'

Trevor laughed shortly. 'My God, Ernesta,' he snorted, 'you and that tongue of yours!' He turned back to Benedict. 'Nobody could beat Houston after his victory at San Jacinto. No, I'm interested in local politics. I want to see the city of Galveston incorporated. Hell's fire, we're not even a city yet, and we've got the biggest port in the Southwest!'

'Enough, enough!' Aunt Stark cried. She stepped between the two men. 'My brother is president of the bank here, Mr Benedict, and one would think he had enough already to occupy his time. But no more of this!' She again grabbed her guest's arm. 'We are here to have fun, aren't we? That's what parties are for!' With a toss of her head, she resolutely led him away and into the salon, where she spied her niece at once. The girl was surrounded by several young men, each vying for her attention. Aunt Stark made her way through the crowd to Laura's side and tapped her on the shoulder with her lilac fan. 'You remember Mr Benedict, love? The gentleman who led you back to safety this morning.'

Laura turned to face him. 'Led me?' she said lightly. 'As I recall, I managed the journey back to the pavement quite unassisted.'

'Well said; and so you did.' Benedict bowed over her

extended hand, noting that even in this brilliant gathering Laura Trevor sparkled like a rare gem. Colour was high in her cheeks, and her deep blue eyes flashed no less than the circle of diamonds at her neck. It was the same necklace, he noticed, that Amanda Trevor was wearing in the portrait he had just seen. But now, the diamonds, which had only increased the coldness of the woman in the painting, were warmed and brought to life by the girl's radiance.

'Ladies and gentlemen,' a voice rang out from the orchestra at the other end of the salon, 'please take your places for the waltz.'

One of the men at Laura's side stepped forward eagerly to claim her as his partner. 'Heavens, no!' Aunt Stark exclaimed as she shooed him away. 'Just this once we will disallow the names on her dance card. My niece must dance with our visitor from South Carolina!' She threw Laura an approving smile before she bustled the disappointed young man off the rapidly filling dance floor.

Laura's eyes followed them, and when she turned at last to face her partner, the music had already begun. Benedict put his arm lightly about her waist and they moved quickly into the dance. His first few well-executed turns brought a cry of surprise to her lips. 'Why, you dance quite well,' she told him, as if she had expected him to be unfamiliar with the steps.

'My dear Miss Trevor,' he said, amused, 'even savages dance! Whirling dervishes shriek and swallow hot coals when they dance, but still they dance.' He thought he detected a flash of amusement in her eyes, but it was gone in an instant. They had circled the floor several times before he spoke again. 'I see no acknowledgment of recognition in your eyes, Miss Trevor, as I was gratified to see this morning on the Strand.'

Laura looked at him, surprised. 'We have met before? Ah . . .' she tilted her head prettily to one side, 'was it perhaps at the Murrays' soirée last week? Dear me, I thought those dreary charades would never end! I dislike them, perhaps because I have never been very good at them.'

'I find that hard to believe,' he told her, 'for you are singularly adept at this one.' He watched her for a reaction, but she appeared not to have heard him and had lowered her shadowed lids to fasten her gaze on his cravat.

'Yes, it must have been at the Murrays',' she said brightly. 'There are so many parties, and I am notoriously forgetful about faces and names! Ours is such a busy town, and new people arrive with each tide. I find it impossible to sort them all out! Do you come here to Galveston often, Mr Benedict?'

'Only as often as necessary, Miss Trevor.'

'Which tells me nothing, of course,' she laughed, as she moved light as a feather in his arms. 'But then that is the purpose of any conversation, is it not?'

'Yes,' he agreed, 'if one's purpose is to conceal rather than reveal what is on one's mind.'

'I have nothing whatever on my mind!' she was quick to assure him. Then, as the absurdity of her remark struck her, she stiffened in his arms.

'I would prefer not to believe that,' he laughed, 'although our conversation thus far would seem to bear it out.' He went on, drawing her closer to him, 'But then I learned only tonight that you once considered a life as a nun. That shows a modicum of thought, certainly.'

'Come, now,' Laura pulled away from him, 'we live only in the present here, and that is exciting enough to keep our minds occupied.'

He smiled down at her. 'I can see that. But I also see a great deal that you would prefer me not to see, Miss Trevor.' He had no chance to say more, for the music stopped and she spun away from him in a whirl of emerald silk.

Just before she was caught up in the arms of a youth who waited to claim her for the next dance, she turned back to Benedict and warned him mockingly, 'Do be careful, sir. If your purpose here tonight is to seduce all the young ladies, you had best be prepared to pay the consequences!'

Benedict watched her as she and her new partner joined the couples already forming for the next dance. When she did not look at him again he walked off the floor, puzzled by the girl's superficial observation and false exuberance. Her last remark, so meaningless and flippant, was precisely what he might have expected from any of the painted ladies here tonight. He found himself standing in the doorway of the salon next to a gentleman in sombre black evening clothes who was running his fingers thoughtfully over his sandy moustache. He studied the older man, who seemed pained to be a part of this rowdy assemblage.

'Deucedly close in here,' Benedict drawled, as he removed a lace handkerchief and dabbed at his forehead.

The older man said nothing as his pale eyes surveyed the dancers in front of him.

'Permit me to introduce myself. Sloan Benedict's the name, sir.'

There seemed nothing for the other man to do but acknowledge his presence. 'Skelton . . . Lord Skelton,' he said shortly. A young man who had stood half-hidden behind Skelton moved forward to be introduced. 'And this is my secretary, Michael Norton. Norton,' Skelton snapped, 'make yourself useful. Bring me some brandy.' The young man hesitated, reluctant to take his eyes off Benedict's handsome embroidered waistcoat. 'Do it *now*,' Skelton insisted, 'there's a good chap.'

Benedict watched, amused, as Norton snaked his way carefully through the dancers on his way to the dining-room. 'Your secretary, eh?' He tucked his handkerchief away. 'Would it be presumptuous of me to ask, sir, what business it is that brings you to Galveston?'

'I am here on behalf of a friend's shipping concern.'

'Oh? And might I ask what it is you do on your friend's behalf?'

'I—I scout the cotton market,' Skelton said, then turned away as though unwilling to pursue the subject.

But Benedict persisted. 'Cotton, eh? I'm a cotton-planter myself. I know a little something about that commodity. What is it you look for here in Galveston, sir?'

'Look for?' Skelton's mouth tightened. 'What do you mean?'

'In cotton. Do you favour long staple or short?'

Skelton's eyes shifted warily. 'Ah . . . Long.'

'Oh?' Benedict pulled out his gold monocle and tapped his cheek thoughtfully. 'You come all the way to Galveston, which deals only with the short staple, an inferior grade, when our port in Charleston has the finest long staple available? I would think you'd do better there, especially since Charleston is closer for your ships by several days' sailing. I find that baffling, sir.' It was apparent that he had finally succeeded in getting the man's full attention, for Lord Skelton turned to face him.

'I find it none of your damned business, sir!' he said.

Benedict raised his eyeglass before his face as if to ward off a blow. '*Touché!*' he laughed. 'And my apologies, for I have told you nothing of my own business here, have I?'

Skelton frowned. 'I see no reason for it.'

But Benedict went on as if he had not heard. 'A tiresome chore, really, for I must return four runaway slaves to my father's plantation in South Carolina. Fortunately they were caught before they could cross the border into Mexico.' He replaced his monocle in his pocket. 'Those blacks!' he sniffed. 'No appreciation of what we do for them! They're a constant source of irritation to us. I just wish we could ship the whole lot of 'em back to Africa!'

Skelton drew himself up. 'We British abolished the abhorrent practice of slavery in our colonies fairly recently,' he said.

'Yes, just three years ago, I understand, and most commendable of you,' Benedict told him in an agreeable tone. 'I also understand that all slave trade between Africa and America on British ships was forbidden by an Act of Parliament as long as twenty years ago. We have not done away with slavery, as you know; only banned further import of African blacks to our shores. But I find it an amusing paradox, sir, that while you British consider the practice of slavery immoral, some of your countrymen still risk severe penalties by illegally smuggling black Africans here for *our* slave markets.'

Skelton's pale eyes registered indignation. 'You dare to accuse . . .'

'Tut tut,' Benedict said quickly. 'You must know how indebted we are to those intrepid merchants of yours —Thomas Ripp of the Monarch Lines, for one. Without their help in replenishing our workforce, we in the South would soon face economic ruin!' He lowered his voice. 'Now, as for that deuced Abolitionist who regularly boards your vessels on the high seas and pirates your cargos of black ivory only to set them free, be assured, sir, he causes us immeasurable concern. I only hope they catch the renegade. Crusty old salt! I understand that he's a doddering little dwarf of a man, old as the hills.'

'He is nothing of the sort! He's a young, hot-headed . . .' Skelton stopped.

'You've heard of him, then?'

'Of course! Everyone has. But, see here, I find this entire conversation distasteful.'

'Again, forgive me, Lord Skelton. I seem to be

touching a few exposed nerves here tonight, and I must humbly apologise.'

It was at this very moment that Skelton's secretary joined them, balancing two brandies in his hands. Benedict took the glass that was offered and raised it high. 'To your health, gentlemen!' He drank it down, noting with amusement that Norton was again admiring his waistcoat.

'Paris,' he told the secretary. 'Beau Brummell has one like it, though I doubt he finds many opportunities to wear it now, languishing away in the asylum at Bon Sauveur. If you like, I can give you the name of my tailor in Paris, Mr Norton. I so infinitely prefer the French couturiers with their sprightly imagination, don't you?' He placed his empty glass in the secretary's hand with a bow. 'With your permission, gentlemen. There are a few beauties here tonight who have caught my eye.'

He moved away, and Skelton glared at his retreating back. 'Bloody simpleton,' he said under his breath. He turned to his secretary. 'I don't like him. I don't like him at all.'

Norton's eyes too followed the young planter. 'Well, I do,' he said. 'He's a fine-looking fellow, Edgar, and I'd give a king's ransom to have a waistcoat like his!'

'Enough of that. You seem to forget why we are here, Michael. We have a job to do.'

Norton sniffed. 'You're the one who seems to have forgotten, wasting so much time on that foolish chit of a girl. You know she won't marry you, Edgar. And how will you explain to Monarch Lines that you were so wrapped up in Lucas Trevor's rich daughter that you've let six months go by and still haven't a clue to the identity or whereabouts of that Abolitionist?'

Skelton fought to control his temper. 'These things take time. And I'll thank you to let me handle this in my own way. *I'm* the one Thomas Ripp hired to find the man, not you! And, in the process, if I win a wealthy wife to ensure my future, so much the better. Now get to it. Keep your eyes and ears open. And . . .' he rasped, 'your mouth shut!'

Laura had no appetite for the raspberry ice brought by the young man seated next to her at the foot of the stairs. She had danced every dance so far tonight, moving from one eager partner's arms to another, but she could not dispel the memory of her waltz with Sloan Benedict. When she recalled their conversation on the dance floor she was infuriated at her own inability to match his wits. He had made no effort to speak to her since, and each time she saw him he seemed to be enjoying himself immensely, lavishing his attentions on every pretty girl.

'Are you ill, Miss Trevor?' The voice at her side startled her. She threw the young man a smile as she got to her feet. 'I need a breath of air,' she told him. When he quickly rose to accompany her, she handed him her untouched ice. 'Please, if you don't mind, I'd really rather be alone.' She dropped her fan on the step beside him, and walked towards the front of the house.

Once through the open door and into the deep shadows that filled the balcony, Laura put her hands on the wrought-iron railing as if by concentrating on its solid unyielding surface she could steady the pitch of her thoughts. A melancholy moon hung low in the night sky and traced a narrowing path of shimmering silver across the calm channel water. But she was too upset to notice the beauty of the night. She remembered her plans, so lightly made that afternoon, to tease the pirate and taunt him; but instead, he had confounded her! What a fool I am, she thought, for even as she had whirled in his arms, she had felt the familiar surge of excitement at his nearness, the sound of his voice, the touch of his hand on hers. She heard a step behind her, and knew with a sinking heart whose it was.

'I was hoping to find you alone, Miss Trevor.' His

voice had lost the Southern drawl and was again the voice of the pirate.

Her hands tightened on the railing, and she did not look round at him. 'You are a fool to show your face in this house again!' Her words startled her, for she had not planned to say them.

'I see the lady's memory improves,' he commented, his voice quietly amused.

'I need only cry out, and they will take you off to prison like the thief you are!'

Benedict moved past her to stand at her side. He put his hands on the railing and looked out over the channel. Only now did she turn to look at him and was struck again by the strength and beauty of his profile.

'Any thief worth his salt would be sure to take his hard-earned booty with him, I should think,' he said drily.

'It makes you no less a thief because in your haste to escape you accidentally drop our guests' valuables on the pier!' she cried.

'Think what you will. But I'm willing to wager that your guests still speak of that night. A pirate raid is surely more diverting than a dreary game of charades, don't you agree?' He gave her no time to reply as he turned to face her, a slow smile tugging at the corners of his mouth. 'But I *am* flattered to see that you remember me after all, Miss Trevor.'

'Remember you!' Laura said, angered by the amused indifference in his tone. 'I have tried with all my heart to forget that night!'

'Oh, come now. Besides, if you knew the reasons for my actions, you would understand.'

'Oh, I don't expect you to explain anything!' Laura fought to control her voice. 'You can probably justify all your actions, your heartless indifference to the treatment of your slaves today, your disguises and your reason for—for everything you do, since you hold the truth so lightly, Mr Benedict . . . or whatever your name is!'

'I know it confuses you, but the nature of my business makes it necessary sometimes to create an occasional diversion . . .'

'Diversion?' Laura cried. 'Is that what you call forcing yourself on a sick, delirious girl . . .'

'Wait a minute!' Benedict held up his hand. 'Sick? Delirious?' He leaned closer to her and the playful note was again in his voice. 'You didn't appear to be incoherent, although your observation about my muddy boots took me by surprise. As for forcing myself on you, it was unfortunate that I had to take your cross as I did, but you exhibited a marked unwillingness to part with it, if you remember.'

'You know I don't speak of *that* night,' Laura said hotly. 'I dare you to deny climbing up on the balcony and coming to my room!'

'Oh, *that* night. But surely you can't recall me being in your bedchamber that night!'

Laura tensed with anger. 'I remember it very well,' she whispered.

He stared at her, his face puzzled. 'But you were fast asleep. Even my kiss—a chaste one, here,' he touched her forehead lightly, 'failed to rouse you.' He pulled back in mock dismay. 'But you look surprised! You certainly wouldn't expect me to return your cross in broad daylight and risk a noose round my neck, would you, Laura?'

When she heard him speak her name, Laura's last bit of strength dissolved. 'My name,' she whispered. 'You said my name that night; only my name. Over and over again.'

'Did I?' He peered at her. 'That would have been exceedingly clever of me, since I learned your name only this morning on the Strand.' There was a trace of concern in his voice.

It took a moment before the significance of his words got through to her. When they did, Laura drew back against the railing, her eyes blazing at him. 'You're lying!' she cried.

'I have no need to lie, I assure you.' He reached for her, but she drew away.

She saw his lips move but heard nothing more, only a small voice inside her that cried, You *fool*! It was you who created the fantasy of his kisses, the urgency of his embrace! *Had* it all been a dream then, that night he held her to him in the moonlit bedchamber? But no, she thought wildly, it was too real! Yet, if what he said was true . . . She stared at him, appalled at the realisation that what she had carried in her heart these many months was only a dream-induced hallucination. Turning away from him, she said stiffly, 'Leave me now. Leave me alone!'

'That's your gratitude, is it?' His voice was suddenly angry. He put his hands on her shoulders and turned her to face him. 'I won't leave until you hear me out!' His grip tightened. 'In all my years,' he told her sharply, 'I have managed to keep my heart to myself, for there was no one I wanted to lose it to. And then one night I saw the girl I had always hoped to find. She was brave, witty, with fire in her eyes. The beauty and depth of her soul was laid bare just for an instant, and in that instant I knew I loved her. She has haunted me ever since. I'd wake to see her face in the morning sky. I'd hear her voice in the soft breeze that filled my sails. She was everywhere, but she was nowhere, for she belonged in my arms. When I saw her run into the street today to help a wounded man, I thought I saw that girl again, yet tonight . . . How wrong I was!'

'Don't, don't!' Laura cried, pulling herself free. 'Why do you come back to torment me? Can't you see, I *am* that girl! I am!'

He stared at her and the moonlight burned gold in his

eyes. Slowly his arms went round her and he drew her close against his chest. 'I want to believe that, Laura, more than anything in the world.' His voice was soft in her ear.

In the circle of his embrace Laura could fight no more. She leaned against him, not daring to think, to move, to breathe, her mind incapable of reason at the nearness of him. Slowly in the darkness his lips found hers. She pulled away, but only for a moment. When their lips met again she felt the earth dissolve under her feet, and the heavens seemed to lift them up, up, until they soared together like a single star through the night sky.

They did not hear the heavy footsteps just behind them on the balcony. 'Laura!' Trevor's voice sliced between them like a jagged shard of glass. He pulled his daughter roughly from Benedict's embrace. 'By God,' he roared down at her, 'what's the meaning of this?'

Benedict stepped forward to come between them. 'Your daughter has no blame in this!'

Trevor pushed him away with surprising strength. 'Leave this house!' he thundered at Benedict, taking Laura's arm. 'What I have to say to Laura is of no concern to you!'

'Mr Trevor, I give you my word . . .'

'Your word? The word of an overdressed young fop?'

'Do as my father says,' Laura cried. 'Please!' She struggled against the hand that held her, but his fingers only tightened on her arm. 'Can't you see, you must leave! It will only make things worse if you stay!'

Benedict hesitated still. Then, seeing that his presence could only further incite Trevor's wrath, he turned and crossed the balcony to take the steps two at a time down to the path. He never looked back.

When he had disappeared into the darkness, her father's fingers dug deeper into Laura's arm. 'It isn't enough that you flirt shamelessly with every man in my house tonight! Now I find you in the arms of a stranger you met only today! How many other men have you brought out here for a stolen kiss?'

'Father, you're hurting me!' Laura cried, trying to twist away.

He pulled her roughly to his side. 'I'll put an end to this, once and for all!' With one arm firmly round her waist, he dragged her along the shadowed balcony to the open salon door. Once across the threshold, in the blaze of bright light, he signalled to the orchestra leader, motioning to him for silence. Laura stared at the faces of the startled guests, all turned towards them now in the sudden hush.

'Ladies and gentlemen,' Lucas Trevor's voice rang out in the big room. 'I know you've all been expecting to hear this, so I won't waste words. Tonight I want to announce the engagement of my daughter to Lord Skelton! It's official. Now, get on with the music.'

Laura turned to look at her father's face, hard as stone beside her. She tried to speak, but could not. As she watched him, stunned, a sound of rising voices began to roar in her ears. The bright lights blurred together, the faces round her melted into blackness as she felt herself slide slowly to the floor.

CHAPTER FOUR

'FEELING BETTER now, Laurie?' John Messersmith sat at the side of Laura's bed, patting her hand gently. It was he who had carried her upstairs following the surprise announcement of her engagement to Edgar Skelton. Now, seeing how small and vulnerable her hand looked in his huge one, he found it difficult to find words to comfort his old friend's daughter. 'Your aunt is tickled to death over this,' he said. 'Ernesta's got everybody believing you keeled over with joy at hearing your name linked publicly with Skelton. But,' a frown deepened between his thick brows, 'you sure fooled me, honey. Frankly, I didn't think you even liked him!' Damn it, he had not meant to say that, even if it was the truth.

Laura stirred and opened her eyes. Encouraged by some response, Messersmith tried again. 'I'd like to say a few choice words to your daddy, though, for the way he went about it, as though he were announcing the highest bidder at a cotton sale on the quay.' He stopped and took a deep breath. 'Laurie, I wish you'd say something to me . . . Anything!'

'Please, Uncle John. There's nothing to say.' Anger flashed in her eyes as she looked at him.

Still Messersmith made another effort to console her, despite her reluctance to talk to him. 'You'll make a beautiful bride, my girl—maybe even prettier than your momma.' He saw a shadow of sadness in the dark blue eyes that watched him.

'I wish . . .' she began haltingly, her face pale in the candlelight, 'I wish I'd known her.' She stirred restlessly under the coverlet. 'Things would be so different if she were alive.'

'I know,' Messersmith said. 'I know, honey.'

'Father never even mentions her name, did you know that?' Laura's eyes wavered for an instant. 'What was she like? What was she really like?'

'Well, she was a beauty, all right.' Messersmith smiled, remembering. 'When Luke first built this house for her, she seemed to take to the life here fine. But I used to wonder how a gal like that could settle down out here.' He shook his head. 'Galveston was a rough place then, Laurie, mightly different from what she'd had in New Orleans. She was spoiled, I guess you could say, and she loved to spend money. But, hell, it was mostly her money, after all. She loved to give parties,' he grinned, 'like Ernesta. One party after another. And Luke never denied her anything, you understand. He went out of his way . . .' He paused, his eyes deepening in the soft light. 'That's why he pretty near went berserk the night she died.' He rubbed his chin thoughtfully. 'He locked himself in his room, wouldn't eat, couldn't sleep, and it went on like that for weeks. He even stayed away from you, Laurie, his own baby . . . He wouldn't go near you! I've never seen anybody so—so . . .' Words failed him.

'But it was my birth that killed her, Uncle John!' Laura cried. 'Do you suppose he blames me for my mother's death? That he blames me still?'

Messersmith drew back. 'Good God, if he blames anybody, he blames himself for putting Amanda through . . .'

'No, no, wait a minute!' Laura pulled herself higher on the pillows and stared at him. 'That would explain so much, don't you see? Every time he looks at me, he's reminded that if I had never been born, she might still be alive!'

'Stop that, Laurie!' Messersmith told her sternly. 'Don't go thinking things like that. Luke loves you!'

'Does he?' She sank back on the pillows. 'He never

shows it! Didn't you see his face tonight when he made me stand up there with him in front of everybody . . . as if he wanted to shame me! And every time I go near him or try to touch him, he draws away. I have never known a kind word from him, a gentle touch.'

'Whoa! I don't want to hear any more of this foolishness. That's not so, and you know it!' Messersmith pulled himself to his feet.

But Laura had closed her eyes. 'I never dreamed,' she whispered, turning her head away. 'I never dreamed . . .'

Messersmith waited for a moment. 'Now, Laurie,' he said. 'Now, Laurie . . .' But she had shut him away. 'Well, I'll say goodnight to you, honey. You just get some good sleep, you hear?' He leaned over and kissed her lightly on the cheek. Then, picking up the candle, he made his way out of the room, sick at heart, for having unwittingly put such an idea into the young girl's head.

When he had left her, Laura lay motionless in the darkness, listening to the sounds from downstairs where her father's guests were finally leaving. Carriages came and went on the street below, the light from their lanterns throwing soft patterns across the ceiling. The night air was full of laughter and sleepy farewells. Then all was quiet once more and the big house settled down for the night. She stared wide-eyed at the lacy canopy above her head. Why had she not seen before the reason for her father's constant rejection of her? Is it any wonder, she thought, that I have never felt at home here at Crosswinds, the house he had built for his beloved Amanda? Laura's very presence in it was a constant reminder to him that her birth had caused his wife's death!

She tried now to think of something in the past which might have indicated to her the depth of resentment she stirred in her father at the sight of her. Slowly, a childhood incident emerged from a mist of blurred memories.

It was something that she had not thought of in years, yet now it was as clear to her as on the day it had happened. She had been only eight, she remembered, sitting alone under the Judas tree tending her small garden behind the house. Maria had come to tell her that Señor Trevor wanted to see her at once. Laura had run to the parlour, and when she saw the anger in her father's face, she tried to think of what she might have done that day to earn it.

'I forbid you to play under the Judas tree,' he had shouted at her. 'If I ever find that you have disobeyed me, I'll take the strap to you!'

Laura had stared at him, not understanding. She had tried to explain to him about the camellias. She had found the dried cuttings under old Ned's tools in the potting-shed and wanted to plant them, but the gardener had told her that the fragile flower would never grow in Galveston's sandy soil. It was from Ned she learned that camellias had been Amanda Trevor's favourite flower, and since he had been unable to grow them here for her, the young bride ordered fresh blooms shipped in from New Orleans each week during her few short years on the island.

But maybe, Ned had told Laura, if she found a shaded spot and kept them well watered, the cuttings might put out new growth. The twisted Judas tree at one side of the carriage house afforded the only shade in the big back yard, and it was there that she had nurtured her private garden, each day looking for tender young shoots to appear in the soil.

'I forbid you to go near there!' her father told her again. 'Now go and get Maria to wash your filthy face and hands. Don't just stand there! Do as I say!'

Laura had flown from the room, bewildered, incapable of understanding the reason for her father's violent outburst. Aunt Stark found her later, curled up on the balcony outside her bedchamber, and provided a ready explanation for her brother's anger.

'You look like a little rag-picker, love, with dirt on your face and your hair every which way!'

'He hates me! But why? What have I done?' Laura remembered sobbing against her aunt's ample bosom.

'Mercy, no such thing,' Aunt Stark had assured her. 'How could he hate his little princess? But he wants to see you always clean and pretty, the way little girls are supposed to be.'

Laura stared dry-eyed now into the darkness. It had been the camellias, she realised. The mention of Amanda's favourite flower must have brought all the painful memories back to him. And that his daughter, who had caused Amanda's death, should be so anxious to cultivate the delicate plant . . . 'Oh,' she whispered, 'why didn't I *see*? How could I have been so blind?' She closed her eyes only to open them again, knowing that if sleep came at all, it would not come easily. It was not until first morning light paled the sky that her mind drifted off and she fell into a deep, dreamless state of unconsciousness.

Maria woken her at ten o'clock next morning with the news that a gentleman was downstairs in the courtyard with Aunt Stark and had asked expressly to see her. 'Oh, no,' Laura exclaimed as the events of the night before crowded in on her. 'Is it Lord Skelton?'

'No, I don't know who it is. Come, *niña*. Señora Stark insists. I'll help you to dress.'

Laura offered no more resistance as she let her maid minister to her. She was careful not to meet Maria's eyes. She surely knew of the announcement of her engagement the night before and Laura's unseemly collapse afterwards, but gave no indication of any knowledge of it.

Once Maria had helped her into her simple morning gown and brushed and pinned up her hair, Laura made her way slowly down the stairs and into the hall. She heard her aunt's high bubbly voice coming from the enclosed garden at the back of the house.

'Of course I knew all along that my niece intended to accept his proposal in her own good time,' she said. 'No one knows Laura as I do. Not that I get any thanks for my troubles. Do you know that my brother has never forgiven me for persuading Laura not to return to that foolish little convent, Mr Benedict?'

Upon hearing the visitor's name, Laura stepped quickly behind the doorway and held her breath. But her aunt had already spied her. 'Ah, there she is!' She flew to her niece's side and, putting her arm about Laura's waist, led her over to Benedict. 'Look who has come to pay us a visit, love!' She went on excitedly. 'Did you know that Mr Benedict had to leave our party early, so he didn't hear of your engagement? Mercy, he would not have learned of it at all, had he not returned here this morning to pick up his hat. He is quite as surprised as everyone else was last night, to hear your exciting news!' She reached out to straighten her niece's collar. 'Dear me, I wish you'd worn the rose plissé, love. That gown is so plain.' She turned to Benedict standing attentively at her side, strikingly handsome in a dove-grey morning coat. 'I shall have my work cut out, you may be sure! Still, there will be ample time, for the wedding date is not yet set. But what with Laura's trousseau, and plans for the reception here at Crosswinds,' she lamented, 'all of it falls in *my* lap, you know.' If the prospect of the many preparations distressed Aunt Stark, it was belied by the liveliness of her manner. 'Yes?' She frowned at the sudden appearance of the Mexican cook standing in the doorway. 'What is it now, Josefina?'

'It is the fisherman, Señora, Cayo Aristo. He is in the kitchen to see about the week's order.'

'Mercy!' Aunt Stark shook her head impatiently. 'If it's not one thing, it's another.' She glanced flirtatiously up at Benedict. 'You will remember to come see us again next time you're in Galveston, won't you, Mr Benedict?

Just because our Laura will be living in England does not mean that you will forget Crosswinds, I hope.'

The young man smiled down at her as he took her hand and raised it gracefully to his lips. 'There is no chance that I shall ever forget Crosswinds, dear lady. You may be assured of it.'

Aunt Stark smiled winningly at him, then turned to Laura. 'You must get some rest today, love. You look positively peaked, and we don't want your future husband to see you so pale, do we, when he comes to call this afternoon?' She smiled again at Benedict, and with a rustle of her full skirts, she was gone.

When her aunt left the garden, Laura moved quickly to sit by the small fountain in a corner, and stared at the stream of water as it splashed softly on the rocks below. 'You took a chance coming here today,' she told Benedict evenly, 'after seeing my father's temper last night.'

For a moment he said nothing, then he strode to her side, his hands clasped behind his back. 'Since the accepted practice is to wish the bride-to-be good fortune,' he said coolly, 'I now do so. Your aunt was correct in saying that I came back to pick up my hat. I shall say nothing of what else I had hoped to accomplish by seeing you again.' He paused. 'Now that I have extended the required courtesy, I take my leave. Good day to you.'

He turned and would have left the garden, but Laura called to him. 'You give me no chance to say anything,' she cried, 'and you call that *courtesy*?'

After hesitating for a moment, he retraced his steps. 'It would seem that each of us is guilty of rudeness, then, for what do you call it when you encourage a man to pledge his heart to you on the very night you plan to announce your engagement to another?'

'I gave you no encouragement!' Laura cried, shocked at the cruelty in his tone. 'You made no pledge to me last night, nor I to you.'

A wry smile played at Benedict's lips. 'To me, our kiss was a pledge. Apparently it meant nothing to you, though.' His voice was heavy with sarcasm. 'You certainly deceived me. You are an excellent actress, Miss Trevor!'

'How dare you speak to me like this! I said nothing to you last night of any feelings for you.'

'You *have* feelings, then? Am I to assume that you entertain feelings for Skelton, since your engagement to him was announced last night?' He leaned closer. 'Or do you?'

'It is none of your business! Besides, it's my father who wants this marriage. But this is no concern of yours!'

'But I want to know,' he told her. 'Don't you see, I have a right to know.'

She looked up at him, appalled. 'What right have you? You come into my life from nowhere, telling me nothing. One minute you are a thief, the next a fine gentleman, and you say you have a *right* to know about me?' She saw his eyes change as he watched her, deepening, softening as they searched hers.

He knelt down before her and took her hands. 'Perhaps I have no right, but for a moment last night, when I held you in my arms, I thought I was sure that you felt something too.'

She could not take her eyes from his. 'Who are you?' she whispered. 'What are you?'

At her words, he released her hands and got slowly to his feet. 'I can tell you nothing. How I wish I could!' He turned and walked to one of the iron benches and sat down heavily. When he finally spoke, he did not look at her and his voice was barely a whisper. 'Do you know what it's like to lose control of your senses, your own heart and soul? Do you know what it is to *love*?'

She did not answer him. She could not. She sat still, her hands warmed where he had held them.

Suddenly he jumped to his feet and walked again to where she sat. 'You ask me who I am, what I am. Well, who are you? There are two of you: the girl I fell in love with six months ago, and the painted flirt you pretend to be. I love them both, for they are both you. I just wish that one day you might feel the same about me, Laura. That no matter who I am, you could love me.'

He waited for some sign, some word from her, but she kept her eyes lowered and could not speak. Her heart pounded, yet still she could say nothing. He stood silently beside her for a moment more. Then, without another word, he turned on his heel and left her alone. She heard his quick steps down the hall and the sound of the front door closing behind him. She wanted to run after him, to feel his arms round her, to bury her head against his shoulder, to tell him that she was haunted by his kiss, his touch. But, instead, she let him go, feeling as empty now as she had on that first night she met the pirate, as if a part of her—the best part—had left with him. But why? What was it she felt for this arrogant, self-assured stranger? Just his physical presence alone sent tremors through every part of her. The touch of his hands, everything about him, filled her with an excitement she had never dreamed possible. Never had her spirits soared, then plunged like this! When he was with her, she knew only peaks of elation or valleys of despair.

Laura looked now at the patch of blue sky reflected in the water of the fountain and put her hand in its coolness and watched the image break apart into a hundred shimmering pieces. When she heard her aunt's footsteps returning from the kitchen, she did not know how long she had been sitting there, numb to the world around her.

'Oh dear, Mr Benedict has left,' Aunt Stark said. 'And I did so want to . . . Laura dear,' she exclaimed as she hurried to her side, 'why such a long face?' She eased her ample body next to Laura's. 'Listen, love, I know your father's announcement last night came as a surprise, but he did the right thing. You would have shilly-shallied until Edgar had given you up, you know. Remember he is the best catch in Galveston, and there are lots of hooks baited for him if you let him get away!'

'Aunt Stark,' Laura did not look up. 'I don't love Edgar Skelton, and I cannot marry him.'

'My dear little goose!' her aunt protested. 'I was just as hesitant when my father promised me to the late Herbert Stark. But he was right, you know. Love grows with time. We had a—a good marriage, when all's said and done. My father knew what was best for me, just as Lucas knows what is best for his little girl!' She patted Laura's hand. 'Now we must start planning. June would be a lovely month for the wedding, don't you think?'

'I know how much this means to you, Aunt. And I am truly sorry. But I will not marry him.'

Aunt Stark jumped to her feet. 'You are an ungrateful girl! After all I have done for you! Well, we'll see what your father has to say about this. Edgar must not see you while you're in this mood! I'll send William round to the Pelican Inn to say you don't feel well and can't see him this afternoon.' She tossed her head indignantly. 'By tomorrow, let's hope you have come to your senses!'

Laura did in fact have a headache later in the day and would have asked to be excused from dinner that night, had not Maria told her that her father had especially requested that she be present. She dressed slowly, dreading what was to come, for by now Aunt Stark had surely told him of his daughter's rebellious declaration earlier that day. She took her place quietly at the dining-room table, steeling herself for an angry outburst, but nothing was said until the meal was almost over. Then, after a strained and silent dinner, Trevor put down his crystal water-goblet with a heavy hand.

'Laura,' he said firmly, 'I have decided that your

wedding will take place in exactly four weeks. I have told Father Renaldo to begin announcing the banns this Sunday.'

Laura looked over at her father with dismay.

'Four weeks?' Aunt Stark cried. 'But that's impossible, Lucas!'

'And, Laura,' he turned his full attention on his daughter as his sister jumped up in horror, 'I want to have a few words with you after dinner. It will be brief, for I have an important meeting tonight.'

'Lucas, I won't have this!' Aunt Stark cried, her face crimson.

'Four weeks!' Lucas Trevor said again as if that was the end of it.

His sister glared at him, then turned and, still protesting loudly, bustled out of the room.

Only moments later, he rose from his chair and motioned to Laura to follow him into the parlour. Once he had closed the door firmly behind them, he strode to his humidor and picked out a cigar. With his back to her, he spoke slowly and deliberately. 'Your aunt has told me that you do not intend to go through with this marriage. Is this true?'

Laura watched him, as he lit his cigar and the smoke began lazily to circle his head. She took a deep breath. 'You know perfectly well, Father, that I have all along refused Edgar Skelton's proposal of marriage. Had you once asked me how I felt about him,' her voice quavered, 'you could have spared us both the embarrassment we suffered last night. You must know that I will never marry a man I don't love.'

'Love?' The word exploded from her father's lips. 'I suppose what I saw on the balcony last night—letting that overdressed young dandy kiss you—I suppose you call that love?' He made a conscious effort to control his temper, and when he continued, his voice was cold. 'Once before, you defied my wishes when you refused to go back to Santa Clara with Father Jiminez. But that was the last time. You will now do as I say.'

Laura, too, fought back her anger. 'Is this to be a test of wills?' she asked evenly. 'For you must know that I also am strong willed. You cannot force me to do anything I know is wrong, Father.'

'You are still young.' Trevor did not look directly at her but examined the end of his cigar, turning it over slowly between his fingers. 'You have no idea what is best for you. I am your father. I have always advised you, supported you.'

'Supported me? When have you ever asked me what I want?' Laura cried. 'If you persist in this, Father, I shall pack up and go. I'll leave, but you may be sure it will not be as Edgar Skelton's wife!'

'That's enough!' Trevor strode angrily across the room and threw his cigar into the empty fireplace. 'We will not discuss this any more.' He walked quickly to the door, but as he reached it, Laura hurled at him,

'Father, I know now why you want to be rid of me!'

He froze, his hand still on the doorknob, and turned slowly to face her. 'Get rid of you? What are you talking about?'

Laura moved towards him. 'I never knew why you wanted to send me away to Santa Clara, or why you want me to marry Edgar Skelton. Either way would serve your purpose, I see that now. I would be miles away from Crosswinds, and that is really what you want, isn't it?'

'What nonsense is this?'

'I know everything now, Father, and I understand.' She came closer to him and held out her hands. But he stood there, staring down at her as if ready to spring away if she touched him. 'Please, we must talk about it. Don't you see? I know now that when you look at me you are reminded of what happened here that terrible night. Please, Father, you must talk to me! There is so much I need to know. Let me help you to share the pain and the guilt.'

'Wait! Wait a minute!' He shook his head as if to stop the rush of her words. 'How—How did you find out?'

'That's not important. But we mustn't let something that happened so many years ago come between us still!'

He moved away from her, his face suddenly drained of colour. He looked wildly around the room, seeming uncertain where to go. Then slowly, unsteadily, he went over to the divan and sank heavily on to it as though the weight of his years had suddenly fallen on him.

'Father, what is it?' Stricken at the sudden change in him, she ran and knelt before him. 'I'm sorry to bring it up to you now, for I know how much you loved her,' she whispered, her hands on his knees.

It seemed an eternity that he sat there, not moving. Then he lifted his eyes to her, but they were curiously unfocused and empty, as if he were looking at a ghost. She reached over and gently touched his cheek. His hand moved up to cover hers, then he grasped it tightly and held it. Laura dared not breathe at the unexpected tenderness of the gesture, the sudden closeness between them, unlike anything she had dared to hope for.

He sat perfectly still until, as though waking from a sweet, long-ago dream, he lowered her hand to his knee, where he cradled it with the other. He turned it over slowly in his own. At last he spoke. 'I wonder how many miles of pink ribbons . . .' he said softly. 'They were always pink ribbons . . . How many miles of them did she thread through those pieces of lace . . . those petticoats. Her hands—they worked so surely, so quickly.'

'Oh, you must have loved her so,' Laura whispered. He looked straight at her, but the vacancy in his eyes frightened her. 'Father?'

'Every time you speak, it's her voice I hear.' He

released her hand and reached out to touch the loose waves of her hair. 'Your hair, so like hers . . . You have her dark eyes, full of fire. It's her step on the stairs I hear. The way you move, she moved. Her skin, like silk under my fingers, your skin. God help me, when I come into the room and see you, I start to call her name.'

Laura listened, moved by his unabashed sentiment. Yet slowly, as she began to comprehend his halting words, she tensed. 'Father, look at me.' For, although his eyes were still on her, he was not seeing her. 'I don't understand. Mother's hair was not black like mine. She was fair.' Laura raised her eyes to the portrait of Amanda Trevor over the mantelpiece. 'I don't look anything like her. I've always wished I did, so that you might have loved me more. But . . . who are you talking about?'

Slowly a change came over him as he sat there. His eyes sharpened. He seemed actually to see her now, kneeling before him. He drew his hand away from her hair and stared at it as if noting the reality of it for the first time. A look of total bewilderment crossed his face.

She drew back, then quickly got to her feet. As she stood looking down at him, her eyes were wide. 'I remind you of someone else, is that it? Are you telling me that—that Amanda Trevor was not my mother?' Trevor tried to get up, holding tight to the arm of the small sofa. 'Is that what you're saying?' Laura persisted.

At last he managed to pull himself up, and stared at her, his eyes hard. The fear had left them, and she saw outrage there, a rapid return to the harshness she had seen so many times when he had dismissed her from his presence. 'I thought . . . you said . . . you knew,' he said coldly.

'I think I do now, Father. But, if that is true, you must tell me why? Why have you let me believe . . . ?'

'Get out,' he said. 'Make me say no more.'

'Who was she? You owe me that! Who was my real mother, for the love of God?'

'I will not say it again,' Lucas Trevor told her. 'Leave this room this instant!'

Laura, stunned, stared at him. It was obvious that the door between them, which had opened so briefly, had slammed sharply shut again. She no longer existed for him. With a cry, she fled from the room.

Laura did not sleep that night. At first morning light she was still sitting bolt upright on the needlepoint stool of her dressing-stand, where she had spent the black hours holding fast to her silver cross. She had gone to her bedchamber after her father's unwitting revelation in the parlour and had searched desperately for the memento left to her by her mother. She had finally found it tucked away in a drawer where Maria had laid it months before. As she turned it over in her hand and felt the rough inscription on the back—'Defend, O Lord, this child'—she remembered how many times she had stared at the portrait in the parlour, puzzled that the cool and elegant Amanda Trevor, with a wealth of handsome jewellery, had left her child such a simple legacy as a crude silver cross.

Maria had told her that her mother had herself etched the brief prayer on the back of it. Laura could not imagine those pale, bloodless hands in the portrait capable of doing such a thing. Nor could she understand that same woman telling the maid of her dearest wish —that her child keep the cross always with her. None of this had made sense to Laura, and in time she stopped studying the portrait and formed her own, warmer image of the woman who had given her life. But who was her mother, then? How could she find out? As she sat there, the significance of Maria's words to her months before came clear: 'When your mother gave this cross to me to keep for you . . .' The maid had received the cross from her mother's own hands . . . she had promised to keep it until Laura was old enough to wear it—of course! Maria had known her. She would certainly be able to tell her who she was!

Laura jumped up, slipped the cross back among the handkerchiefs where she had found it, and made her way quickly downstairs in the quiet house. The light in the wide hall was grey, for the morning sky hung leaden above the island, and there was an eerie stillness in the air that usually foreshadowed a squall later in the day. She moved through the dining-room and heard the sound of Maria's voice in the kitchen. She let herself quietly into the pantry, then hesitated at the kitchen threshold, for the maid was arguing with a man at the open back door. They spoke in Spanish, and discussed a basket of oysters which sat at Maria's feet.

'You can indeed charge other people too much money,' came the maid's voice, 'but you know I will pay you only a fair price, so save your breath!'

The man shrugged, and kicked the basket so that it slid past Maria and into the room. 'I cannot argue with you,' he said.

Her laugh was light. '*Por Dios*, if we do not argue, what will we talk about?'

For just an instant Laura saw the face of the man as he leaned forward through the door. One of his eyes stared white, opaque and sightless. She backed away quickly. She had seen him before. But where? Then it came to her. He had been on the quay the night of the pirate raid, and had picked her up in his arms as the small boat pitched against the piling. He had been one of them —one of the pirates! She held her breath while Maria paid him and sent him on his way. When she was sure that he had gone, Laura walked into the kitchen.

Maria was surprised to see her. 'Up so early, *niña*? My, what a way to start a day, fighting with the fisherman!' She smiled. 'He is such a scoundrel! He charges too much money, but not here. He knows he cannot fool me!'

'I have seen him before. What is his name, Maria?'

'Cayo Aristo. He would have you believe he is the best fisherman on the island, and that is perhaps the only truth to pass his lips. He was born knowing these waters. But I can understand how you might fear him.' She shook her head. 'He lost his eye, as a boy, when it was pierced by a fish hook.'

'But he was one of them,' Laura cried. 'One of the pirates! I saw him that night!'

'Pirates?' Maria smiled. 'But no, *niña*, you are mistaken. Your memory of that night is blurred, for you also thought they had taken your cross, remember? Now——' she bent to examine her purchase '—are these not fine oysters?'

'Maria,' Laura put a hand on her shoulder. 'You must help me. You knew my mother! Tell me, who was she?'

Her words startled the maid. 'Who was she? *Madre mía*, but of course Señora Trevor . . .'

'Stop! No more lies, please! I learned last night that Amanda Trevor was not my real mother, Maria. I must know who she was, and you are the only one who can help me!'

Maria's eyes widened in astonishment. 'You were . . . never to know. But who told you of this?'

'My father, last night. I doubt if he even knows what he said, but he described another woman he loved . . . my mother! It was not Amanda Trevor. That's all I know. Please, for the love of God, you must tell me who she was! You knew her!'

But Maria looked away. 'I . . . can't. I have made a vow before God never to say a word to anyone.'

'Who made you promise that?' When Maria did not answer, Laura pressed her. 'Was it my father?' The Mexican woman nodded slowly. 'Is she . . . still alive? At least you can tell me that!'

'Yes,' Maria replied, 'but you must not . . . Please!' She turned beseeching eyes on her mistress. 'You must not try to find her. It would only bring pain. And, believe me, *niña*, your father made sure that she was well provided for. He was very generous.'

Laura stared at the black eyes of her maid. 'Generous? Do you mean . . . that he *paid* her for me?'

'She loved you! She loved you more than life, *niña*, and she would have done anything, anything to keep you. But she had nothing—only a silver cross—to give you, while your father had so much!'

'But she gave up her own child for money! What kind of love is that? What sort of woman was she, who would sell her own child?'

'No! I have said it all wrong. Please, you must listen! Don't turn away from me. I only thank the Holy Mother that you will soon be far away from this house to start a new life. It is full of sorrows here, *niña*. There are things I cannot tell you—so many things!'

But Laura had already walked across the kitchen to the pantry door. Maria called after her, 'You would not ask me to break my vow! Oh, please, forgive me . . .'

Laura stood at the threshold, then turned back. 'It is my *mother* I cannot forgive,' she said. Then, in a voice suddenly cold, she added, 'When William comes in, send him to me. I have an errand for him.' She said no more, but disappeared through the doorway without a backward glance.

Aunt Stark discovered her niece seated at the dining-room table when she came downstairs half an hour later. 'I knew you'd come round, love,' she trilled happily at Laura. 'William tells me you've sent a note to the Pelican Inn asking Edgar to come here this morning. You're a sensible girl, and I'm delighted that you listened to your father's good advice.' She sat down in her chair at one end of the table, careful to fold back the frothy ruching at the cuffs of her yellow morning gown as she cut into the fruit of her mango. 'When Edgar gets here—poor dear! won't the early date surprise him?—we'll get him to help us with the wedding plans. But what was Lucas thinking of? Only four weeks!'

Laura said nothing, but sat as cold as stone, determined to push all thoughts and questions aside for ever about the identity of the woman who had deserted her—had *sold* her! She had made up her mind, sitting here in the quiet house, to concentrate now only on her present plight—Edgar Skelton! Besides the fact that she did not love him, she now had the added knowledge of her illegitimacy to put before him: surely two compelling reasons for him to agree that the marriage must not take place? She no longer cared what her father might say. It was clear to her now that he wanted to be rid of her; not because she was a painful reminder to him of Amanda Trevor's tragic death, but of an illicit love affair! She was even prepared to put up with Aunt Stark's fury at the change in plans. For now, she had only one duty—to free herself from the engagement that had been forced on her.

When Lord Skelton arrived just an hour later, the early date of the proposed wedding was indeed a surprise to him. It did not unduly upset him, however, as Aunt Stark was pleased to note. 'Come,' she said as she led the way into the parlour. 'We can start on the list of guests.'

Laura put a restraining hand on his arm. 'I must speak to you,' she told him. And to her aunt, she said, 'Lord Skelton and I are going out for a walk.'

Aunt Stark was quick to protest. 'A walk? My dear child, have you seen the sky? Mercy, Laura, there's a storm coming!'

But Laura was already fastening her bonnet under her chin, and Maria had been sent to fetch her cloak. 'We won't go far.'

'Well, if you must,' her aunt fretted. 'But stay close to the house and return quickly! We have so much planning to do!'

Once alone out on the Strand, Lord Skelton made known his displeasure at Laura's stubbornness. 'I should not give in to you,' he told her, holding tight to the brim of his hat against the rising wind. 'You are an impetuous child, Laura, and will not always get your own way, you know.'

'I am not a child,' she said, but he did not hear her as he bent further into the wind. Perhaps it is just as well, she thought, for I need his patience and understanding today, not his censure. When they had walked along the sea wall for a short distance, he suggested that they turn back. 'Just a little further, and we'll be on the beach!' she called.

'No!' he protested. 'This is quite far enough, and it's beginning to rain.'

She turned back to smile at him. 'You need not humour me after today, Lord Skelton, I promise you.'

In a few minutes they reached the eastern end of the wall, and he helped her down the steps to the sand. She saw a sheltered spot behind an overturned boat, where they could be out of the rain, and pointed to it. 'We can sit over there.'

'Good Lord!' he cried. 'Do we have to sit at all?' Still, he followed a few reluctant paces behind, then stood uncomfortably watching her as she gathered her billowing skirts close to her and sat down in the lee of the derelict vessel. His hesitation in joining her signalled his profound disapproval, but in time he moved next to her and sat stiffly at her side.

'There,' she said. 'Isn't that better?'

'Certainly not,' he said shortly. 'It smells of fish!'

'And so it should, since this is a fishing-boat!' Laura said lightly, hoping to defer for a little while the declaration she must make to him. She looked out at the churning sea only a few yards away, where each new wave that crashed on shore sent up fine sprays of foam. She filled her lungs with the clean pure air that blew in on them, and felt again the strong kinship with sand, sea and sky she had always known, as if only in this special environment was her spirit set free.

Finally she turned to Lord Skelton. 'I don't know how to say this to you, my lord, so I will simply say it outright. You know that my father's announcement of our engagement last night was made without my consent. I cannot marry you. I have already told my father that there will be no wedding.'

He appeared to find her words amusing, for he laughed thinly and tugged at one corner of his moustache. 'And what did your father say to that?'

'It's not between my father and me,' she told him. 'It is between the two of us.'

'You're wrong, my dear,' he told her. 'It is very much his business and mine. We made an agreement, an irrevocable pact, which will not be broken.'

'If you're speaking of my dowry, a dowry is certainly not an irrevocable pact!'

'It's a bit more than a dowry, Laura. If you must know—and I think now that you should—your father has settled a substantial amount of money on me to take you to England as my wife. It's done all the time. Rich Americans seem to enjoy buying old titles for their daughters. Come, you mustn't look so horrified! The papers are signed and were duly sealed yesterday. The thing is done.'

Laura stared at him. 'Then it must be undone!' she cried.

When he merely shrugged, she went on slowly, deliberately. 'You should know, Edgar, that I was . . . born out of wedlock. I am not my father's legitimate daughter. Amanda Trevor was not my mother.'

She waited, astounded to see that Edgar seemed to

find this amusing. 'Well, well!' he said lightly. 'And I suppose you'll tell me next that you have eleven toes on one foot and three on the other? Believe me, this is a matter best left to your father and me to decide. Look, it's raining harder.'

Laura jumped to her feet. 'I'm telling you the truth!' She glared down at him. 'How *could* you marry me, knowing the truth about me?'

'Oh, come!' Edgar too, pulled himself up slowly to face her. 'If this is so, then tell me who was the woman who brought you into the world? Her *name*, Laura!'

Laura faltered. 'I—I don't know.'

'There! It's truly extraordinary, my dear, to what lengths you will go to try to put a stop to our marriage. In no way can you change anything. It will take place in four weeks, so spare yourself any further concern. Ah, see, it's raining hard! I've really had . . .'

'But you don't love me! And I don't love you.'

'Love has nothing to do with this! Now, come, I've had quite enough.' He held her arm.

She wrenched away from him. 'But . . . I love another man!' she blurted out, not knowing where the words came from, but knowing only that she spoke the truth. She knew it now, as she must have known it from the first moment she looked into the pirate's eyes. Suddenly she turned and began to walk quickly up the beach, wanting to get as far away from him as she could. She heard his voice: 'Come back here this instant!'

She began to run now on the slippery sand, the wind behind her. She did not feel the warm rain that poured from a leaden sky. The ribbons at her throat came loose and her bonnet blew off, releasing her hair to the rough mercy of the gale. Still she ran faster, her tears mixing with the rain. She lost first one slipper, then the other, but did not stop. As she ran, her cries lost in the thunder of the surf and the screaming wind, she felt herself slip out of time into another dimension, as though the present had collapsed in an instant and she was a child again.

She had been running like this then, too, away from the sight of a wounded rabbit struggling to free itself from a trap. She had come upon the terrified creature in an isolated *arroyo* outside the mission school at Santa Clara, and had seen the fear and helplessness in the animal's crazed eyes and been unable to do anything to help. She had turned and fled then as she was fleeing now, only now it was *she* who was trapped just as surely as the rabbit had been! She pushed on through the lashing rain, struggling to breathe against the whipping wind, and all at once her feet stumbled on an outcrop of rock jutting out of the beach. She fell face down, her cloak tumbling about her, and lay there, her cheek against the roughness of the sand. Her fingers dug deep into it as if to find some surface she could cling to, but it fell away in her fingers. She did not know how long she lay there, overwhelmed with despair. She might have lost consciousness. She did not know.

But suddenly she was roused by a voice carried on the wind. It was the pirate's voice: 'Laura, Laura!' She opened her eyes and searched the foam of the angry waves as they crashed on to the beach below her. His voice came again. She struggled to her feet, and looked around. For a moment she thought she saw him, just as he had looked on the night he had first burst into her life through the balcony doors at Crosswinds. With a cry she ran towards him, but he had vanished. There was no one there—only the stinging rain which, with the quickening darkness, had obscured even the sand dunes behind her. Oh, heaven, she thought wildly—so this is madness!

She pulled her wet cloak tightly round her and set out again, turning this time away from the sea towards the town, her breath coming more quickly. It was impossible to close her ears to the roar of the wind as she leaned into it, pushing her way into the darkness, her face stinging as the rain, driven almost horizontally in the wicked gusts, pounded her unmercifully. There was no feeling in her hands or feet, but she ached in every other part, her body deathly cold as though the blood had congealed in her veins. She had no idea where she was going. She did not care. She only knew that she must keep moving. Over and over again she lost her footing in among the dark sand dunes, pulling herself up only by the sheerest will-power, not daring to rest for fear she might be caught up in a swirling eddy and washed out to sea.

At last she felt herself on more solid ground, and paused for a moment. The rain was lessening now, and she could see that she stood at the eastern end of town. It was only a few hundred yards to where the pavement began. She pushed on, and once she had reached it, she made her way past shop-fronts shuttered against the storm. Nothing appeared familiar to her. It was a ghost town, the small buildings huddled together as though cringing from the recent fury of the elements.

She kept close to the boarded-up shops to keep out of the wind. The street still churned with an angry flume of water, and she stumbled on a hard object. It surfaced for a moment, and she saw that it was the wooden sign that had hung outside Madame Georges's shop. In an instant it was swept along in the receding water, and she watched as it rose and fell in the swift current. As the sky began to brighten, she saw that she was just outside the dressmaker's front door. The wide bow window had been boarded up, but she was able to make her way to the door, and leaned gratefully against its familiar panels until her breath returned. When she was able, she lifted one hand and rapped sharply. Then again, louder this time, when there was no answer. At last she heard the click of a latch against the noise of the wind. The door opened slowly, only a crack, then swung wide as the wind caught it.

Madame Georges stood there, her black hair tumbling loose to her waist. When she saw Laura, she reached out and pulled her inside. Quickly together, they managed to shut the door behind them. 'Oh, Mademoiselle,' she cried. 'What are you doing out in this storm?'

Laura fell into her arms. 'Please,' she gasped, 'Madame, help me!'

'Stay here,' Madame said. 'I'll get you a blanket.'

'The fire, Madame. Let me warm myself at your fire!'

'No,' Madame protested. 'Stay here.'

But Laura had already broken away and run back into the small apartment, where a bright fire crackled on the hearth. She went to it and knelt down, holding her hands out gratefully to the flames which sought to survive the sharp gusts of wind that blasted down the chimney.

'Thérèse?' A man's voice called from the stairs at one side of the hearth. 'Where the devil did I leave my boots?'

Startled, Laura looked up to see a tall figure emerging from the darkness of the landing, and as the light fell on his face all the breath left her body. Sloan Benedict stood there, his hair tousled, his chest bare as he pulled on his shirt. For just an instant, their eyes met and held. Then, quick as a cat, he stepped back into the shadows. Paralysed with disbelief, Laura could not take her eyes from where he had been.

Madame Georges spoke from just behind her. 'Please, Mademoiselle,' she said, 'you do not understand. It is not what it appears to be!'

Laura jumped to her feet, and with a cry she gathered up her wet skirts, pushed past the dressmaker and ran back through the shop. She threw open the door and began to fight her way blindly back to Crosswinds, unmindful now of the cold wet cobbles under her feet; unmindful of a voice, *his* voice, calling to her, 'Laura! Laura!' over the howling of the wind.

CHAPTER FIVE

AUNT STARK was in her glory. The October day was bright under a cloudless sky, perfect weather for John Messersmith's boating-party to honour the engaged couple. Her new navy and white costume had been extravagantly admired, and she was pleased to see that her niece was behaving quite as a young bride-to-be should. Only the day before, she had told her brother over the breakfast coffee, 'Laura has been such a lamb, Lucas!' As indeed she was, for she had shown a docile willingness to comply with the many demands which must be met to prepare for the nuptials only one week away. Aunt Stark stood at the railing of the small river steamer as it ploughed its way through sparkling blue waters of the Gulf. The voyage so far had been smooth. They had passed small shrimp-boats, large cargo vessels from all parts of the world and now, as Laura joined her aunt at the starboard rail, a school of porpoises plunged playfully in the wake of the boat.

'Aren't they dear little things?' Aunt Stark exclaimed. But because she always experienced a feeling of disquiet whenever she found herself on the water, she added, 'I hope the captain knows what he's doing, love. I should hate to be washed up on some foreign shore in a storm!'

At the prospect of such peril befalling them on a short forty-five minute crossing from Galveston to Port Bolivar on the mainland, Laura laughed aloud. The sound of her own laughter startled her, for she had not heard it in a long time. In truth, the festive air of the day's outing had lightened her spirits. She listened now to the raucous cry of the seagulls which had followed them, wheeling and dipping, all the way from the pier at Galveston. Bright green and yellow pennants festooned the awninged deck behind her and snapped and fluttered in the soft breeze. Sprightly music drifted in the morning air as a small orchestra hired for the day sought to entertain the guests.

Laura loved the broad waters of the Gulf in any kind of weather, and welcomed the change it effected in her mood. For three weeks now she had moved numbly through her days, prepared to let her marriage to Edgar Skelton take place. The part of her that mattered—the thinking, feeling and caring part—had diminished to only a small enclosed corner next to her heart, which she kept securely locked. Edgar Skelton's constrained manner with her since the morning she had run from him up the storm-swept beach demanded nothing of her, she supposed, but a contrite heart. He did in fact treat her like an unreasonable child who had misbehaved, been properly chastised and, it was to be hoped, had learned a lesson from it. Aunt Stark's scolding of her on her return to Crosswinds that morning, soaked and shivering, was predictable. 'Imagine setting off like that, alone,' she had cried. 'Poor dear Edgar was worried sick! I told him what a young gypsy you used to be, Laura, going off like that when you were young. Well, marriage will settle you down. Edgar will see to that!'

Her aunt spoke suddenly beside her. 'I wonder where Edgar is. He should be here at your side, I should think!' She studied with approval her niece's pale apricot *gros de Naples* bonnet, which framed the lovely face so becomingly. 'Now, you must be nicer to him, Laura,' she whispered. 'Make more effort. You're such a pretty thing, dear, and can be so amusing when you want to be. Just look around you!' She made a rapid sweep with her bright eyes at the elegant ladies who strolled up and down with their escorts on the crowded deck. 'There is not a woman here who will not still try to steal him from you. I will feel easy only after Father Renaldo bestows his final blessing on your union next week!'

Laura nodded absently, for by now she was tending to ignore her aunt's continuous prattle. She was aware that Edgar's secretary, Michael Norton, had joined them at the rail. The young man had been much in evidence today, stalking through the crowds, speaking to everyone as though he shared the host's duties.

Aunt Stark made no secret of her dislike for the 'young cockle-burr, permanently affixed to poor dear Edgar's side', as she had called him. At the sight of the secretary in his spruce coat and carefully tied cravat, Laura's aunt was quick to ask, 'Where is Lord Skelton? Have you seen him, Mr Norton?'

He managed a strained smile for the ladies, and when he spoke his voice was smoothly condescending. 'Edgar is pretending an interest in local politics with Mr Trevor and Mr Messersmith,' he replied. 'I can't think why, for I know he finds the subject tiresome.'

'Well,' said Aunt Stark sharply, anxious to be rid of him and seeing from his languid stance at Laura's side that he had no intention of leaving, 'I shall go and fetch him!'

She bustled off, and Laura was left alone with the young secretary. She liked him no more than did her aunt, but made an effort to be polite. 'This has been a long stay for you, Mr Norton. I suspect you are anxious to return to your own home in England?'

'My home,' he told her archly, patting at his cravat, 'is Edgar's home. I, too, live at Olney, you know.'

'Oh?' Laura was surprised. In Lord Skelton's few allusions to his ancestral home, he had failed to mention that his secretary lived in the big house with him.

'You'll find it so different there,' Norton said, watching her. 'Perhaps very different from what you expect!'

'I'm sure of it,' she told him. 'When over five thousand miles separate our two countries, there is bound to be a difference.'

'Yes,' he went on. 'Our pleasures at Olney are simple ones.'

'Good,' said Laura, shielding her eyes from the brilliant play of sun on sparkling water. 'I look forward to it.'

'And,' he ran his eyes up and down Laura's figured chintz gown, 'in the matter of dress, too, you may be in for a surprise. We dress rather less . . . er, flamboyantly than seems to be the case here.'

'Better and better! Now, if you will excuse me.'

He laid a restraining hand on her arm before she could turn away. 'You surprise me,' he said, 'for your own taste in gowns is rather extravagant, I've noticed.' When she made no comment, he went on, 'Speaking of dress, I've been meaning to ask if you know how I might get in touch with that planter from South Carolina. I saw you dancing together, so I assume you know something of him. Benedict, I think his name was.'

Laura felt her cheeks flush. 'Why do you ask?' she said evenly.

'He was wearing a waistcoat I greatly admired, and I meant to get from him the name of his tailor in Paris, but had no chance.'

'I cannot help you, Mr Norton, for I know nothing about him. Nothing!' In an effort to be normally conversational despite the quickening beat of her heart, she went on, 'But didn't you think that Mr Benedict's taste in clothes was perhaps too ostentatious, since, as you say, you prefer more simple dress?'

'Listen, *I* don't!' the young man protested. 'It's Edgar. He's just like his father used to be. The old earl dressed in such dreary, old-fashioned attire. But, as I keep telling Edgar, he shouldn't go to London looking like a vicar in a country parish, should he?'

'London? Lord Skelton and I will be spending time in London, then? He has not mentioned it to me.'

'I doubt that you will be obliged to accompany him there. Such a dirty town,' Norton announced primly. 'No, we keep a small set of rooms there, he and I, for when his presence is required in the House of Lords.'

At Laura's expression of surprise, he went on smoothly, 'You would not expect him to go there without his secretary, would you?'

Before he had a chance to continue, John Messersmith's big voice rang from the back of the deck. 'Friends,' he called out, 'we'll be putting in at Port Bolivar pretty soon so that you can all stretch your legs. Be sure to watch for our sailing in one hour's time, for otherwise you'll have to swim the two miles back to Galveston!'

A ripple of amusement passed through the assembled guests. Edgar Skelton, who had been only briefly at his fiancée's side since the excursion began, appeared just in time to help Laura down the gangway. Remembering Aunt Stark's admonition to make more effort with him, Laura suggested they join half a dozen of the guests who planned to venture to the top of the lighthouse, a handsome edifice newly built at the point of land that separated Galveston Bay from the Gulf.

But Lord Skelton declined. 'I have seen enough water in my time,' he told her briskly.

There, thought Laura, I have tried to be nice! 'I'll go alone, then,' she announced, and when he did not protest, she gave him her parasol to hold, then made her way to the foot of the tower. She slowly climbed the narrow, twisting stairway, holding her full skirt to one side, and at last reached the top. As she moved to make way for those behind, she found herself surrounded by a wide window of glass that stretched across all four sides of the small room, and gasped at the breathtaking expanse of water and sky that shimmered as far as the eye could see.

Towards the south, the tiny island of Galveston lay like a grey smudge on the horizon, barren and featureless. It seemed so small and insignificant, a bit of débris in the calm basin of the Gulf. She would not miss that thirty-two-mile stretch of sandbar, she knew. Nor, God help her, would she miss anyone on it. Certainly not her father, for he was more distant now than he had ever been. She would not even miss Aunt Stark, for although the little woman had been kind and singularly attentive, her frivolous interests and constant chatter had become increasingly irksome. As for Madame Georges—the one person on the island whom Laura had truly liked and respected—how could she ever feel the same way about her after what she had seen in her small apartment only three weeks before? And Sloan Benedict—no, she dare not even think of him! It was enough that he still haunted her dreams; she would not let him invade her conscious thoughts, for the pain *he* had caused her was the cruellest hurt of all.

She felt a nudge at her elbow, and turned to see Michael Norton again at her side. 'Pretty ladies have no business looking sad, Laura,' he said.

Not for the first time, Laura resented his overly familiar manner with her when they were alone. She looked away from him. 'It would almost appear that you are following me, Mr Norton.'

'I only hoped to conclude our conversation,' he said.

'I thought we had.'

Her abrupt manner did not deter him, for he went on, 'You will miss all this, won't you?' He swept one arm in a wide arc.

'I suspect I shall,' Laura agreed, trying to soften her earlier sharp tone with him. 'But I look forward to seeing your country, too.'

'I hope you won't feel out of place, my dear,' he said.

'Our ladies don't go strutting around in feathers and ribbons, and no dark banditos swagger up and down our main streets with guns in their belts. And as for cut-throat pirates bursting into an English drawing-room, why . . .'

'Pirates?' John Messersmith had moved up behind them and put his arm lightly round Laura's waist. 'That's a mighty romantic notion, my boy! We haven't had a pirate in these waters since Jean LaFitte, and he's been pushing up six feet of Galveston soil for ten years now.' He mopped his red face, still glowing from the exertion of climbing the steps.

'Have you forgotten that pirate who forced his way into Mr Trevor's house last spring?' Norton demanded. 'Surely you remember him, Mr Messersmith. I understand he made off with your solid gold watch!'

Messersmith laughed heartily. 'God, yes!' he bellowed. 'I thought I'd never see it again. But they were a butter-fingered lot, leaving everything behind the way they did!'

Norton smiled knowingly. 'That pirate wasn't interested in a few paltry trinkets. He was after bigger game by far that night!'

'Oh?' Messersmith studied the young man with amusement. 'You seem to know a lot about that young scallywag, my boy!'

'Scallywag? He's a thief, a conniving thief, and the hangman's noose is waiting for him, my friend.'

Messersmith, who did not consider himself a friend of Michael Norton by any stretch of the imagination, was suddenly aware that Laura had taken his arm and leaned now against him. He looked down at her. 'What's the matter, Laurie? You're white as a sheet!'

'I—I suddenly feel faint,' she whispered.

Messersmith was all concern. 'Come along, I'll get you back down on solid ground. A lot of people feel queasy, being so high up, honey.' Laura let herself be led slowly down the narrow twisting stairs, holding tight to the railing. 'A few more steps,' he assured her. 'Just lean on me.'

He circled her waist with his arm, and Laura welcomed his strength for she had lost all of her own. But why, she wondered, furious with herself, had Michael Norton's words upset her so? Why should the mere confirmation of what she had known all along make any difference? Had she not known from the very beginning that Sloan Benedict was a thief? Still, when she and John Messersmith reached the bottom, her knees had turned to water and she leaned her full weight against him.

When Messersmith spotted Edgar Skelton standing alone at the edge of the water, he tucked Laura's arm in his and together they strolled across the grass to the stone embankment. 'Here, Skelton,' he called. 'Take care of your lady! She pretty near fainted up there.' He waited while Skelton climbed the slippery rocks and joined them. When he did, he was quite out of breath. 'I'll leave you with her now, Skelton,' Messersmith told him. And to Laura, he said, 'You'll be all right now?'

She assured him that she would, and in truth, the fresh air and brilliant sunshine had somewhat restored her strength. Just before John Messersmith turned to leave them, he said to Skelton, 'That young secretary of yours seems intent on scaring the ladies half to death, with his talk of pirates and hangings!' He stooped down to kiss Laura lightly on the cheek, then left them.

Skelton moved instantly to Laura's side. 'What did Michael say up there, Laura?'

'It isn't so much what Mr Norton said,' Laura lied, 'but he really is a most unpleasant man. I don't like him.'

'Come now,' Skelton began, his pale eyes probing hers. 'He can be a nuisance at times, I know. But what did he say to upset you?'

'Everything he says upsets me! Is it true that he will live with us at Olney?'

'He told you that?' Laura nodded. He opened her parasol and held it over her head to shield her from the hot sun. 'It's a big house. I doubt you'll even know that he's in it. What else did he say?'

'It doesn't matter,' Laura told him, taking her parasol from him.

'All right, we'll say no more about it, then. He's not a bad lad, really. He just needs a little straightening out now and again. You go on ahead, but be assured that I shall have a chat with Michael.'

Laura, glad that the subject was closed, turned from him and walked slowly away to join the others on the quay.

At that moment Michael Norton emerged from the door of the lighthouse. Skelton called to him immediately, and motioned him over to his side. 'What in God's name have you been saying to Laura?' he demanded.

'Nothing!' The secretary drew back, instantly on the defensive and no little annoyed. 'Why? What lies has she been telling you?'

'Keep away from her, do you hear? We've come too far to let anything go wrong now.'

'I don't know why you had to become involved with that girl, anyway!' he retorted sulkily.

'*That girl*, as you call her, is our insurance for the future, and you'd do well not to forget it! It's the present we have to concern ourselves with. We've only one more week to accomplish what we've set out to do!'

Norton snorted. 'We've done all we can, it seems to me. The bait is set. The fisherman is to let us know the instant that thief comes ashore. God knows, you crossed his palm with enough Judas money!'

'Hold your tongue,' Skelton whispered harshly. 'And just mind yourself, Michael. Keep away from Laura. She dislikes you intensely.'

'Well, for that matter, I can't say I'm fond of her!'

'Enough! Now, it's time we joined the festivities.' He gave his secretary a push, and together they walked across the grass to the pier.

CHAPTER SIX

AUNT STARK had managed to do the impossible, she was fond of saying, to plan the wedding and reception in only four short weeks. The chancel at St Ignatius was to be banked with lilies brought in from New Orleans, and Father Renaldo would christen the new vestments made for him by his parishioners, the linens and brocade donated by Lucas Trevor himself. The formal French furnishings of the salon at Crosswinds had been re-covered in palest aquamarine silk, the floors waxed until they gleamed, and the house stood ready for the grand reception the following day. Caterers had already begun to crowd Josefina out of the kitchen with their preliminary preparations for the extravagant buffet that would be set up in the dining-room, the musicians' gilded chairs had been put in place at the far end of the salon, and the Big Day, as Aunt Stark called it, was nearly at hand.

It was not surprising that, on this day before the wedding, she took to her bed with a headache. 'Close the shutters,' she told Laura from under her pale peach coverlet. 'The light hurts my eyes.'

Laura went quickly to the wide windows, untied the braided satin cords that held the rose portières in place, and closed them tight against the bright morning sun. She had been summoned to her aunt's ornate bedroom by Maria, who found her mistress already dressed and working her embroidery down in the open courtyard by nine o'clock. Today was to be the final fitting at Madame Georges's for the wedding gown.

'I can't go with you, love,' Aunt Stark moaned into her cologned handkerchief, 'but just make sure that those little side panels aren't puckered at the seam. Tell Madame . . .'

'Aunt,' Laura protested, 'there's no need for a final fitting! The gown is finished. There'll be no puckering, I know.' She was suddenly stricken at the prospect of being alone with Madame Georges. Since the night she had seen evidence of the dressmaker's romantic tryst with Sloan Benedict, she had mercifully been accompanied by her aunt to the many fittings required to complete her trousseau, so there had been no opportunity for any communication between herself and Madame. 'I'll certainly stay here with you today,' Laura told her aunt. 'I refuse to leave you when you're feeling so wretched!'

'Nonsense,' said Aunt Stark. She looked very small in her chiffon-draped bed, propped up against a mountain of lacy pillows. 'Who ever heard of such a thing? Of course you'll go. I can't stand the thought of that expensive gown being any less than perfect. Oh,' she moaned again, and turned her face into the pillows, 'my poor, poor head! I know Lucas doesn't appreciate all I've done to prepare for tomorrow! Mercy, I'm not even sure I'll be able to be downstairs tonight for the bridal party dinner!'

'Of course you will,' Laura assured her. 'But I must insist on staying here with you today.'

'Laura, Laura,' her aunt pleaded, 'don't cross me! Do as I say. And tell William to pick up the flower order after he brings you back home. John Messersmith promised that the packet from New Orleans would be in by three o'clock. Oh, and send Maria in to me before you go. There are a million things I want her to check. I hope you appreciate what a sacrifice I'm making in allowing Maria to go off to England with you? Mercy, why did this happen to me today, of all days? My poor, poor head!'

Laura saw the futility of further argument and said no more. But it was with a sinking heart that she kissed her aunt lightly on the forehead before she went to fetch her pelisse and bonnet. This is the last full day I shall have to spend in this house, she thought, as she slowly descended the wide staircase. Morning sun flooded the big salon across from her now, and washed the high-ceilinged hall with a shimmering gold light. The graceful oak banister that slipped so easily under her hands had been polished until it shone. The vivid colours of the oriental rug that stretched down the length of the hall glowed with jewel-like clarity in the soft filtered light.

When she reached the bottom step, Laura stood for a moment, looking through the shadowed dining-room into the brightness of the open courtyard beyond. The flat fleshy leaves of the plants that grew in such abundance there under the open sky had been oiled and rubbed, and shone now like giant satin medallions. It was so quiet in the big house that she could even hear the gentle murmur of the garden fountain.

This is the way I shall try to remember Crosswinds, she told herself. But in her heart she knew that always, always when she thought of it, she would see the pirate standing there in the doorway to the salon, with his muddy boots on her father's fine carpet. And in the courtyard she would see Sloan Benedict close to her, his eyes dark, his voice low: 'Who are you? What are you?' She held the curved newel-post and stepped carefully down on to the floor. I shall leave it all, she thought, and gratefully shut the door behind me, blot it all out as if it had never been! Yet, as she made her way to the front door and stepped out on to the balcony to William waiting for her below in the coach, she could almost see the man who haunted her dreams standing in the dark shadows, his arms round her, his lips on hers . . .

She took a deep breath, and called out, 'Here I am, William! I'm sorry I have kept you waiting!'

Laura was relieved to see, upon her arrival at Madame George's shop, that the dressmaker was occupied with another customer. 'I will be only a moment more, Mademoiselle,' she told Laura briskly.

'No matter,' Laura was quick to reply. 'I am in no hurry, Madame. Please take your time.'

'Your gown is hanging behind the screen,' said Madame Georges. 'I shall be in directly to help you into it.' Neither woman looked full at the other during their brief exchange.

Laura slipped behind the Chinese silk screen and slowly began to remove her bonnet, hardly conscious of the soft voices of the two women in the shop. Her eyes fell on her wedding gown, which hung on a silk hanger at one side of the full-length mirror. She stood, transfixed, by the glowing yards of ivory satin skirt, with narrow lace inserts set in panels at the front, the bodice cut low and trimmed with a graceful tucker of French lace. All along the train, which was caught up on another hanger, were dainty clusters of satin rosettes. Laura put out her hand to touch the glistening fabric, when she heard the bell over the front door announce the departure of the customer. In a moment Madame slipped quietly in beside her. Their eyes did not meet as Madame Georges began to take off Laura's pelisse.

'The gown is magnificent, Madame,' Laura began, 'but my aunt expressed some concern about these side panels here . . .' She stopped at the sound of a sudden sharp burst of gunfire from the little alley beside the shop and turned to stare at the dressmaker, who had pulled away, her dark eyes wide. Both women stood listening, and almost immediately heard the back door of Madame's private apartment thrown open, then slammed instantly shut. The bolt was slid quickly into place. Then—silence.

'One moment, Mademoiselle,' Madame Georges cautioned. 'Please stay where you are.'

She disappeared, and Laura stood rigid, listening. When she heard nothing more and feared for Madame's safety, she slipped quickly round the screen and pulled back the curtain that separated the shop from the living quarters. 'Madame?' she whispered.

In the flickering light of the sputtering fire and a single candle above it on the chimney piece, she could at first see nothing in the little room, where the only daylight came from the small curtained window in the back wall. But slowly her eyes were able to distinguish a fallen figure on the floor—a man's figure, lying on his side, his knees drawn up as if in pain. Madame Georges was kneeling beside him, gently pulling open his torn shirt. Laura gasped as she saw a bleeding wound in the man's chest. He was a black man, his dark skin glistening in the half-light.

Madame Georges looked over at her. 'You must leave here immediately, Mademoiselle,' she whispered urgently. 'It is dangerous for you to be here.'

Laura stood frozen in the doorway, as the injured man's head turned in her direction. Their eyes met. She had seen the same expression of pain in the eyes of the kneeling slave out on the Strand. With a cry, she moved to the dressmaker's side. 'Let me help,' she said as she knelt down at Madame's side. 'I've tended patients at the convent hospital, Madame.' When she saw the severity of the wound in the man's chest, however, and the many lacerations on the bruised body, she fought back a wave of dizziness.

'No, no!' Madame insisted. 'Go into the other room!'

At that instant the bell above the shop door rang loudly, and a man's voice cut into the silence. 'Hello! Where's the proprietress here?'

Madame was quickly on her feet. She moved to the curtained doorway where she turned, her eyes seeking Laura's in the semi-darkness. 'Stay here,' she whispered, 'and say nothing!'

When she had disappeared through the door, Laura rose and crept closer to the curtain, hardly daring to breathe. Suddenly a hand was clapped across her mouth from behind, and an arm roughly circled her waist and held her firmly. Terrified, she could not cry out. When she tried to break free, the strong arm only tightened round her.

Madame Georges's voice came from the next room, cool and precise. 'This is a ladies' shop, sir. How dare you burst in here?'

'Where are they?' the man demanded. 'Them runaways! We shot one of them, and they turned into your back alley here.'

'Runaway *slaves*?' Laura could hear the contempt in Madame's voice. 'Here? Do you think for a moment that I would shelter runaway slaves here?'

'They musta come in here, lady,' he went on. 'Step aside, and I'll have a look.'

'Who do you think you are, sir?'

'Town Marshal's office, ma'am. Now, if you'll let me by . . .'

'Indeed I will not!' Madame Georges hurled at him. 'I have a customer in the back room in a state of undress! I shall see to it that you are severely reprimanded if you dare to trespass into my fitting-room. Now—go!' She launched into a furious tirade in rapid French, and it was only a moment before the little bell rang again, and Laura heard the door close firmly behind the intruder.

Slowly the arm loosened around Laura's waist, and the hand came away from over her mouth. She felt the figure behind her step back, and in an instant the curtain parted and Madame Georges reappeared.

A man spoke from the shadows behind where Laura stood. 'I'm sorry we had to put you through this, Thérèse, but there was no other way.'

Laura's heart leapt in her breast, for she recognised that voice! It was the pirate—Sloan Benedict!

'If you can find me a horse,' he went on, 'I'll go and get the ship's doctor.'

'No, you are in no condition to go, *mon vieux*. I will go. The stableman is accustomed to my comings and goings, and he can have my equipage ready for me in a moment. On the way, I'll drop Mademoiselle Trevor at her home.'

'No.' Benedict's voice was faint with exhaustion. 'Let her stay.'

Madame Georges, surprised at his order, none the less moved quickly to pick up her cloak. Without another word between them, she slipped out into the alley and was gone.

Only now did Laura turn to search the shadows, to see the tall figure of Sloan Benedict, his eyes on her. His skin was coloured to a dark mahogany and a deep cut bled profusely on one cheek. Like that of the injured man on the floor, his rough white shirt was muddied and torn, his breeches in tatters, and his feet were bare. Laura watched, bewildered, as he crossed the room and slid the bolt on the door, then strode to the chimneypiece. He took a lucifer from a metal box, struck it on a piece of rough paper lying beside it, and returned to light a lantern on the work-table in the centre of the room. As the small apartment slowly brightened, he dropped to his knees beside the slave and gently removed the blood-stained shirt. Without looking up, he spoke to her at last.

'You said you wanted to help. We'll need clean cloths. You'll find some in the trunk at the top of the stairs.'

Laura hesitated for only a moment. Then she went to the chimney piece, picked up the lighted candle and, gathering her full skirts about her, went up the narrrow steps to the floor above. At the top, she held her light high and peered into the shadows. It was a small room, the ceiling so low that she could not stand erect. Boxes and bolts of fabric were piled ceiling-high everywhere, leaving scarcely room to turn round. She held her candle higher and saw on an opposite wall, neatly arranged on hooks and hangers, several articles of masculine attire. A part of her mind registered startled recognition of a finely tailored burgundy evening coat, and next to it the embroidered waistcoat Benedict had worn on the night he had taken her in his arms and told her of his love for her!

She looked away quickly, and discovered a wooden sea-chest, its brass fastenings catching the light. She leaned to undo the leather straps, then threw it open. Instantly she recognised the faded red bandana the pirate had worn to cover the lower half of his face when they had first met. A stab of pain went through her at sight of it, but it was not allowed to remain long. She searched further and found a pile of soft cotton shirting, which she pulled out, and clutching it to her, made her way down the steps again.

Benedict stood at the bottom, waiting for her, his eyes glowing dark in the light of her candle. He was holding a basin of water. 'It's too late,' he said quietly. 'The man is dead.' He moved away to set the basin on the table, then came back to where she stood, still stunned by his words. He took the candle and set it back on the mantelpiece. 'Thank you,' he said. 'You knew nothing of what is happening here, yet you were willing to help us.'

His strong shoulders suddenly dropped forward, and he might have fallen but for Laura's quick movement to support him. With an arm about his waist she guided him to the dressmaker's narrow cot, recessed in the back wall of the small room, and lowered him on to it. 'You must rest,' she told him. 'Perhaps a cup of tea?'

'No!' He managed a weary smile as his head touched the pillow. 'There's brandy in the cupboard next to the fireplace. Better bring two glasses. You could do with some yourself.'

When Laura returned to the bedside and each had taken a sip of the warming spirit, Laura lifted the basin of water and sat down with it at the side of the cot. With a piece of shirting, she began to cleanse the wound on his cheek. At first he winced at her touch and kept his eyes closed as she bent to him, then he relaxed as her hands moved gently across his face. The little room was silent but for the whisper of the dying embers still casting a flickering light on to the body of the slave, covered now with a blanket.

Laura knew that Benedict watched her, but she did not dare to meet his eyes. She continued to pat gently at his gash with the wet cloth, wringing it out, then re-applying it. Finally, when she could bear his silent examining no longer, she looked squarely into his eyes as if to tell him she did not fear the exchange.

A slow smile lighted up his face. He caught her hand and held it. 'That's better,' he said.

She pretended to misunderstand. 'Yes, the bleeding has stopped.'

'I don't mean that, Laura.'

She dropped her eyes and his hand tightened on hers. 'Please don't look away from me,' he said quietly. 'I need your strength.'

She could not speak, and he too was silent. When she could again look at him, his eyes were still on her, but now they were filled with sadness. With a groan, he turned his head away on the pillow. 'My God, the last one, and to think he never made it!'

Laura leaned closer, her heart full; not understanding his words, only knowing that once again she rejoiced at the nearness of him. She watched the play of light and shadow on his face as the sunlight filtered through the curtain at the window above.

At last he turned back to look at her. 'I want to tell you everything. I must. First of all, what you saw here that night of the storm was not what you think. Thérèse Georges and I are only old friends who share the same . . .'

'Don't tire yourself out with talking,' she said softly.

But he went on. 'Everything I've ever wanted to do, I have been able to do, Laura . . . But at what a cost to others! You must realise that when I tell you what I do, and the reason for my disguises, your own life will be in danger.'

'Don't tell me what you do, for it doesn't matter!' Laura heard herself saying as she took his hand in hers. For suddenly it didn't matter! Nothing did. Only that the man she had been unable to banish from her heart and dreams was only inches away, and gazed now at her with his green eyes clear and fine, acknowledging his love for her.

Instantly he raised himself on one elbow off the pillow, his eyes questioning hers. 'Not a tear shed here today?' he said. 'No word of recrimination, no questions? You only—*love* me, is that what you're saying, Laura?'

'Oh, yes.' Laura brushed his hand with a kiss. 'You said once you hoped I could love you, whoever you are, whatever you do,' she told him quietly. 'I—I can't fight it any more, Sloan. Loving you is all that matters to me now.'

He hesitated for only a moment, then pulled himself up off the cot and, taking both her hands in his, drew her gently to her feet to face him. 'Laura,' he whispered, 'if you knew how often I've dreamed of hearing those words from you! Oh, my love . . .' His arms went round her and held her tight. At that moment the bell over the shop door jangled.

'Miss Laura?'

A man's voice called from the next room. 'It's William, ma'am, come to fetch you home.'

Laura drew away, her eyes suddenly filling with tears. 'Miss Laura . . .?'

She knew she must speak, for the coachman was coming closer to the curtained door. 'Yes, William,' she called out, 'I'm coming.' She backed slowly away from

Benedict, his face blurred now in front of her. Still watching him, she moved to pull the curtain aside and quickly stepped into the shop. She left him standing there—his arms, where she had been a moment before, still outstretched for her.

Laura sat, flushed and silent, at the dinner-table that night. She had scarcely touched the rich lobster parfait or the young squab placed before her and sat quietly, her hands in her lap. Flickering light from the heavy candelabra glistened on burnished silver and sparkling crystal, and all up and down the length of the table several of the bridal party had already proposed humorously suggestive toasts to the couple. Laura had smiled when it was expected of her, but found herself now staring down at the arrangement of crimson hibiscus and baby's breath that comprised the graceful centrepiece. The airy bouquet sat like a burst of precious jewels on a mirrored stand beneath it. When she lowered her gaze to the mirror, she was startled to see a face reflected there, and it was a moment before she realised that Michael Norton's eyes, cold and insolent, watched her.

She looked quickly away to see her father at one end of the table, his spirits heightened and his face flushed from too much fine wine. Aunt Stark's voice, high and excited, rose above all the others. 'Doesn't our little bride look beautiful?' She had made the same remark more than once tonight. It was hard to believe that she had been so ill that very morning, for now she was enjoying herself enormously. John Messersmith, seated next to Aunt Stark, caught Laura's glance and winked broadly. He had hardly been able to take his eyes off the bride-to-be, which was true of most of the guests, for the glistening royal blue of Laura's low-cut satin gown matched exactly the melting warmth of her lustrous eyes. Her hair was swept high in soft shining curls, with plumes and brilliants tucked expertly here and there, and her creamy complexion glowed in the soft candle-light.

'You really must try to eat something, my dear,' Lord Skelton said solicitously at her side. Laura supposed that her response was adequate, for he said no more and did not comment on her withdrawn manner. Truly she had separated herself completely from the confusion, the bright laughter and the chatter all around her. Her thoughts lingered in a silent world a universe removed from here. Her spirit—indeed her soul—had never left the dark little room behind the dressmaker's shop where she had at last told Sloan Benedict of her love for him. She still saw his eyes as they revealed, more clearly than mere words could ever say, what was also in his heart.

'Your attention, friends,' Lucas Trevor's voice rang out from his end of the table, where Laura's maid had bent to whisper a message. 'I have just been told that there's somebody here to see Lord Skelton. Maria tells me it's urgent, Edgar, so you'd better see to it.'

He smoothed his moustache with his napkin, then nodded across the table to his secretary. Both men rose, and with a polite word of apology, made their way out of the dining-room. It was only a moment before they reappeared, but not to take their place at the table, for Skelton went quietly to his host and spoke to him while Michael Norton waited in the doorway.

Trevor nodded, then announced to his guests, 'Edgar finds that he must leave us. Something important has come up.' He gestured briefly to excuse his future son-in-law, who came round the table to where Laura sat and took her hand in his. 'Forgive me, my dear,' he said. 'I'm sorry that tonight, of all nights, I am called away.'

Laura looked up at him with unseeing eyes. She did not even watch the two men leave the room, and it seemed only a few minutes later when she noticed a stir at the table as Aunt Stark signalled that the time had come for the ladies to withdraw and leave the men to their brandy and cigars. She followed the others into the parlour, where her aunt had already settled her ample figure in front of the coffee service.

The little lady had spread her lavender taffeta skirts so widely that there was room for no one else to sit beside her on the divan, and her voice already filled the room. 'Laura will miss her piano, of course, but one of the first things she'll do, once they're settled in Edgar's ancestral estate of Olney is to send to Paris for one of the newest and most expensive instruments. Isn't that so, Laura?'

Laura stood just inside the doorway, still numb, removed from reality.

'Isn't that so, love?' her aunt said again.

Laura took a deep breath, then walked over to the divan. 'Aunt,' she said quietly, 'may I be excused? I'm awfully tired.' She kissed Aunt Stark lightly on the cheek as she clucked sympathetically.

'Of course, we do understand, love,' her aunt said.

As Laura made her way slowly up the stairs, she heard her aunt's words: 'Did you see the light go out of Laura's eyes when Edgar was called away? Mercy, they're so in love!'

When she reached the top, she saw Maria coming out of her father's bedroom, where she had turned down the covers for the night ahead.

'*Niña?*' She came closer to her mistress, holding her candle high. 'Why aren't you downstairs with the guests?'

Laura managed a smile. 'There's been so much excitement! I'm going to rest for a while.'

Maria quickly went across the hall to open the door to her mistress's bedchamber. 'You'll perhaps feel more like joining the party again when Lord Skelton gets back, yes? I cannot think why the fisherman came to fetch him tonight. Now, just go in and stretch out.'

'Wait,' Laura put a hand on her arm. 'The fisherman, you say?'

'Cayo Aristo, yes. I can't imagine what possible business he might have with Lord Skelton, but he said it was important. Take this candle with you, *niña*.'

'No, thank you, I really prefer the dark. I'll call you if I need you, Maria.'

Laura indeed welcomed the darkness when she reached the sanctuary of her own room and closed the door behind her. Moonlight washed the walls in broad shifting bands, diffused and set in motion by a soft breeze that stirred the silk curtains at the open balcony door. She leaned against the wall, and her glance fell on the wedding dress that hung from a corner of her wardrobe. In the half-light it shone ghostly grey—like a funeral shroud!

The horrifying thought sent chills through her, for only now did the inevitability of her fate finally penetrate to the secret place in her soul that she had so persistently kept shut away. No longer could she deny the stark actuality that, this time tomorrow, she would be the bride of Edgar Skelton! Slowly, as if in a dream, she began to pull out the plumes and brilliants that held her hair, and laid them on the dressing-stand. Then she slipped out of her gown and let it fall to the floor. She stooped to gather it up, but all at once her body began to tremble with an unearthly cold, and she buried her face in its fragrant folds, sick to the bone with emptiness. For just a few precious moments in her life she had been made whole in the arms of the man she loved. But now—God help her!—she was back, her soul fragmented, her body empty, as though she had returned to a forlorn hovel after travelling on wings across the width of the world.

She was abruptly wrenched from her thoughts by the sound of a footstep outside. She raised her head, wondering what madness had taken hold of her now. When it came again, she peered uncertainly through the darkness to see a shadow—a man's shadow—standing just behind the thin veil of curtains. She dared not breathe, but stood frozen, and watched as the shadow lengthened and the curtains were pushed aside. With a burst of joy she called his name—only there was no sound from her lips as the cry came from her heart.

He did not see her standing there in the shadows, and neither of them moved, until at last Laura could bear it no longer. She dropped her gown and ran to him. His arms opened instantly to take her in, to hold her tight to his chest. They stood there as if nothing could ever come between them again. Then, quickly, he released her. When he spoke, there was a harsh urgency in his voice.

'Thérèse has just told me that tomorrow, *tomorrow*, you are to marry Skelton! Is this true?'

She could only nod, struck dumb by the nearness of him.

He pulled her again into his arms, and spoke in a whisper against her hair. 'Do you love me as you said you did, Laura?'

'Oh, yes, yes!' She clung to him. 'With my whole heart!'

'You must be very sure of this.'

'I am! Oh, I am! Look at me. Can't you see?'

He held her away from him. 'Perhaps I see a bitterly unhappy woman who would grasp at anything to escape a marriage with a man she does not love.'

Laura recoiled as if he had struck her. She turned away angrily, and clasped the bedpost for support. 'Is that what you think?' she whispered. 'Is that what you really think of me?' She felt the tears begin as a painful pressure in her throat, and in a moment she could not hold them back. She felt him move up behind her.

'I had to be sure,' he said softly. Then, gently, he turned her to face him and looked deep into her eyes. 'You must know, Laura, that I can promise you nothing but my love.'

'That's all I want, that's all I ask for!' she said, her voice trembling.

His arms went round her and he found her lips in the darkness. Slowly, she felt the fire start deep within her, the fire only he could breathe to white-hot flame. He, too, felt it, for his kisses became more urgent as the heat spread through both of them as if fanned by a raging wind. His hands moved insistently on her, and there was no turning back now as their two bodies seemed to fuse as one.

Benedict lifted her up and laid her gently on the bed. When he leaned down to kiss her again, she caught his shoulders and pulled him closer, closer, clinging to him. He lowered himself slowly until he lay beside her, his arms encircling her. For a moment they lay there, not moving. Then she felt the urgency of his hands on her again as he slid the camisole from her shoulders. He bent to her, his kisses hot on her breast. She moved against him as if to hold him there, and felt the surging muscles of his back as she helped to strip away his shirt.

She explored the wonder of his shoulders, the strong cords of his neck, breathing deeply of the clean salt-sea smell of him. His hands were tongues of flame as he found her breasts, her thighs, running over her skin as if eager to know every part of her with his touch, and she pulled him ever closer in response, wanting to share the secrets of her body with him. At his persistent touch Laura was suddenly a wild woman, tuned to the wildness in him. There was nothing here of the delirium-induced embrace. This was solid, taut, and beyond any control.

His body moved across her and for the first time she knew the power and force of his manhood. She shuddered with surprise and ecstasy to know it at last, to feel the fiery brand enter her, to give herself to the glorious rhythm of their two bodies as, first gently, then in a frenzy, he made the excitement mount. She cried out at a momentary spasm of pain, which was instantly dispelled by the raging need for more, more. Then the heavens and earth exploded in a blaze of white light all about her. Laura felt herself lifted out of her own body, as he had left his, and they rose together into a whirling funnel of wind that roared in her ears. She cried out, and he covered her mouth with a kiss.

Afterwards, she did not know how long she lay nestled in the circle of his arms, her face buried in the hollow of his shoulder. 'Laura . . .' he whispered. 'My love.' She felt the quick beat of his heart against her, then it slowed, slower and slower, until she thought at last he slept. With her fingers still tangled in his hair, her mind drifted off, content to lie as still as her body. As long as he is here with me, she thought, no harm will ever come to us. Together—for ever. I shall never be unsure again, never frightened, never alone.

Suddenly she felt Benedict tense beside her, and before she knew what had happened, he leapt on to the floor and began pulling on his clothes. 'What is it?' Laura whispered. But now she, too, heard them, running footsteps on the street below. They came to a stop directly outside the front of the house.

'In here,' a voice shouted in Spanish. 'Quickly!'

'Aristo!' Benedict said. 'What's he doing here?'

'The fisherman?' Laura jumped up and reached for her dressing-gown. 'He came here earlier to get Lord Skelton.'

'Here?'

'What is it?' Laura cried. 'What does it mean?'

He put out a hand to warn her to be silent. 'Is there a back way?'

'Yes, stairs lead down to a side door into the alley. But what is it?'

'I'll have to run for it!'

'I'm coming with you!'

'No! Don't you see, it's not safe!'

'I'm still coming with you,' she said again.

Benedict took a few long strides to the door, and when he felt her at his side, he opened it and scanned the dark hall. He paused for only a moment, then he took her hand and together they crept silently to the small door across the landing. He led her down the dark stairs to the outside door, slid back the bolt and opened it only wide enough to check the alley. 'Now,' he said. He held tight to her hand as they slipped outside into the darkness. The alley was empty and silent as they made their way past the kitchen wing of the big house and towards the back street. A broad ribbon of moonlight lay ahead. They crossed it quickly and were nearly into the sheltering shadow of the carriage-house when a shot rang out.

Laura felt herself lifted off her feet as Benedict picked her up and placed her just inside the shed door. He slid in beside her. She heard his quick breath in the darkness. 'Stay here,' he said. 'Stay exactly where you are!' Before she could stop him, he stepped out again, pulling the door closed behind him. The latch clicked into place, then came the sound of running footsteps out on the street. Another shot rang out! Laura felt frantically for the latch in the darkness. At last she found it, threw the door open and stepped outside, straining her eyes in the blackness.

Then, oh, God, she saw him! He lay sprawled in the centre of the narrow alley, the moonlight full on him. She screamed his name, and ran to where he lay. With a cry, she fell on her knees beside him. She reached out to touch him, sick with dread. Already a dark stain widened on the white of his shirt. 'Sloan, Sloan!' she sobbed. 'Oh, please, someone help him! Help him!' She was suddenly grabbed from behind and pulled to her feet. She tried to break free of the arms that held her, and a man's voice spoke in Spanish at her ear.

'It's too late, he's dead!' He dragged her away.

'Let me go!' she cried. 'For God's sake, let me go to

him!' She turned to fight the man whose arms were pulling her, and saw the cold, white eye of the fisherman staring down at her. She beat at his chest with her fists.

But all at once the sound of her own sobs faded in her ears, and she felt the darkness close in on her as she sank helplessly into unconsciousness.

CHAPTER SEVEN

'LADY SKELTON? Ma'am?'

Laura roused herself from the book on her lap. She closed it, and looked up at the rugged features of the ship's steward who had been trying to attract her attention. His dark face broke into a grin.

'I'm sorry,' she said. 'I must have been dozing.'

'I only wanted to know, ma'am, if you'd like a steaming cup of broth about now, seeing as how you've been off your feed, as you might say.'

Laura shook her head. 'Perhaps later,' she told him. 'But thank you.' He smiled politely and left her. Her eyes followed him as he disappeared down the companionway, and she looked about her to find that she was alone on deck.

Maria had placed her chair by a hatchway, out of the wind, just an hour before, with explicit orders to send for her immediately if Laura experienced a return of the nausea that had racked her during their first ten days at sea. Only this morning, the maid had lost patience with her mistress. 'You are better now, *niña*, and you have been confined in this dark cabin too long. The sun is going to shine later on. See, the sky is already brightening.' Laura had submitted to Maria's coaxing with only mild protest, her body moving as it was bid, feeling nothing; her thoughts registering nothing, as if she had been turned to stone.

She lay her head back now against the chair and watched the shift and play of tattered clouds that scudded fitfully about a timid sun, then darted away to regroup and head across the sky. The storm had abated last night, but the restless sea still rolled with the spent fury of it. A stiff breeze had come up again and the ship shuddered as she faced into it. Wind-driven whitecaps crowned each rise of grey water that licked up, to be sent flying off in feathers of spray. Above her the giant sails ballooned and strained, then emptied to fill again. A loose rope had set up a strumming as it wrapped itself around the mast, then broke free to coil again at the next gust. She was conscious that one of the ribbons on her bonnet fluttered gently at her cheek as the breeze caught it.

She closed her eyes, trying desperately to keep the world of sight and sound away, and the memories. Oh, she thought—the memories! But Sloan Benedict's face was everywhere she looked. She had seen him in the kind eyes of the captain when he came to enquire about her health during her illness. He was in the gentle touch of Maria's hands as she tended her in the dark little cabin. He was in the smell of the sea, the grey wash of sky overhead, the gentle motion of the ship, the noise just now of the rope whipping above her head, the roughness of the coarse woollen blanket over her knees . . . No, no! she thought, panicking, Sloan Benedict is dead! Why can I not let go of him? She must not let thoughts of him flood back to her like this, for with their return would also come the nightmare image of his lifeless body lying in the alley, his white shirt darkening over his wound . . .

She pushed back the blanket Maria had tucked round her, and got shakily to her feet. She made her way to the port rail and clung to it, staring out at the open ocean, like tarnished pewter now that the sun had moved behind a cloud. She looked down at the churning water far below, and her eyes filled with tears. It would be so easy—so easy! She had only to climb over the railing and let go . . . A short drop, and then blessed oblivion!

Suddenly she drew back, seized with cold dismay at the depths to which she had allowed her spirits to plunge. I must come to grips with the unalterable fact that I shall never see him again, she told herself firmly. It was easier in the dark cabin to resist that truth. Here, with the salt sea spray in her face and the cool air filling her lungs, with the sea and sky beginning to work their magic on her, she must finally accept the reality of her loss. She had known the miracle of his love, and she had those few stolen moments to hold on to for the rest of her life. Other memories of that night must fade with time. She did not know how she had got back into the house, back to her own room after the fatal shot was fired. She remembered seeing the fisherman bending over her in the alley, and knew only that Maria found her in her own bed next morning. As she had bathed her mistress and made preparations to dress her for her wedding, the maid told her of the shooting the night before.

'The shots did not wake you, *niña*? We heard two shots outside—probably a bandit—but we didn't go out to investigate. After all, the sound of gunfire in the streets is something we have heard on other nights, no?'

Laura had walked through her wedding day as though it was happening to someone else. Afterwards she had stood on the deck of the *Triton* before the little packet pulled away from the dock, and seen below her the face of Aunt Stark, of her father, of John Messersmith. She had felt the touch of Skelton's hand on her arm, but it had nothing to do with her. She had gone early to her cabin, and by then the ship was already headed south into the Gulf, to be caught in the turbulent waters that presaged the storm which would batter them for ten days.

Now, with determined resolve, Laura gathered up the blanket and book from her chair and walked briskly towards the companionway. I must find Maria, she decided. I must not be alone like this ever again!

Maria took pains with her mistress's coiffure that night. She could not conceal her joy that Laura would at last put in an appearance at the evening meal. 'You must look especially well tonight,' she told her as she smoothed the raven hair back from its centre parting and made sure that each shining ringlet was in place. 'Everyone, especially Lord Skelton, will be happy to see that you are well again!'

Laura caught her maid's eye in the small mirror set up on one of her trunks. Maria's expression did not change. She knows that I have slept alone these many nights, Laura thought, and, like the good and practical woman she is, she expects, now that I am recovered, that the marriage will begin. The long confinement below deck had taken its toll. Laura had lost several pounds, and Maria shook her head as she tied the pale green sash at her waist.

'A husband's two hands could easily close round it,' she said, 'but a few more days out in the fresh air, and you'll be yourself again.'

Laura found her way to the dining-salon, wondering if she was overdressed for dinner. The *Triton* was a merchant vessel, and the accommodation for the dozen passengers she carried was cramped and rough. But on letting herself into the long narrow room, she was pleased to see that she was properly attired. Two elderly gentlemen who sat at the long rectangular table in the centre of the room were in evening clothes, as was the lady between them.

'Hooray! If it isn't Lady Skelton!' the woman called out at sight of Laura, and waved her over to join them. 'At last another of our lady passengers is heard from. I'd begun to think I was the only female on board, and certainly the only American. Welcome, fellow countrywoman!' She introduced herself as Dilly Kemp, and she was extravagantly gowned in low-cut scarlet taffeta, with diamond brilliants topping her ornately coiffed red hair.

One of the gentlemen, who introduced himself as Oliver Trumbull, held Laura's chair for her as she sat down, then drew his own close to her side. He was lean and distinguished-looking, and his grey eyes smiled at her through thick spectacles. 'We had almost begun to wonder whether Skelton really was hiding a bride on board ship!' he told her in a clipped British accent.

The other man, also an Englishman, quite obese and stooped with gout, moved to her other side. He gave his name as Sir Patrick Norse, and indeed he could have been Nordic with his mane of white hair and scarlet visage. 'I can see why he wanted you all to himself, my dear,' he said gallantly.

Even before she had taken her seat at the table, Laura had been aware that her entrance had interrupted a heated discussion among them. 'Please don't let me interrupt,' she told them all. 'Do go on with what you were talking about just now.'

Dilly Kemp, bright-eyed and heavily rouged, seemed only too happy to continue. 'Men,' she groaned. 'If I live to be a hundred, they'll never cease to amaze me! You should hear these two . . .'

'Now, Dilly,' Sir Patrick cut her off. 'Lady Skelton couldn't possibly find our subject entertaining, for she knows none of our cast of characters. I'm so sorry,' he leaned closer to Laura, his breath strong of whisky, 'that your husband cannot be with us tonight. I understand that he has finally succumbed to the *mal de mer*. The captain, too, I regret to say, will not join us, as he suffers from dyspepsia this evening.'

'Dyspepsia, ha!' Oliver Trumbull said drily. 'More like that excellent brandy we all tucked away here last night. It would appear that Sir Patrick and I alone survived.'

'A pity, too,' laughed Dilly Kemp. 'For had you both kept to your cabins, Lady Skelton and I might have enjoyed an intelligent conversation!'

At that moment a steward appeared with the first of several dishes to be set before them. Two solitary lanterns swung from heavy ceiling beams, affording the only illumination in the dark salon, but Laura could see that the fare looked heavy and unappetising.

Sir Patrick seemed not to care, for he helped himself generously as the platter was passed round. 'Maybe we should put our little question to Lady Skelton,' he said blandly, his mouth full of fatty mutton. 'Perhaps she may decide it for us.'

'Pshaw, she'll feel as I do!' Mrs Kemp assured him. 'But, all right. Lady Skelton, whom do you consider the guilty party when . . .'

'Wait, wait!' Sir Patrick protested. 'You'll go about it all wrong, Dilly dear. Lady Skelton, let me fill you in before we ask you to decide. The three of us share a mutual friend in London, Cedric . . .'

'No last names!' shouted Dilly Kemp.

'Well—fair enough! But a year ago, he brought an American bride back to London with him. Today the damn fool's on trial for murder!'

'For shooting his wife's lover *in flagrante delicto*,' snorted Mr Trumbull.

'Precisely so,' said Sir Patrick. 'But after all, when a gentleman finds a stranger in his bride's bed, shouldn't he have the right to do him in?'

'Wait a minute . . .' Mrs Kemp waggled her ringed fingers at him.

'No!' Sir Patrick stopped her. 'Do you agree with us, Lady Skelton, that a husband has a responsibility to defend his honour in his own bedroom?'

Laura, surprised at the indelicacy of the subject, said quickly, 'I would have to agree. Yes.'

'Wait, there's more!' Dilly Kemp jumped in. 'Cedric should have known the kind of girl he was marrying! I have no sympathy for a man who buys a pig in a poke. Anybody in Philadelphia could have told him that Moira was not the pure, virginal little lady she pretended to be! Despite the fact that she wore pristine white all the time—she even had a white *dog*! Why didn't he ask one of her friends what kind of woman she was before he married her? Why didn't he ask *me*? I've known Moira for years. Everybody knew her reputation. She'd been kept by several rich young dandies by the time she was eighteen! Once a trollop, always a trollop. Leopards don't change their spots.' She shrugged apologetically at her own use of a cliché, then went on. 'Besides, it's in her blood. She's illegitimate, my dear, a *bona fide* bastard, and her mother was notorious for her sexual appetites, they say. No, Moira was rich, beautiful and available, and that's all Cedric cared about. He never looked further than his nose. He didn't want to, because he liked what he saw!'

'Tush, tush,' Oliver Trumbull admonished her. 'He is a gentleman, Moira, and a gentleman does not pry. Cedric also happens to be one of the cleverest men I know.'

'Which one is cleverer,' Dilly Kemp cried, 'Moira, who is scot free today, or Cedric, who is behind bars? And which is the *guilty* one, Lady Skelton, the deceiver or the deceived? Be careful; we ladies must stick together on this!'

It was apparent that all of them waited for Laura's answer, with Mrs Kemp the most impatient to hear it. Laura was hesitant to take sides but finally, relieved to be rid of the subject, and with all eyes on her, she said evenly, 'I think the lady herself owed her husband the truth when once she saw that his intentions were serious and honourable.'

'Bravo!' Oliver Trumbull hooted.

But Dilly Kemp was outraged. 'How many women do you know who would have done that?'

'If she had had a shred of decency in her,' Sir Patrick declared, 'that is precisely what she would have done!'

'There!' Mr Trumbull murmured. 'That's the end of it, then. She did not, and poor Cedric will hang for it.

Now, Lady Skelton, we'll speak of other things. I understand that you and your husband will be living near Wyckham. That's not far from London, you know. We must all be sure to get together, mustn't we, when once you've settled in?'

Laura did not linger long in the salon after the evening meal was over. She had eaten almost nothing, and her head throbbed. 'You'll get your sea-legs soon,' Dilly Kemp had assured her, her manner abrupt. The older woman was not entirely pleased with the outcome of their earlier discussion, but they parted amicably enough. Laura made her way back to her cabin, where Maria had left a candle burning. She undressed herself quickly, then blew out the light and climbed gratefully into her berth. The heated conversation in the salon had upset her. Too many voices, too loud, too argumentative.

She drew her pillow over her head to shut it all away. Exhausted, she concentrated on the roll of the creaking ship, and soon managed to fall into a deep sleep. No sooner had she drifted off, however, than she was caught in a dream. She was walking through what appeared to be a village fair, with the sound of festive music all around. Bright merchandise was being hawked for sale in gaily-striped tents on every side. She could hear the rattle of their canvas flaps against the tent-poles, although the air was still.

She moved lightly through a crowd of laughing faces, her head held high, her hands clasped at her breast, fingering the silver cross that hung round her neck. Only now did she notice with distaste that the hem of the simple white gown she wore was stained with the thick mud that covered the trampled ground. She walked on, and found herself in an open area where a group of women whirled dizzily in a frenzied dance. The music grew louder as they spun faster and faster. She watched, fascinated, as their ballooning skirts circled about them. One of the women, garishly painted and arrayed in scarlet, with brilliants flashing in her red hair, gaily beckoned to her to join the dance. Then another—this one in white, holding a small white dog against her hip—gestured to her. And the third—Laura thought she knew the third woman, and realised that it was her own face that looked at her! The woman's hair was jet black and threaded with pink satin ribbons. She, too, bid Laura join them and called out, 'You are one of us! Come and dance with us!'

For an instant Laura hesitated, wanting to be a part of the gaiety, but she looked quickly away and would have passed them by, but they separated themselves from the others and set upon her. They began to claw at her with bawdy remarks, and she saw that their fingers tore at her dress, ripping it from her in shreds, then throwing the filmy fabric into the mud. All the while the sound of their laughter echoed in her ears, and she put up her hands to cover them.

She realised all at once that she stood naked now, and from out of nowhere a man stood before her, his face dark and accusing. It was Edgar Skelton. 'Here,' he said, throwing a garment at her. 'Cover yourself with this!' She caught it and held it close. But instantly she recoiled at the touch of it, for it felt wet and cold against her skin. When she looked down she saw that it was the pirate's shirt she held, covered with the dark stain of his blood . . .

She woke with a scream and sat up, terrified, staring into the darkness. At first she did not know where she was, conscious only of the rapid pulse in her throat and that her body shivered uncontrollably. She threw back the coverlet, stepped out on the rough flooring and found her way in the dark to the door of her cabin. She loosed the latch, opened it and looked out at the shadowed corridor. Everything looked as it had earlier, the normality of the heavy beams and dark panelling infinitely reassuring to her. Further up the hall and across from her, she saw a thin thread of light glowing under another door—the door to Edgar's cabin. Her husband's cabin.

She closed her own door silently and bolted it. Trembling still, she made her way back to her berth and again climbed into it and pulled the coverlet over her. The dream haunted her! She knew that the woman all in white and holding a white dog was Moira, the same woman who had so deceived her husband. And the one in red, surely Dilly Kemp, with the rouged cheeks and brilliants in her hair. And what of the one whose face was Laura's own? 'Come and dance with us!' she had cried. Was it Laura's *mother* that came to claw at her, to tear off the virginal white gown her daughter wore so sanctimoniously? 'You are one of us!' she had called out. Laura burned with shame now as she remembered her own overpowering urge to join the dancers, and her husband's accusing face as he threw her the shirt stained with her lover's blood!

There was to be no more sleep for Laura that night as the dream revealed to her the depths of her own hypocrisy. Who are you, what are you? Sloan Benedict had echoed her own words in the courtyard at Crosswinds. Who, what, indeed? How easily she had exchanged her dedication to serve her God for the frivolous life of Galveston society! And now! She had married a man she cared nothing for—nor could she ever learn to love Edgar Skelton when she had already given her heart and soul to another. Her body, too, she had given to Sloan Benedict—joyously, wondrously—so no longer could she pretend to be the unsullied virgin Edgar had every right to expect his bride to be. She would never be whole again, having lost the half of her, the best half, that existed only in Benedict's arms. Her love for him had been the one true and honest emotion she had ever experienced. With him gone, she was only half a person, and Edgar—indeed *any* man—deserved better than a phantom wife.

She decided, lying on the narrow berth in the small cabin that night and during the early morning hours, that the time had come to put an end to the masquerade. She could not go to England and play the part of a chaste, dutiful little wife! Before the sun was fully up, she threw her covers aside, put on her velvet dressing-gown and let herself quietly out of her cabin. The narrow corridor was lit only by a single lantern at its opposite end, and she made her way past the closed doors that separated her cabin from Edgar's. When she came to his, she rapped softly. She could hear nothing from the other side of it, as the gleaming wood panelling of the dimly-lit corridor sighed and groaned with the gentle motion of the ship. At last she heard a bolt slipped aside, and Michael Norton's face peered out at her. She had not expected to see Edgar's secretary at this early hour and in her husband's cabin!

He was as surprised as she, but managed a thin smile. 'You've come to see Edgar?' he asked. His face was very pale in the shadows, and for a moment she thought that he, too, might be ill.'

'I have,' Laura told him.

'He's sick, you know, and he's still asleep.'

'Let me in please, Mr Norton, and then you may go back to your own cabin.' She stepped aside to let him pass. For a moment he hesitated, then edged past her, gathering his loose bathrobe about him.

The little room was quite dark, but despite the dim light, Laura could see disarray everywhere. Edgar's clothing was thrown carelessly on the backs of two small chairs, across the top of his half unpacked trunk—even on the floor. A rancid smell of whisky and stale cigar-smoke was heavy in the air. She moved quietly across the short distance to Edgar's berth and looked down at the jumble of bedclothes.

'Edgar!' She put her hand on his shoulder and gently shook him. He did not come awake at once, so she called his name again. 'Edgar, it's Laura. I must speak to you.'

At last he roused. His body shifted and his head appeared. He stared at her with blinking eyes. 'What are you doing here?' he said sleepily. 'Why, Laura . . .' He sat up slowly, and she saw that he was clean-shaven, his beard carefully trimmed and his nails newly buffed.

'I must speak to you,' she said again.

'Now?' He frowned at her. 'Can't you see I'm sick? Surely Michael told you?'

'Yes, he did. But it may be because you lie here in this unpleasant little place with no air, no light. You need to get out on deck.' I sound like Maria! she thought. 'And this cabin is a mess! Surely Mr Norton could take better care of things.'

Edgar, seeing that she intended to stay, finally pulled himself higher on the pillows and faced her. 'I hate to have you see me like this.'

'You look surprisingly well, Edgar.'

'What is it you want? Do you realise how early it is?'

'I do.' Laura sat lightly on the side of the rumpled berth. 'We must talk, Edgar,' she said evenly. 'I have decided what I must do when we arrive in England.'

His eyes widened. 'Do? What do you mean, you've decided? Why, we'll go straight on to Olney, of course.'

'No. I intend to take the first available vessel back home.' When he began to protest, she put a hand on his. 'Hear me out, please. There is . . . something you must know. I have deceived you, Edgar. You have played the game fairly, and I have not. You were honest with me. You told me of the marriage settlement from my father; you made it perfectly clear that you didn't love me. Now I must be as straightforward with you. There are— things—about me . . . Well, when I tell you of them, you will see that I am unfit to be your wife—anyone's wife.'

'You're not going to bring up that nonsense of your illegitimacy again, are you?'

'Since you are determined not to believe that, I shall not. But there is something else. I have . . . There has been . . . someone else in my life, Edgar.'

'You wake me up at daylight to tell me this?' He appeared to find her halting confession amusing, for he smiled at her. 'You're not a child, and I certainly hope by now that you have some knowledge of the world, Laura. I am not altogether without my own—ah, experiences, you know, but there's surely no need for either of us to unburden our souls to the other.' He took her hand. She looked down, and saw that the early morning sunlight, only now slanting through the porthole, glowed warmly on her plain gold wedding band.

Edgar's voice went on. 'My dear, anything from the past is dead and buried. I am not one to go around poking through ashes to find a hot coal. Nor must you be. Now, I'll forget what you said here, and we'll go straight to Olney as we planned.'

Laura shook her head. 'I can't do it, Edgar,' she told him. 'If it's Father's settlement that worries you, you'll still keep it, of course. But—I can never be your wife.'

Edgar frowned at her. Then, as if a new idea suddenly occurred to him, he shifted his weight under the covers. He leaned closer to her, a small muscle working at one side of his temple. 'Be assured of one thing, my dear. I will never—*never*—force my attentions on you. I mean that. You will have your own friends as I have mine. You will pursue your life at Olney doing all the things you do best. There is need in the town of Wyckham for someone to help the poor and needy. There are tenant farmers on the place to be visited, their children tended when they are sick.' He watched her closely. 'Do you realise it has been thirty years since my mother died, and Olney has been without a mistress for all those years? Olney needs you, and . . .' He squeezed her hand. 'And I . . . Look at me, Laura! I am almost fifty years old. I am alone in the world. *I* need you, my dear.'

His plea was so impassioned that she stared at him in surprise. She had never dreamed that Edgar Skelton was so capable of feeling. 'Still,' she said slowly. 'It isn't fair that you don't know . . .'

'I need only to know that you are my wife.' He gave her a wan smile, then settled back against his pillows. 'Forgive me, but my strength is gone.' He turned his head towards the wall, and released her hand. 'You will be doing me a great kindness, Laura,' he said, 'if you never mention this again. We have a full life ahead of us, I promise you.' His voice trailed off, and he appeared to have fallen asleep.

By now, misty sunlight was flooding the small cabin, warming the old timbers in a clear yellow light. Laura stood and looked down at her husband. Dilly Kemp's words the night before came back to her. 'Cedric never looked further than his nose,' she had said. 'He didn't want to, because he liked what he saw!' Laura closed her eyes for just a moment, then turned and quietly left the cabin.

She had not been gone for very long when Edgar's door opened silently. Michael Norton came inside and shut it behind him. He went straight to Edgar's berth. 'Well?'

Skelton's head turned quickly to look up at his secretary. His smile now was genuine. He pushed the covers away and swung his feet to the floor. 'I could use some brandy, my boy. Fetch the bottle!'

'What did she say?'

'Never you mind, Michael. She's my business, not yours. Just rest assured that she'll cause me no problems.'

'*Us!* She'll cause *us* no problems, Edgar. We're in this together.'

Skelton smiled thinly at him. 'So you keep reminding me! Now, get the brandy, like a good chap, and we'll drink a toast to the end of that damned pirate, and to riches even beyond your greedy little imagination, my boy!'

CHAPTER EIGHT

LATE AFTERNOON sunlight slanted through blackjack oak and scrub pine to lie in broad bands of shimmering gold dust on the forest floor. As the big chestnut gelding plodded heavily through the tangle of dead leaves and roots underfoot, a shaft of diffused light picked out the copper-coloured hair of the rider. Every inch of these South Carolina woods was familiar to the man. He had climbed many of these tall cedars as a boy. He had swung on looping vines that trailed out over the water, then dropped into the sparkling river below, to swim far up to where the banks curved sharply to the left and out of sight. He had gathered Spanish moss to fortify the dams he had built on the small stream he crossed now, that fed the river. His heart had been filled with contentment and discovery. There had been no room then for sadness.

He headed the big horse down towards the river bank, thankful that he had chosen Banner from his father's stable, for, with his left arm still in a sling, the ageing animal was as much horse as he could handle. When they reached the water's edge he dismounted clumsily, then threw the reins over the horse's head and sat beside him as Banner drank deeply. A shrill warning cry from a crow high in a treetop startled him, for it was strangely quiet all around as though the woods slumbered in the heat of a dying day.

He reached into the pocket of his breeches and pulled out the letter. It had been read, folded and refolded so often that the creases in the heavy paper were weakened and tearing. He knew the contents of it now by heart, as he scanned the neat spirited writing:

Mon ami,

I write this in hopes that your health continues to improve. Until today I knew only that you were gravely wounded when Cayo Aristo rowed you back to the *Liberty* that terrible night. Then, just today, your ship put in at Galveston again after a successful run, and Mr Merritt brought me word that you convalesce at your father's home in South Carolina. He tells me your ship will berth at Charleston before Christmas, and he and your men will await further word from you there. I learned too that Cayo works for you again, a contrite, chastened man since his betrayal. He swears he was told only that Skelton planned to send you back to England in irons, and was certain that you would again outwit them. But it was, after all, the fisherman who saved your life, and I doubt that he will ever again let his greed override his loyalty.

That night when Skelton and his secretary came to my shop looking for you, it was Norton who searched upstairs, found your embroidered waistcoat and recognised it as belonging to you, whom they had met at Crosswinds. It was he who went there while Skelton stayed here guarding me. The man Laura married may be many things, but at least he is no assassin, for it was the secretary who shot you. I told Mr Merritt that I can no longer be of use to the operation now that I am known to be your accomplice, and gave him the name of someone on the mainland who is anxious to help and can be trusted. I will miss you, *mon cher*, and our work together. I pray that your wounds heal. I speak also of your heart, for I know how much you loved Laura. I would give so much if things had turned out well for you, but you must try to forget her and get on with your life. *Courage, mon brave.*

Thérèse Georges

The big gelding had drunk enough. Banner shook his head and stamped impatiently on the soft ground. But Sloan Benedict was not ready to go back. Not yet. 'Hold it, boy,' he said quietly. The silence here, with the whispering woodland behind him, should have brought solace to his melancholy spirit. Instead, his thoughts went to somewhere far across the sea; to England, where Laura was. For just a moment he closed his eyes and could almost feel her sitting here beside him, her knees drawn up under her chin, gazing out at the opposite river bank, savouring the silence with him. He had imagined her to be everywhere with him these last six weeks as his chest wound slowly healed. He had sometimes thought it was her light footstep he heard outside his bedroom door—but it was only Matty, the house girl, coming to change his linen. There were echoes of her voice in the evening breeze that cooled his feverish forehead, and he had wakened more than once to sit up in bed, ignoring the pain, to call her name. But only the dark night outside whispered an answer.

When once he left his bed—the doctor announced only this morning that he might—he found himself looking for her in every room of the big house. Sometimes the image of her standing there in a shadowed corner of a room was so real that he had to rub his eyes to confirm that it was a mirage after all. He had dreamed he held her close, as he had on the night it had all come to an end. He could remember about the night only that they had wondrously consummated their love and then been wrenched apart. It was not until the *Liberty* put in at Charleston, with his fever broken and his mind cleared, that he realised it was too late for them—for him and Laura—for by now she would be far out at sea, married to another man.

Benedict got to his feet and winced at the stab of pain in his shoulder as he swung his leg across the saddle. He headed slowly back towards the ridge, determined to put his mind to something else—to someone else. He had had a run-in just this morning with Westerly's farm manager, and the memory of it still angered him. Preston Ames was a cocky little fellow who had done things pretty much the way he had wanted to since Benedict's father's infirmities kept him from checking on field operations. Because of Ames's laziness, the cotton yield on the sprawling five-hundred-acre plantation had fallen off sharply during the last few years. Just this morning, the first opportunity Benedict had had to head down to the farm office and storage sheds to see for himself why production had suffered, he had had words with the foreman. 'You're going down too deep,' Benedict had told him. 'You're letting them set the ploughs at nine inches, Mr Ames, which is all right for the heavier soil, but four inches is plenty for sandy soil like this.' They had stood together at the edge of the field, watching the mule-teams at work. Ames had mentioned coldly that he had had no complaints in the fifteen years he had been supervising the planting of cotton at Westerly. 'During the latest of those years,' Benedict had reminded him, 'our yield has dropped off a third. I've seen the ledgers, Mr Ames.'

Ames had later stood beside him outside the seed-shed, his face red with anger. 'When those last fields are picked,' Benedict ordered, 'send your people in there to destroy every last trace of green plant. The ground is infested with disease.' Ames had watched him darkly. 'Those fields that are clean, we'll plant with soybeans, cow peas and corn, which we'll turn under next spring before planting time. Do it, Mr Ames. You've let the soil go. We've got to bring it back. And another thing, damn it, these men are not to be treated like animals. If I hear of another mutilation of a slave, for *any* reason, you'll answer to me!' He had ridden off, leaving Ames standing on the ramp, grumbling. Serves him right, Benedict thought. The little bantam rooster has had it too easy here. It is time somebody cut him down to size.

Banner plodded heavily now up the rise and in a moment, through the trees, Benedict saw his father's graceful old house gleaming white in the setting sun in its lacy collar of live oaks. He found Henri Benedict where he expected to find him—in the library huddled over his ledgers, his spectacles perched at the end of his authoritative nose. The old man's concentration was so intense that he had not heard his son's footsteps in the hall. Benedict stood just inside the door and coughed—just once, but it was not enough to attract his father's ear.

'Father?' he finally said aloud.

Henri Benedict's head turned slowly. Again his son was saddened to see the difference the years had made in his appearance. His hair had thinned, and snow-white side-whiskers all but obscured the lower half of his face. His big-boned figure was stooped and seemed to have shrunk inside his clothes. But it was his hands that had most noticeably aged. They were bent and stiff with gout, the skin on the back of them stretched like transparent parchment over the strong bones. Henri Benedict looked his son up and down as if he was surprised—not to see him downstairs at last after six weeks of confinement in the sick-room, but at his appearance. He studied the rough cotton shirt, the faded breeches, muddy boots and month-long growth of beard.

At last he spoke. 'I'm glad you're finally able to move about, Sloan. But go and shave off that loathsome beard, bathe and put on decent clothes. If you plan to dine with me tonight, you can at least look like a gentleman.' He turned again to the open ledgers on his desk.

There seemed nothing else for Sloan to do but to obey

him. He, who had commanded thirty men aboard the *Liberty*, turned obediently with a smile to do as he had been told.

'That's better,' Henri Benedict said as his son appeared in the doorway of the dining-room where the old man was already seated. 'I didn't know that young ruffian who was here before! Come over here and let me look at you.' His eyes smiled as Sloan came to stand before him. It was always in Henri's fine green eyes that a smile began. 'You have your mother's hair; the same red in it. How tall are you now, my boy?'

'A full three inches longer than my berth aboard the *Liberty*, sir,' Sloan said wryly.

'Sit down, sit down.' His father waved him to his place at the table. The two were silent as their dinner was put before them. It was apparent that his son's mention of his ship still stayed with Henri, for in time he spoke again. 'I suppose, since that English shipping company didn't manage to kill you this time, you'll be going back to give them another chance? You plan to continue to break the law, do you? Yes or no?'

'Yes, sir. I can't do otherwise.'

Henri threw down his napkin. 'You young fool!' he said. 'If you're so dead determined to set slaves free, why don't you start here, instead of pirating them on the high seas? At least then you'd operate from home. We've got upwards of a hundred and fifty negroes at Westerly you can run up to Canada on the damned underground railway! You can be an Abolitionist right here, and not risk the wrath of the biggest merchant line in Britain by commandeering their slaves!'

'Those men and women are not slaves when we take them off those Monarch Lines ships, Father,' Sloan said hotly. 'They haven't yet learned what it's like to be sold at auction, to be another man's property. They've been forced from their families, their African homeland. You of all people should understand the unfairness of that! You've always beaten the drum for blood continuity, the importance of families sticking together—why should these things be less important for them? Why should they be denied the human rights we take for granted?'

'Goddam! I treat my people well, and you know it. They're well fed, well clothed, they're a hell of a sight better off . . .'

'Is Christopher better off? I went down to the quarters this morning to see him. Here he is in the prime of life, and he'll never again walk.'

'Ames will not commit such an atrocity again. I have his word on it.'

'His word? You'd believe the word of a man capable of cutting off another man's foot to teach him a lesson?'

The old man grumbled into his wine-glass, which he proceeded to drain at a single gulp. The two men finished their dinner in silence, and it was not until they had settled themselves before the library fire with their brandy that Henri spoke again. 'You're like your mother, you know, my boy,' he said. 'She was so concerned. She *cared* so much what happened to our blacks. She'd probably still be alive today if she hadn't set out in that storm to bring a negro child safely into the world. I've lost one of you, Sloan. I don't want to lose the other.' His eyes misted over at the memory of the woman his son knew only from a faded daguerreotype that sat on his father's dressing-stand. 'There's never been another woman for me. I hoped one day you'd have a love like that.'

'I have,' Sloan said quietly, his eyes fixed on the apple logs that hissed in the fireplace. 'There was a girl in Galveston.'

'A *Texas* girl? Bah!' Henri sat straighter, and frowned at his son. 'Is she the one who sent you the letter? I didn't know Texans knew how to write!'

Sloan winced at the caustic remark. 'No. The letter

was from a dear old friend in Galveston. She's one of us.'

'One of . . . What's a woman doing in a foolhardy operation like yours?'

'After we drop off the Africans in south Texas, they're picked up by sympathisers along the way. With luck, they escape to freedom in Mexico. It's Thérèse Georges who handles all our overland contacts for us.'

'Wait a minute! Freedom? In *Mexico*?'

Sloan nodded. 'Some make it, others don't. Those who do are put aboard Quaker ships for the voyage back to their homes in Africa.'

The old man's head dropped back against the pillow behind him. Silence lay heavily between them while each man stared at the fire. Finally Henri asked, 'Is Laura the girl, then? Matty said you kept calling that name during your delirium.'

'She married another man,' Sloan said simply.

'Good.' Henri studied the strong profile of his son, finely etched by the firelight. 'Forget her, son. There are plenty of pretty girls here to choose from. I ran into Brace Hanes's youngest the other day. She's turned into a real beauty.' He stopped when he saw the young man's jaw harden. 'I want only one thing before I die, Sloan,' he went on softly. 'To have you living here with a wife and fine family of your own. You are all I have in the world, and Westerly is your home.' He turned his head away and closed his eyes. 'We'll say no more about it tonight.'

When next Sloan looked at his father, the old man had fallen asleep. He got up, fetched a rug from one of the sofas in the big room and laid it gently across his father's knees. How thin he was; how frail. He stood for a moment looking down at him, wishing he could tell him how much he loved him, how much he had missed him, but Henri Benedict was a man who had no time for sentiment—or so he pretended. Sloan made his way quietly out into the square hall, lighted by a lamp that sat on the centre table. He walked out through the open front door on to the veranda, where he sat down at the top of the curved stone steps that led to the wide path below. He gazed, unseeing, into the blackness, his spirits as shrouded and heavy as the night.

My father was right, of course. I am needed here at Westerly. Yet how can I give up my work when there is still so much to do? God knows, though, he told himself, there are other good men aboard the *Liberty*, as capable as I am. Merritt, for instance. The first mate was a splendid man. He had been with the young Abolitionist since the beginning; had helped to pay for and outfit the speedy little frigate, which had played such an important role years before in the 1812 conflict. He and Merritt had hand-picked each man who served with them. Not all were Southerners, but each was dedicated to abolishing the practice of slavery. That they had managed their clandestine operation so smoothly was due in large part to Merritt. Together, he and the first mate had perfected their complicated strategy. Never once, during these years, had they suffered any loss of life on either side during the dangerous boarding of those Monarch Line ships known to be carrying black Africans to American shores. Always they operated at dead of night and usually in calm waters.

But the weather had not held for their last foray, and it was then that Merritt's mettle had been put to the test. The first mate saw to the lowering of their longboat into turbulent seas, his boarding party at the ready. These ten men, each armed with a pistol and dagger tucked into his belt, had been carefully coached on their duty when once they had made their way over the side and on to the decks of the sleeping British ship. Each man knew which of the seaman standing watch was his responsibility. Then, a quick stunning blow to the head, and each lookout slumped to the deck, senseless. It was Benedict himself who always took care of the man at the helm and stayed to lash the wheel to keep the big ship on its course.

But, on the last trip, they had found three seamen taking their ease on the afterdeck, wide awake, smoking and talking among themselves. One of their own men was spotted, and it looked for a moment that they would be unable to proceed as planned. However, Merritt himself took care of the extra men, and afterwards made short work of prying open the grille over the hold and slipping below into the putrid bowels of the ship. He had set about calmly, disregarding the added peril to their mission from the delay, cut the chains of the black men imprisoned there and led them, wide-eyed, up the ladder. There, others of their band waited to help the prisoners silently over the side. Some blacks were in such deplorable physical condition that they had to be carried, and as Benedict lowered each one down into the *Liberty*'s longboat, he saw that their own ship was moving away too quickly in the gusting wind, putting too much distance between them and the British vessel to effect a successful transfer.

Mr Merritt, too, saw it as he emerged from the hold. Instantly he gave the signal for the little boat to cast off without him. His men blindly obeyed, as they had been taught to do, and many thought they had seen the last of the first mate. However, as the boat pulled away, Merritt jumped the thirty feet down into the turbulent water to swim powerfully after them and at last to catch up with them. He was hauled safely into the longboat, where he manned one pair of oars himself, pushing aside the younger, less experienced man who was visibly shaken by the close call. It was thanks to Merritt, with his great strength and determination, that they had managed the safe trip back to the *Liberty*. Afterwards, with the dazed blacks stowed in warm, dry quarters and the ship's doctor tending them while Cook handed round hearty fare, Benedict had commended his first mate.

'It's all part of the job,' had been Merritt's reply, for with all his quick thinking and courage, he was a modest man.

He had even refused to share credit with Benedict for the daring raid on Lucas Trevor's house in Galveston, a diversionary tactic that drew the authorities away from Port Bolivar and the newly-landed captives. Since that night, over a year ago, the *Liberty* put in at isolated coves along the mainland where they could remain hidden. God knows, Benedict thought, the first mate knew every possible anchorage along the Texas south shore, where they could safely transfer their negroes to the wagons waiting to take them overland to the Mexican border. Indeed—he smiled at the memory—Merritt had even acted the role of a cruel overseer in pretty respectable fashion as he had first set free, then led, four of their cargo who had been captured at the border back to the safety of their ship. He himself had made the decision to chain them together and parade them down Galveston's main street, while Benedict walked beside them, prepared to acknowledge the four men as his own recaptured slaves. Convincing, too, for had not the town—and Laura—believed it? Benedict had been far less successful months later in his efforts to free three men who had been taken prisoner. Of the three, only one had survived the gruelling overland journey. That man's fate was to be shot almost at their destination, and finally to die almost at Laura's feet in Thérèse's small apartment!

Yes, he thought now, Mr Merritt was amply qualified to handle each phase of the operation himself. He was a born leader. Thérèse Georges's letter had said that the *Liberty* would lay over before Christmas in Charleston, where his men would await him. So. One last trip for him with that gallant little band, Benedict decided. He would put Merritt in charge, and he himself would return to Westerly to shoulder his responsibilities.

Slowly, now that his eyes had become accustomed to the darkness, he saw the outline of live oaks bordering the lane all the way to the main road, as they arched softly against the lighter sky. As if they had been hiding, the stars began to appear one by one. Now, too, a cloud moved aside to let the crystal crescent of moon bathe the sweep of lawn in front of him. A lone whippoorwill's plaintive song came from somewhere deep in the woods, and he was conscious of the whirr of night insects and a far-off shout from the slave quarters at the foot of the gentle rise to his left. He realised again how much he loved Westerly, how much he had missed its beauty, its tranquillity. Oh, how he had dreamed of one day bringing Laura here! But, as Thérèse Georges had so wisely counselled him, 'try to forget her and get on with your life.'

Forget her? He gazed up at the moon and was struck with the thought that in just a few hours that same moon would be looking down on Laura, on the place where she slept. Benedict groaned, then lay back against the cold stone of the veranda and threw one arm across his face. 'Oh, God,' he whispered, 'take care of her!'

CHAPTER NINE

FATHER DENNIS MCLUCHLY called out encouragement to his little mare, who was finding it difficult to keep a steady footing. 'Just another mile, Sally—we're almost there!' There had been a hard frost the night before, not unusual for late November in England, and the hedgerows that stretched on either side of the frozen road to Olney had already been touched with the first icy fingers of the winter that lay ahead. Nearly every yard along the way was piled high with the year's accumulation of golden straw, for the rethatching had already begun on many of the cottages he passed. Yellowed leaves of oak, ash and elm, which had not been scattered by passing traffic along the lane, lay ice-crusted under the horse's hooves, and the footing was treacherous. 'Pick up your feet, lady,' the priest called out as the trap swerved dangerously under him.

The air was raw and cold, and the priest was grateful that Mrs Wetherill had insisted he wear his woollen cape, though he would not tell her so. His housekeeper mothered him shamelessly, and he tried not to encourage her. The big man, already a familiar figure in the countryside around Wyckham, although he had served the few Catholic parishioners at St Jude's for only a little over a year, could often be seen flying by in his shabby little gig, his cloak flowing out behind him, his wild red hair blowing free in the wind, his smile ready, his voice booming out greetings in his jovial Irish lilt.

At last the mare found herself on a dry stretch of road, where pale afternoon sunlight had melted the icy surface. He ran his eyes appreciatively over the long blue vistas of wooded slopes and gentle valleys that stretched on each side. 'Just a little further,' he called out. 'Round this bend up ahead.'

Father McLuchly looked forward to this call today, for he was curious. Like everyone else, he knew that Lord Skelton had put an end to his long bachelorhood by bringing an American bride to his home at Olney. It had not yet been the priest's pleasure to meet the sixth Earl of Skelton, as he was often abroad on business, and when he was in residence he was not inclined to put in an appearance at St Jude's. And no one, as far as he knew, had seen the bridegroom's lady. Speculation was rife in Wyckham—what was she like? The priest had met only Lady Skelton's maid, a Mexican woman who had twice been to his services. He had asked her just last Sunday when he might hope to welcome her mistress, and the maid seemed uncertain how to answer. 'Tell her I shall come to see her,' he had told her, but he could read neither approval nor objection in the maid's dark face.

Mrs Wetherhill, he knew, would demand a full report on his return. She had already gleaned some information about the situation there from her grandson, Eugene Nettles, Olney's coachman. The young man was often to be found sharing a pot of tea with his grandmother in the kitchen of the presbytery. 'But he doesn't tell me anything,' she had assured the priest. 'He's not a prying lad. But you, Father,' she had begged him when he had left that afternoon, 'try to remember what she's wearing, and what she looks like. Is she very rich? Pretty? Young?' She was happy only when he kept her supplied with information about his small congregation, a practice he frowned on.

'You're always looking for gossip to pass along,' he had scolded her. Which was not altogether true. Mrs Wetherill was privy to many of the distressing stories she overheard in his office, but as far as he knew, she kept them to herself.

'There!' he called out to his mare. 'See, just up ahead.'

The rolling hills and woodlands of Olney had at last come into view. Father McLuchly guided his gig into the overgrown lane that led up to the big house, and shook his head at the state of neglect that was so apparent. No one had attempted to clear away the choking weeds and brambles that all but obliterated the fine old wings of stone that marked the entrance. He had heard it said that Lord Skelton's secretary had been busily contacting carpenters and stonemasons in Wyckham, preparatory to repairing the big estate when once spring arrived, and as the priest drove up the rutted lane and saw the wild fields on either side, he felt that a flock of sheep might not be amiss either.

As the fine old house came into view, he half closed his eyes and tried to imagine how it must have looked many years before when it was carefully tended. The lines of the old Georgian mansion were excellent. Of massive stone, it stood like a shabby old aristocrat who had been shorn of her last bit of finery. Its windows, half overgrown with ivy, gave back no reflection of the sun's feeble rays on this dull day, and the grey stone of the house itself was mottled with moss and dead tendrils of vine that had dug deep into the mortar and pulled it away. Some chunks of wall hung precariously in place, and the ground at the base was littered with evidence that many of the building stones had already become dislodged and had fallen. The central part of the house faced on the remains of a paved courtyard, which was weed-grown and uneven. Father McLuchly was glad to know that steps would soon be taken to restore it before it mouldered away altogether.

No servant appeared to take his horse, so he tied her to a rusted hitching-post at the foot at the stone steps that led to the handsomely carved oak door. When, after repeated pulls at the bell, he still received no answer, he pounded on the heavy panels and at last the door opened just a crack. A manservant surveyed him with suspicion.

He introduced himself. 'I should like to see Lady Skelton,' he told the stony butler, then added jauntily, if not altogether truthfully, 'She's expecting me.' Finally, and with stolid reluctance, the servant admitted him.

He was led through a dark hall to a library at the back of the house, and was left there to wait, with only a meagre fire burning on the hearth to bid him welcome. It was a comfortable enough room, with a wide window seat before a bow window that looked out on to what had once been a formal garden, but was now overgrown. Rows and rows of books climbed to the ceiling on two sides, and the remaining walls were panelled in the same dark depressing wood that lined the hall and the broad stairs. There was a dank and musty smell about the place. After some time, he was conscious of a figure standing in the doorway, and turned at once.

'Lady Skelton!' he boomed. 'This is a pleasure.' He charged forward, took the hand she offered, and was instantly struck with its icy coldness. Holding on to it, he led her to the fire, crackling more brightly now. 'Might I be allowed to build up the fire for us?' He pointed to a basket of small logs.

She thanked him as she sat down in one of the two chairs he drew closer to it. Her slender figure (he began to make mental notes for Mrs Wetherill) was attired in a simple lightweight gown of a becoming soft rose, but surely not heavy enough for this climate, he thought. He marvelled at the luxuriant radiance of her ebony hair, drawn back from her face to fall in soft curls to her shoulders. Her face was pleasing in all its aspects, from her finely-chiselled nose to the graceful curve of her chin. She was certainly a beautiful young lady, but it was her eyes that especially caught him. Set wide apart in a clear forehead, they glowed like the deep amethyst of a summer twilight sky, of a depth and intensity . . . He was studying her, he realised, so he looked away, for he had seen something else in her eyes that puzzled him.

Was it sadness? Or fear? He found himself trying to bring a smile to her face, rambling on about the town of Wyckham, politics in the English countryside, and how delighted he was to welcome such a charming addition to his small band of parishioners.

Lady Skelton appeared to be only mildly interested in all that fell from his lips, and remained silent. She seemed removed, somehow, as though her mind were a thousand miles away. He had noticed, on entering the room, a handsome sword that hung above the fireplace, and in an effort to spark her interest and perhaps to break down her reserve, he jumped up and went over to it.

'Ah,' he said, 'I have heard this treasure described by the villagers. The flaming sword of Philip IV of France!' He took it carefully down from its supporting brackets. It was heavy, three feet in length, with a curiously serrated blade and a magnificent hilt of intricately chased steel. He clucked appreciatively as he studied it. 'You know the history of this, of course?' he asked. She shook her head. 'One of your husband's ancestors, I'm told, wrested this sword from the hands of King Philip during an unsuccessful war with England in the thirteenth century. It's a grand weapon. I've been anxious to see it for myself.'

His hostess managed a faint smile, and Father McLuchly replaced the sword with a sigh. He sat down again. 'An impressive history, my lady! I'm sure that you and Lord Skelton hope that many stalwart sons will pass on the tradition of his respected title. But I have been doing all the talking. Tell me about your family, your home . . .' He stopped at a sudden sound from Lady Skelton's lips that he could not interpret. Was it a sob, a sigh? He looked at her and could not tell. She had covered her mouth with one hand. Was it his mention of her home? Of course, the lady was homesick! Transplanted here with an ocean between her and her loved ones, perhaps rich, pampered and popular there, and to come to this dismal place! He reached out and took both her hands in his. An extravagant gesture, but the situation seemed to call for it.

'My dear child,' he said quietly. 'I think I know what you're going through. You are many miles from home and sorely miss your family. Added to that, you face a whole new life here, with so many adjustments to be made; unfamiliar food, climate and relationships. These things can have a disastrous effect at first, both emotionally and physically. 'I've seen it happen often. You must simply try to be patient.'

At last now she looked directly at him, and her eyes glistened with tears. Heartened that he had found the key to her unhappiness, he squeezed her hands, then released them. 'And perhaps there hasn't been time to hear from your loved ones at home. But it won't be long, believe me. And, in the meantime, you have a loving husband to comfort you, and a fire to warm you, and a new country anxious to welcome you. You also have St Jude's, my lady, where we hope to see you next Sunday!'

He rose to his feet (wait until Mrs Wetherill hears that I was never even offered a cup of tea, he thought!), and took his leave. Lady Skelton followed him to the door, her smile forced, he thought. As he let himself out into the chilling air, he none the less counted his visit a success. She is young, and all she needs is time, he told himself. Time, and a newsy letter from her family back in . . . *Texas*, was it? The priest whistled gaily to his mare, and was pleased to see her ears flick in answer.

When Laura heard Father McLuchly's trap pull away from the house, she went back to the fire and stared at it. Never had she wanted so desperately to take someone into her confidence. She had dared not look too long into the priest's kind brown eyes, for surely he would have read there the depths of her misery. Had he called on her yesterday—only yesterday—she thought numbly, she might have been able to conduct herself more amiably. But now, with the frightening possibility that Maria was right, Laura could not pretend that all was well. For just this very morning she had heard from her maid's lips the one thing she feared most. They had been returning from their daily walk, picking their way carefully across frost-stiffened grasses that carpeted the small woodland, when Laura had been swept with a wave of dizziness. She had clung to Maria's arm.

'I must sit down,' she had told her. 'I feel faint. I can't walk another step until I rest.'

Maria had lowered her mistress on to a fallen log. As she untied the ribbons of her bonnet and unfastened the collar of her cloak, she had said, 'It has been too long a walk for you, *niña*!'

'No, no . . .' Laura had leaned against the comforting shoulder beside her. 'Be patient with me, Maria. I've not yet become acclimatised, I suppose. Every morning now for over a week I have felt so—so . . .'

She had stopped, and Maria's voice came softly, full of concern. 'What, *niña*? What?'

'So—ill. It's the food, I'm sure. Cook's heavy gravies, the puddings. But I often feel unwell.'

At a small cry from her maid, Laura had turned to look at her. A smile had spread across Maria's face. 'You cannot guess?'

'Guess?' she had asked.

Maria had reached out to take one of Laura's hands in hers. 'Ah,' she said, scarcely able to contain her joy. 'You are going to have a child, *niña*!'

The words struck Laura like a physical blow. She had pulled away, too stunned to say anything, to do anything but stare at the maid.

'You'll see,' Maria had gone on. 'Things will be happier for you now with a baby of your own!'

Maria could have no means of knowing that if indeed

she was pregnant, it was certainly not Edgar Skelton's child she carried. But was it possible? Dear God, she had thought wildly, is it true? She had turned her face from Maria to hide her astonishment. The pirate's child! Sloan Benedict's child! When she could finally get control of her voice, she turned back to the maid. 'Say nothing of this to anyone—until we know!'

Before they had reached the big house after their walk, the exhilarating prospect of carrying a living, breathing part of her pirate under her heart filled her with a surge of happiness. But later, as she sat alone at luncheon—Edgar was in London and Michael Norton in Wyckham—the full realisation of her plight had overwhelmed her. If it were true, what would happen to her? Edgar would certainly banish her, and what would she do then? Where could she go? By the time the priest arrived in early afternoon, she could not look that good man in the eye lest her guilt at the possibility that she carried her lover's child be all too easily read.

As she stood now before the fire, the sun broke through the overcast sky outside, and the dark library brightened. Determined to close her mind to borrowed trouble—for it could only be borrowed until she knew the truth, she told herself sternly—she walked to one of the shelves that lined the wall. She scanned the titles, then took down a small leather-bound book of Keats's poems, intending to lose herself in it. She was certain of only one thing: that she must suppress this panic that stifled her when she dwelt on what might lie ahead of her if Maria's diagnosis was correct. She curled up against the pillows lined up along the window seat and opened the book at random, to stare unseeing at its yellowing pages. The priest's words had fallen on deaf ears, she had thought, but now as she gazed at the open book before her, she began to recall them. She was only homesick, he had told her. It would take time and patience to adapt to her new environment, to the different climate and unfamiliar diet. Laura thought of the black pudding Meredith had set before her at lunch, which she had pushed away untouched. As she herself had told Maria that morning, the heavy food at Olney could easily account for her frequent surges of nausea. She had once, in the few weeks since her arrival, gone to the kitchen to suggest a lighter diet than Cook's country stand-bys of pigeon pie, ham, cold boiled beef, mutton, steak, kidneys and barley dumplings, only to find Michael Norton confronting her there.

'I have personally managed the kitchen quite satisfactorily,' he told her in front of Cook, 'and until I hear otherwise from his lordship, I shall continue to do so.'

Perhaps another contributing factor to my unease during these weeks, Laura thought now, is the friction caused by having Norton in the house. His manner with her was rudely condescending, his implied authority in all household affairs continually demeaning, as if he sought to make it clear to her that she would never exert any influence here—not even in the kitchen! He was witty and affectionate with Edgar, but only barely civil to her when he found it necessary to include her in a conversation at all. She had spoken to Edgar about it.

'Now, Laura,' he had replied, 'he means well, and he's important to me.'

'What does he do for you here?' Laura had asked him. 'Just what are his duties?'

He had hesitated for only a moment. 'Well, he has managed the estate for years. He handles my correspondence for me, keeps the farm ledgers . . .'

'*Farm* ledgers? I've seen no evidence of a working farm here!'

'Come now,' Edgar said, 'you're being childish. I feel obligated to give him a home. You must learn to ignore him, Laura.'

She had tried to ignore him, but perhaps her complaint had done some good, after all. Not that the secretary's manner had changed, but Edgar himself seemed to show more consideration for her. Just a few days later they had been seated at dinner and Norton had, as usual, monopolised the conversation, all directed at Edgar. He had been outlining his plans for the repair and redecorating of the main drawing-room at Olney, which had been closed off for years.

'Brocade curtains,' he had said matter-of-factly, piling mashed potatoes on his fork. 'Gold, I think.'

'I hate gold,' Edgar had said mildly.

'But those small side chairs would be beautiful upholstered in the same fabric, Edgar, and the sofas at the other end of the room.'

'It's a dark room,' Edgar had remonstrated. 'I think a warmer colour might be better.' Laura, certain that still another of their foolish arguments was beginning, was unprepared when he addressed her. 'What do you think, Laura?'

His question had so surprised her that it was a moment before she answered. 'I agree with you, Edgar. A soft rose might be lovely, and there's already rose in the border of the rug. It would warm the room nicely.'

Norton had appeared to bristle at what must seem a sudden conspiracy between the two. 'Come, now,' he said petulantly, addressing Edgar. 'I have experience in these matters. I believe you would hang crude sacking at the windows, Edgar, simply because you do not care about such things.'

Laura, encouraged by taking a part in the discussion, had spoken coolly. 'Since it is Lord Skelton's home, Mr Norton, he may indeed hang a Union Jack at each window if he chooses.' She thought she detected a glimmer of amusement in Edgar's eyes.

'Well——' Norton had chosen to ignore her, 'I'll send for the decorator later, but I'm going up to London tomorrow to see some new ideas, Edgar. I'll be using our rooms there, of course.'

Laura had looked directly at the secretary for the first time since she had sat down at the table. 'Do you expect to go by carriage?' When he said nothing, she had gone on, 'Whose carriage do you propose to use?'

Norton's fork had stopped halfway to his mouth. 'Why? Edgar's, of course. Whose carriage would I be expected to use?'

'You have received permission from my husband, have you?' Laura had persisted. 'It may be that he has plans of his own.'

It was Edgar who had put a stop to it instantly when he had said, 'It's all right, Laura, my dear. I have no use for the carriage tomorrow.'

So, thought Laura, with Edgar as an ally, I might one day learn to ignore the constant rudeness of the secretary, but it will take time. And meanwhile she must expect that her body would rebel just as surely as her spirit at the continually tense atmosphere in the house. Perhaps Father McLuchly had been correct, and the annoying and persistent nausea was simply a bad case of nervous indigestion. But he had been wrong in assuming that she was homesick, and that a letter from home would restore her spirits. Just this morning she had received a note from Aunt Stark, and the news her aunt imparted—while surprising and causing her concern for her father's health—had none the less left Laura unmoved.

She felt in the pocket of her skirt for the letter, and pulled it out. Her aunt's spidery script leaped across the paper.

> By now you are settled in at Olney, and I know that you are blissful in your married state. I've heard it said that weddings are contagious. Perhaps so, love, for at this very moment

Madame Georges is busy sewing a trousseau —for me! By the time you receive this, John Messersmith and I will be married and living in a new home just outside New Orleans. I worry so about leaving poor Lucas, for your father is not at all well. He is given to attacks of chills, sweats and great weakness, yet still he drives himself at the bank. Gone, of course, are his political ambitions, for his recurring bouts of illness perforce keep him low. I do worry how he will manage with just a housekeeper, once I'm gone! I enclose my new address. Now, be a good girl and write often to your loving aunt,
 Ernesta Stark.

Laura put the letter down, and was conscious that the big house lay around her as quiet as a tomb. The silence seemed almost to crouch like a living thing in the deepening shadows of an early dusk. How could she ever feel at home here at Olney? She had never felt that Crosswinds was her home either, but suddenly she longed to hear again the sharp clatter of wagon-wheels along the cobbles of the Strand, excited shouts from down along the quays, the hollow clip-clop of horses' hooves . . . even Aunt Stark's excited voice crying 'Mercy, mercy!' She missed perhaps most of all the caressing breezes off the Gulf, the broad white beaches and open stretches of sea and sky. But with thoughts of Galveston came the memory too of Sloan Benedict holding her close in his arms, and remembering the warmth of his embrace, she knew that she would truly never feel warm, or at home, again.

She looked down at her hands, trembling now as she folded her aunt's letter and put it away. She was about to close the book of poetry, when a line caught her eye. *'This living hand, now warm and capable of earnest grasping . . .'* The words were familiar. Where had she heard them before? She held the book up higher to catch the waning light, and then remembered. The pirate had quoted those words to her that first night when he had taken her hand in his and studied it as they confronted each other in the hall at Crosswinds. She read on: *'This hand would, if it were cold and in the icy silence of the tomb, so haunt thy days and chill thy dreaming nights that thou wouldst wish thine own heart dry of blood . . .'* She read it again, then again. When the poem's tragic implication became clear, she felt as if a knife had been plunged into her heart. Had Sloan Benedict been familiar with the rest of the poem, she wondered, when he quoted the first line to her? If he had, had he somehow known that death would all too soon separate them for ever? She closed her eyes, and the book fell to her lap.

Half an hour later, when Meredith came into the library to set out the lamps, Laura was still sitting there, staring out at the black night that had silently closed her in.

CHAPTER TEN

As the days wore on, there was less and less uncertainty about Laura's condition. No longer could she pretend that her morning illness resulted from something other than a pregnancy, for she had been careful to restrict her diet to only the lightest fare. There had been no further confrontations with Edgar's secretary to distress her. And she was certainly not homesick. Maria went about her daily tasks humming snatches of Mexican lullabies, and kept her word about not mentioning her suspicions to a soul. Her bright eyes and air of expectancy, however, betrayed her joy at the anticipation of a baby in the house. Already she had begun to unpack her mistress's one remaining trunk in a hall bedroom next to Laura's, which she hoped would soon be used as a nursery instead of a general storage-room.

Laura, her mood see-sawing between moments of rapture at the thought of the child growing within her and depths of dark depression, was not surprised when, a week after the priest's visit, Maria came to upbraid her for not yet having seen Wyckham's doctor to confirm the coming event. The maid was right, of course. Better to know the truth at last, Laura realised, and face the frightening consequences. She chose a day when Edgar had, only the night before, returned from London, to ask him for the use of the carriage that afternoon.

'Oh?' Edgar seemed surprised at the request.

'I haven't yet been to town, Edgar. I'm anxious to make a few purchases.'

'Give Nettles a list, my dear, and he can do your shopping for you.'

'I'd far rather go myself. I feel as though I've been cooped up here for so long!'

He had finally, and not ungraciously, consented, and that afternoon Laura stood with Maria on the doorstep waiting for Nettles, the young coachman, to bring the carriage. As she settled beside her maid, with a lap robe tucked round her, she tried not to think of what might lie ahead. Instead she concentrated on the scenery moving past them. A soft haze blurred the gentle rise and fall of hills and valleys—the result, Nettles told them, of smouldering fires the farmers had set earlier in the week to burn stubble from their fields. Modest stone cottages huddled within their walled-in gardens, each with a plume of smoke poised over its chimney, waiting for a breeze to waft it away. Further on, Maria exclaimed aloud to see a handsome cow stick its great head through the hedge and watch them as they passed. A cock pheasant, all gilded chestnut and fiery green, crossed the road just ahead, then scurried to cover as the horse's hooves came closer.

Just before they reached the town of Wyckham, they crossed a low stone bridge, to see just beyond it, at a sharp bend in the road, the tiny shape of St Jude's. Maria pointed it out, as it was partially hidden within its own concealing woodland. The lane here was overhung with ash and oak trees, skeletons now against the lowering sky, with only a few tattered leaves still clinging to their branches. As they drew nearer to the town, they passed laden farm carts, a carrier's wagon, and farmers trudging by in their stout weather-resisting smocks and corduroy breeches. Nettles waved to a woman who stood in the open doorway of one of the cottages. 'That's me mum,' he told them. The woman waved back, a stolid rosy figure in a dress of coarse linsey-woolsey, with a heavy shawl about her shoulders.

By now they had reached the village, a pleasant little town with its small shops, blacksmith, saddler, wheelwright and mason. At the centre of Wyckham they came upon a large rectangular area of grass, brown now, bounded all around by old half-timbered houses, some gabled, some thatched. Laura had learned, through guarded inquiry of Meredith, that the village physician, Dr Benning, had a surgery in one of the buildings on the square.

She leaned forward and called out to Nettles, 'Just drop us off here at the confectioner's shop, if you please. We'll be an hour or so, and we'll meet you here when you return for us.' She did not look at Maria, but felt the maid's hand squeeze hers gently, as the carriage pulled over to the side of the road to let them alight.

'Where the dickens have you been?' Michael Norton poked his head in at the open carriage door on their return to Olney that night.

It had been dark for over an hour, and the rain, which began shortly before Laura and Maria left Wyckham to head for home, splattered noisily on the carriage roof. Nettles jumped down from the seat to help the ladies to descend the step, and Laura lowered herself carefully on to the wet paving.

It was Nettles who hastened to explain why they were late. 'All manner of troubles, sir, with the horse throwin' a shoe and the smith never there when you need him, and the ladies had to wait donkey's years in the tea-shop while I . . .'

'I've been waiting here since five o'clock! Do you know what time it is now?' Norton grabbed Laura's arm. 'Edgar's already sat down to dinner. I should have left two hours ago! At this rate, I won't get to London until almost midnight—if I'm lucky, with this cursed rain.'

Laura shook him off angrily. 'Mr Norton, hold your tongue!' She tried to move on up the steps, but he held her back.

'Look at me when I'm talking to you!' he shouted in her ear.

'Sir,' said Nettles, 'the lady's gettin' wet standin' here!'

Maria managed, on stepping down on to the ground, to break Norton's grip on her mistress's arm by thrusting herself roughly against him, muttering, in rapid Spanish, what sounded like profuse apologies but were really vulgar allusions to his ancestry.

As the two women climbed the stone steps to the front door, they could hear Norton shouting now at the coachman. 'I don't give a damn if you've not had your supper! Put another horse to this carriage and let me get on my way immediately!'

'Pay no attention to him, *niña*,' Maria whispered to Laura as they entered the cold hall. 'Here, give me your wet cloak, then go in and have your dinner. We must take special care of you now.'

'No one is to know,' Laura said quietly. 'Not yet.'

Maria nodded dubiously, disappointed that the exciting news could not at last be circulated in the house. 'You're trembling,' she said. 'Perhaps you'd better come upstairs first for a hot sponge-bath.'

'I'm all right,' Laura assured her. 'Please . . .' Both women looked up quickly as Edgar Skelton entered the hall. He had obviously been drinking.

'No need to explain anything, my dear,' he said. 'I overheard that little scene outside. But you are very late, you know. I've already begun my dinner.' He led Laura into the dining-room and pulled out her chair. 'Michael didn't decide until after you and your maid had left that he must be in London again tomorrow. He'll be staying overnight.' He went to take his place opposite her at the table, and rang the small brass bell at his elbow to summon the butler. The man appeared immediately. 'Meredith, serve Lady Skelton's dinner at once,' he ordered.

Laura stared at the plate of warmed-over food when it was set before her, only half conscious that the rain, heavier now, pelted at the windows, and wind-driven branches began to whip at the walls of the house. Conversation was difficult over the noise of the rising storm. She looked up once to see Edgar watching her.

'Eat your dinner, my dear,' he said. Although quite talkative, his words were badly slurred. She tried to smile but could not, and picked up her fork mechanically to hold it poised over the unappetising mutton chop. 'I know Michael upset you,' Edgar called out, 'and I'm sorry. But we must give the devil his due. He is so anxious about the downstairs decoration, and sometimes his boyish enthusiasm is wearing. But you are mistress here, and I shall tolerate no further impertinence from him.' His voice went on in a conciliatory manner, but Laura was no longer listening. She laid down her fork and clasped her hands in her lap, watching the candles at the centre of the table, almost mesmerised by the leap and sputter of their flames as they danced in the draught from the doorway.

Edgar's voice droned on. '. . . and when the weather turns pleasant, we'll set about putting the gardens in order, and begin to restore the outside of the house.' He had emptied a decanter of wine and was about to call the butler for another when Meredith appeared from the shadows to stand at Edgar's side.

'We've got trouble, my lord,' he had to raise his voice over the fury of the wind and rain. 'The roof's leaking up in the east wing. The Mexican woman is up there now trying to mop it up, but I think you'd better come to see what's to be done.'

Edgar, annoyed, bade Laura excuse him. Then the two men, each with a candle, made their way from the room and she was left alone.

She had already made the decision, on hearing the doctor's confirmation of her condition, that she must leave Olney at once, without a word to anyone. There was no other choice. She would simply disappear. The dining-room suddenly blazed white as a flash of lightning lit up the sky. Then, almost directly overhead, a deafening clash of thunder shook the big house. She got quickly to her feet and made her way out of the dining-room and up the stairs to her own bedchamber, closing the door sharply behind her. I must think; I must plan, she told herself. There is enough money in my reticule, surely, to get me to London. But once there, what then? She remembered that she had brought all of Amanda Trevor's jewellery with her. She could certainly pawn that when once she reached the city. That is all I shall take with me, she decided. Just the jewellery.

The room was dark; she had not thought to bring a candle with her, but in the intermittent flashes of lightning she moved over to her highboy, opened the drawers one by one, looking for her jewellery box. In her searching, her fingers came across a hard irregular-shaped object tucked in with her lingerie. Even before she opened the embroidered linen case, she knew that it contained the silver cross her mother had given her. Maria must have packed it away with my things, she thought. I have not seen it since the night I learned that Amanda Trevor was not my mother. Oh, so long—a lifetime—ago! She slipped the cross now from its case, and walked to the fireplace, where a fire still smouldered fitfully, coming to life occasionally when quick bursts of wind drove down the chimney.

Only now did she think of insurmountable obstacles confronting her in the prospect of a flight from Olney. If she did manage to get to London . . . How? On foot? What would happen to her there? She had not only herself to think of now, but the child as well! She could perhaps provide for her own needs, but what of her baby's? She leaned her forehead against the cold marble of the chimneypiece and clutching the cross to her breast, ran her fingers absently over the back of it, feeling the rough letters etched there. 'Defend, O Lord, this child.' Thoughts of her own mother surfaced all unwittingly, and she felt a sudden surge of understanding for the woman she had never known, as she laid the silver cross on the mantelpiece. Her mother too had perhaps faced such a situation when she found she carried a child conceived out of wedlock. Maybe she too had wondered what would become of them, and had finally been forced to give up her baby to secure a better future for it. Laura thought back over Maria's words to her in the kitchen at Crosswinds. 'Your mother would have done anything, *anything* to keep you, but she could not.' 'No,' Laura cried aloud, her words lost in the raging of the storm outside, 'I will not give up my child as my mother did! I will do anything, *anything* to keep him!' But what? What could she do?

She heard the sound of heavy footsteps, and knew that it would be Edgar returning to his room directly across the hall. For a moment he hesitated, just outside her door, and she held her breath. Then, over the moaning wind and heavy rain lashing at her windows, she heard the door of his bedchamber slam shut. For a moment she had feared that he might come into her room and perhaps try to calm her fears at the violent storm that seemed now poised directly over the house. Edgar had never touched her during their weeks together, keeping the promise he had made aboard the *Triton* that he would not force his attentions on her. But tonight, alone in the house, with Michael Norton away, and surely excited by all the wine he had drunk at dinner, might not he . . . might not he . . . ?

A quick burst of fire in the sky lit up her room, and it was as though, with the blaze of light, that the solution to her dilemma came. Laura had known the power of her beauty, had read the desire in men's eyes as they looked at her, had felt it in the lingering touch of their hands.

Although her husband had thus far remained immune to her charms, might not she try . . . She shuddered at the thought, but still—it *could* work! It might! And she would try *anything*!

She ran to the dressing-stand in the dark, unpinned her curls and brushed out her hair until it fell softly to her shoulders, then she flew to the door and opened it. She went across the landing, and for one brief moment, hesitated in front of Edgar's door. Then, taking a deep breath, she raised her hand to knock loudly upon it. 'Edgar,' she cried. 'Oh, Edgar, please, please, let me in!'

When there was no answer, she pounded against it with both fists, crying his name louder. 'Let me in, let me in!'

At last the door was thrown open and Edgar Skelton stood there, outlined against a flash of lightning that filled the room behind him. It was instantly apparent that he had been drinking more wine, for he backed away from her unsteadily. 'What's this?' he asked drunkenly. 'What're you doing here?'

'Oh, Edgar, I'm afraid of the storm!' A resounding clap of thunder right over their heads drowned out her words. She flung herself against him. 'Hold me, hold me!' she cried.

He pushed her away roughly. 'What nonsense is this? What're you doing here? Get back to your room!' He turned abruptly from her and stumbled over to a small sofa before the empty fireplace and fell on to it.

For a moment Laura stood there, making no move to go to him, her resolve weakening. But when lightning flared again and Edgar's massive four-poster bed loomed up beside her, its heavy brocade hangings blood-red in the stark white light, she knew she must go through with this. There was no other way.

She went over to the sofa and dropped to her knees in front of him. 'Edgar!' She saw his eyes staring unseeing at her. 'You must not shut me away like this. You are my husband . . .' her voice faltered, 'and I need you. Please let me stay here with you tonight.' He tried to shake her away. 'Edgar, listen to me, please . . '

But he had begun slowly to pull himself to his feet. His body leaned dangerously to one side, and before Laura could reach out to break his fall, he tumbled heavily against the upholstered arm of the sofa, striking his forehead on it. He let out a groan, then slumped to the floor and lay there, his arms stretched wide.

Laura looked over at him, at first too frightened to move. 'Edgar,' she whispered. She heard the distant roll of receding thunder as the storm moved away at last up the valley, and fought back an impulse to run from the room, suddenly overcome with guilt at the depths of her own deceit. But the words came back to her: 'Anything! I will do anything!' She stood up and leaned over him. Then, with a strength borne of wild desperation, she reached down and grabbed him under his arms, and managed to pull him to his feet. He waved his arms drunkenly, but she held tight to him. 'Let me help you,' she whispered. He leaned his full weight against her as she led him over to the bed. He fell heavily on it, and instantly his rasping snores filled the room. With a competence that surprised her, she undressed him and strewed his clothes carelessly on the floor. Then, slipping out of her gown and underthings, she climbed in naked next to him, and pulled up the coverlet. She lay still in the dead dark of his room, willing the long and torturous night to be over.

At some time near dawn she finally fell into a light and troubled sleep. She woke suddenly, aware of someone standing over her, and opened her eyes, expecting to see Maria with her breakfast tray. But it was Michael Norton, his face pale and threatening in the morning light.

'So this is your game, is it?' he whispered, his eyes running contemptuously over her bare shoulders. 'Well, it won't work!'

Laura first thought that she was still in the grip of a nightmare, but as she saw the crimson hangings above her head and realised where she was, the awful reality of the night came back to her. She sat up, clutching the coverlet to her. 'Get out of this room at once!' she hurled at him. He just stood there, watching her. 'I will not say this again. Leave this room!'

Still he made no move, but just looked at her. Suddenly he reached over to take Edgar's dressing-gown from the foot of the bed and threw it at her. 'Here,' he said. 'Put this on and cover yourself.'

Laura's eyes blazed at him. She turned to where her husband lay beside her, flat on his back. 'Edgar, wake up! Wake up!' she cried, but she could not rouse him. He merely grunted and slept on.

Norton leaned closer to her. 'Yes, go on! Wake up your husband and tell him the good news that you're carrying a child. *Another* man's child. Edgar would be interested in that, I'm sure. There,' he said as he saw the blood leave her face, 'perhaps now you'll come with me and listen to what I have to say.'

Laura was at first paralysed by his words. Then, quickly, she slipped into her husband's robe, got out of the bed and walked to the door, with Norton following close behind her. Once out on the landing, she spun round to face him. 'How dare you?' He pulled the bedroom door shut. 'How *dare* you?' she said again. She would have run from him into her own chamber, but he took hold of her arm and held it.

'Don't be so quick to leave, my dear. Aren't you curious to know how I learned of your condition? On the way up to London last night I called in at Dr Benning's for my headache powders, and he asked me to congratulate my employer on his expected heir. Did you really believe you could convince Edgar by climbing into bed with him that *he* had sired your bastard child?'

Laura reached over and hit the secretary hard across the face. He staggered back for an instant, then recovered his balance. He came menacingly towards her, seeming to enjoy her indignation. 'You should have realised by now,' he whispered, 'that Edgar is quite incapable of such a thing. He and I have been lovers for eight years.' He laughed shortly as Laura shrank away in disgust. 'And there's more,' he went on. 'Come, shall we go into your room, where we won't be disturbed?'

Laura, too stunned to resist, felt herself being led across to her own chamber, where she walked in unsteadily and sat down.

'That's better,' he told her, closing the door. 'It so happens that I'm more angry with Edgar than I am with you at the moment.' He began to pace in front of her. 'I found evidence in our rooms in London, when I got there at midnight last night, that Edgar has been entertaining his pretty boys in my absence. I am no longer able to amuse him, it appears. So, you see, it's only a matter of time before he'll discard me, penniless, and bring a new lover here.' He came closer. 'He'll send you away, too, when he learns that you carry Sloan Benedict's child!' He saw her body go rigid. 'You're surprised I know who your lover was? He was still warm from your bed on that night I shot him in the alley behind Crosswinds. I'd found his embroidered waistcoat at the dressmaker's shop, and I knew then that he was the damned hothead we'd hunted for all those months. I remembered meeting him at Crosswinds, you see, so I went there while Edgar waited at the French woman's, and . . . *voilà*! That sly devil, disguising himself as a South Carolina slave-owner when all the time *he* was the one freeing Ripp's shipments of blacks bound for American slave markets. I should have known he was the cursed Abolitionist we were after!'

'Oh, God!' Laura jumped to her feet as an agonised cry escaped from her lips. She pushed past him and ran for the door, but he caught her.

'Don't be in such a hurry to leave, my dear, for you have a deuce of a problem!' He led her to the bed, where she sat down helplessly. 'You're left with Sloan Benedict's child, aren't you? I told Edgar nothing of your little tryst with Benedict that night, for somehow I felt that this information might serve me well one day. And this is the day! There are a few means by which you may work your way out of this. First, as I see it, you could arrange to lose the child. Accidents do happen, after all.'

'No!' Laura cried. 'I *will* have this child!'

'That's touching. Impractical, foolishly sentimental —but touching. I can see how a young lady of your delicate sensibilities would want to keep her only link with her dead pirate. So that's out. Now, let's concentrate . . .' He tapped his forehead lightly. 'There's a second option we might consider. You could go back to Galveston. Your father might even welcome his wayward daughter and illegitimate grandson with open arms —though I doubt it.' He watched her intently. 'No, I can see that idea has no appeal. Number three option, then. You might deceive Edgar into believing that, in his drunken state, he was indeed able to sire a child. But if you think I would remain silent while you secure for Benedict's child not only Edgar's title but his estate and the respectability that attends one in his position, you're quite mistaken. Which brings us to the fourth option. You can leave Edgar, go to London, have the baby, change your name and start all over again.'

Norton had ceased his pacing and now stood close to her, his eyes bright. 'Ah, I thought so! At last we have hit on something. But could you do it all alone? You would need someone, wouldn't you, to arrange for a place for you to stay during your confinement, to see to the annulment of your marriage—which would be accepted in your church, I believe, since the union has never been consummated. In short, you'd need someone to help you in all manner of ways. I think that, so far, you follow me?' A smile had appeared at the corners of his mouth.

Laura could do nothing but stare at him, her heart hammering in her breast.

'I am that very person, my dear,' Norton said, drawing back now, his chest swelling with assumed importance. 'I have friends in London, influential friends. I know what must be done and how to do it. As it happens,' his voice took on a biting edge, 'I, too, must leave Olney, now that I know what Edgar . . . But that's my business. So what do you say? Will you let me help you?'

Surprised at his sudden sympathetic manner, Laura found her voice at last. 'Why—Why would you do this for me? I have nothing to give you . . . no money.'

He frowned at her. 'No? Why, devil take it!' He slapped his forehead. 'You were never told of that inheritance, were you? I couldn't believe it when Edgar said you had been kept in ignorance of Amanda Trevor's legacy all these years, but it would seem to be true after all. Your late mother's estate comes to you on your twenty-first birthday. You'll be rich, Laura! Very rich indeed.' He waited for her reaction, which was not long in coming.

'But Amanda Trevor was not . . .'

'Not rich? Oh, she had a lot of money, believe me. And it will all be yours! Think of it! You have only to send the bank in Galveston your new London address, and everything will be taken care of.' He began again to walk back and forth in front of her. 'Now I think it's time to speak of something else. Were I to exert all this effort on your behalf, I know you agree that I will have earned some sort of remuneration. I would guess that an annual payment of—say, a few hundred pounds might suffice. Each year for the rest of my life.' He stopped and faced her again. 'Is it worth it to you, to be able to shift your considerable burden to someone else? After all, I shall make your welfare my main concern. Yours, and Benedict's child.'

Suddenly feeling very faint, Laura clutched the bedpost for support.

'Realise, dear girl,' Norton went on gently, 'that there is nothing else you can do.' Again he waited, then smiled. 'I take your silence for acquiescence. But, so that there will be no disputing the terms of our little agreement . . .' he strode quickly over to her writing-table, where he opened a drawer, removed a heavy sheet of notepaper and, dipping her pen in the inkpot, began to write, talking all the while, 'I'll spell it out in writing. It isn't that I don't trust you. You're a lady who prays to her Holy Mother every night.' The noise of the pen scratching on the heavy vellum was the only sound in the room. 'There,' he said at last, and motioned for her to come over and join him. 'We'll need your signature, my dear.'

Laura, one hand to her cheek, moved slowly over to the writing-table as if in a dream. When Norton closed her hand round the pen, she signed the paper.

Then he folded up the note and put it into his pocket, and walked quickly to the door. 'We'll leave tonight,' he said. 'We're a team now, Laura. Until death.' He opened the door and stood poised on the threshold, 'Somehow I've always known that beneath that sanctimonious exterior there beats a heart as devious as mine!' With a thin smile, he slipped out into the hall and was gone.

Father McLuchly checked the dwindling pile of religious tracts on the table, reminding himself to replenish it before the Sabbath. Also, he told himself, he must remember to have new rushes strewn on St Jude's earthen floor by then, to warm the feet of the faithful on this first Sunday of Advent. He shivered as a sudden cold draught tugged at the hem of his cassock. While the weather this morning was bleak and cold again—far more normal for the time of the year than was yesterday's unseasonably high temperature and the freak thunder storm during the night—he did not entirely welcome it. He disliked being too long away from the fire in the presbytery study.

He made a mental note to go out later in the morning to assess the storm damage, but his thoughts were interrupted by a quick movement in the shadows behind him. Only the rustle of ivy against the window, he thought absently. There had been small gusts of wind out of the east, and although the sky was dark, the sun had been valiantly trying to break through.

As he leafed through the neat pile of literature on the table, he saw that the church brightened behind him, evidence of the sun's dogged persistence. But something else caught his eye: a hooded female figure. As he watched, the woman leaned heavily against a pew, holding on as if to keep from falling. The priest made his way quickly to her side and took her free arm to support her.

'My child,' he said, 'perhaps you had better sit down.' He felt her stiffen at his touch.

'No—no! Leave me alone!'

'I didn't mean to frighten you,' he said. She turned to look at him, and he recognised at once the extraordinary deep-blue eyes of Lord Skelton's young American wife. 'Lady Skelton!' he cried. She drew away, and he saw that her cheeks were wet with tears. 'I can understand your emotion,' he told her. 'Sometimes, in an empty building, one feels the awesome patience of God, and it can be a very intimidating experience. Come,' he put a hand under her elbow and led her back to the outside door. 'Shall we go over to the presbytery? I have a fire there, and my housekeeper can make us a cup of tea.'

She offered no resistance, and once outside she let herself be guided slowly along the flat stones that led through the trees. The sun had disappeared again in a steel-grey sky as Father McLuchly looked back, surprised to see an empty gig sitting in front of St Jude's. 'You drove here yourself, my lady?' he asked.

She nodded, her eyes lowered.

'Watch your step,' he cautioned her. 'There are icy patches here and there along the paving. Bless my soul, I believe it's begun to drizzle again!'

Once inside the presbytery, he asked Mrs Wetherill to bring them tea, then took his young visitor to his study. Laura would not let him remove her cloak, but pulled it more tightly round her. He set about to stir the fire with a poker, then put on new wood which in a moment crackled brightly on the hearth. Then he pulled up a chair across from her and settled his substantial body into it. 'Now, my child,' he said quietly. 'What can I do for you?'

She kept her head averted, and he could not hear her murmured words. He leaned forward and asked her to repeat them. When she would not, he pressed her gently. 'If I am not to know the purpose of your visit, Lady Skelton, how can I help you?'

'I—I came here because I have no place else to go.'

'H'm.' Not altogether flattering to him, the priest thought.

'I must get away,' she whispered.

Thinking she meant that she must return home, he suggested that he himself drive her back to Olney. 'It's not safe for you to be handling that light trap alone on these icy roads. If you will wait here . . .'

'No!' she said firmly. 'I cannot go back there!'

Father McLuchly's brows lifted. He waited. She made no move to continue. He could see that it would be difficult to get her to speak of what was in her heart, and suddenly he felt very tired. He did not feel up to playing cat and mouse with this unhappy lady. 'Perhaps you would like to make your confession, my child?'

She shook her head. He began to wish for Mrs Wetherill's entrance with the tea. Maybe the hot beverage would loosen Lady Skelton's tongue. He sighed, and decided to take a different tack altogether. 'We have not seen you at Mass. Did you . . . Were you a regular communicant when you lived in Texas?'

At last she spoke. 'I—I was to have been a nun.'

The priest sat up straighter. 'Really? What changed your mind?' He waited again, then decided to answer his own question. 'There is great sacrifice of one's personal life which not everyone is prepared to make. I can understand how you might have felt.'

'No!' Laura stared down at her clasped hands. 'I—I fell in love.'

How simply she said it. The priest felt that he was making some headway. 'But you tell me that you must get away from your husband's house, and in the next breath you inform me that you decided against a life in the church because you fell in love?' A sudden thought stopped him, and he pulled himself to his feet, picked up the poker and began to prod the burning logs. Of course, he thought. It was *another* man she loved. He had heard this story so many times here in his study, and it seemed almost that the little room echoed now with all the sad tales he had listened to, the unchecked tears he had witnessed.

He laid down the poker, straightened and looked down at her. At the sight of her deeply troubled face, he felt his impatience melt away. So much anguish and grief were written there that he turned his anger on himself. What kind of a spiritual adviser was he? He had offered Lady Skelton no comfort for whatever problem brought her, weeping, to the church. Instead, he had asked her why she had not seen fit to attend his services! 'My child,' he said gently, 'I believe that you carry a heavy weight on your soul. Perhaps it will help if you make your confession, after all.'

Her reaction to his words startled him, for she swung round in the chair and raised her tear-stained face to him. 'I must get away from here. Oh, help me, Father! Send me to a nunnery—anywhere—only I must get away from them!'

Mrs Wetherill chose this very moment to enter with their tea, which angered the priest anew. He had at last seen a break in his visitor's reserve, only to see the opportunity destroyed in a whirlwind of domesticity. His housekeeper made a homely little ceremony of setting out the tea-things on his desk, passing the plate of sweet buns under his nose for his approval. Then, when assured that nothing more was needed for his comfort, she finally withdrew.

The priest poured their tea, and handed a cup to Laura. 'Now,' he said, noting that the young woman had somewhat recovered her composure, 'suppose we begin by your telling me something about yourself. I gave you little chance to talk last week when I visited Olney, as I recall.' He noticed the cup shaking in her hand, so took it from her and set it on a table at her side.

At last she began to speak, and Father McLuchly listened intently as her words tumbled out incoherently. She spoke of a Father Jiminez—a priest with warm brown eyes, she said. Suddenly her mind skipped to an overwhelming passion she felt for a pirate—a *pirate*? 'How could I have believed him to be a thief,' she whispered, 'when he risked his live to save others?' She spoke of a small rabbit trapped in an *arroyo*, but where? And why did the memory grieve her so? Then she seemed to travel back to her childhood, and told of planting camellias under a Judas tree, to be cruelly scolded by a father who hated her. She spoke of a mother she never knew, then quickly her thoughts shifted to a narrow alley, a shot ringing out in the darkness, and a blood-stain widening across a white shirt. She would have gone on, but he put a hand on hers. 'Lady Skelton,' he said gently, 'please collect your thoughts. Can you not begin by telling me what brought you here today?'

Laura stared at him for a moment, her eyes too bright, almost crazed with fear. She slipped from her chair with a cry, and threw herself on her knees at his feet. 'Oh, Father!' She clutched the skirt of his cassock like a demented child. 'He made me sign it! He made me promise . . .'

'Who, child, who?'

'Mr Norton. He said he'd help me, but that I must . . . I should never have listened to him, but I am so alone! What could I do?'

The door to the study flew open. The priest looked up, angry that Mrs Wetherill had chosen this precise moment to see that everything was satisfactory. But it was not the housekeeper. A gentleman blocked the doorway, his high-crowned hat and greatcoat glistening with rain, his face crimson. He stood for a moment on the threshold, taking in the scene before him and as if the sight pleased him, his face broke into a smile.

'Thank God!' he said. He came quickly to them, reached down and pulled Laura to her feet. One of his arms went firmly about her waist. 'I am her husband, Father,' he said. 'You cannot know how anxious I have been. When I found that Laura had again tried to run off . . .' He shook his head sadly. 'It is such a pity,' he muttered. 'Such a sadness to see her in this condition.'

The priest stood up slowly. There was surely no doubting the relief that flooded Skelton's face on finding his wife. 'Again?' he asked. 'She has run off before?'

'Many times.' He caught Laura's hands and held them.

'But this is terrible, terrible!' Father McLuchly murmured, his eyes on the struggling girl.

'You must tell me what she said to you, Father,' Skelton snapped.

The priest frowned. 'Since Lady Skelton's words to me were in the nature of a confession . . .'

Skelton had to raise his voice over his wife's cries, as she tried to twist out of his grasp. 'How can we hope to help her if we don't know what brought about this most recent hallucination?'

'Well, she mentioned something about a note she signed—she was forced to sign, she said . . .'

Skelton's eyes snapped wide. 'Forced by whom?'

'I think she said—Norton. Someone named Norton. But truly this is a frightful thing for you, Lord Skelton.'

'Yes. If things don't improve, I fear she may have to be committed.'

Father McLuchly looked at Laura, and indeed, at that moment, she did appear to be deranged. Her eyes blazed as she stared at her husband.

'Come, Laura!' Skelton pulled his wife with him as she struggled against him to be free. 'See,' he tried breathlessly to explain as his wife's fists flailed at him, 'she has the strength of a madwoman when she gets these attacks.'

'But, my dear sir,' the priest followed them out into the narrow hall, 'this is distressing news. Perhaps if she could stay here until she quietens down . . .'

'No, there is only one way to handle this kind of mental disorder. Believe me, I've been through this before.' He called to his young coachman, who ran in quickly from the kitchen, where he had been talking to his grandmother the housekeeper. 'Nettles! Come over here and help me!'

Father McLuchly stood and watched helplessly as the two men carried the fighting woman through the door and out to the waiting carriage. But just before they could put her safely inside, she dragged herself out of their grasp and ran through the rain to where her small gig was still standing. When she reached it, she climbed up on the seat, picked up the reins and whacked them sharply across the horse's back. She moved so quickly that Lord Skelton and the coachman did not at first react.

Then, 'Stop her!' Skelton cried, jumping into his carriage. 'Nettles, for God's sake, come here and go after her!'

Already Laura's gig was hurtling down the lane, her hair flying, her cloak blowing wildly about her. The priest watched as it careered crazily on its approach to the sharp curve in the road, veering to right and left. His own shout was lost in the clatter of Skelton's carriage as it rumbled past him. Laura's light conveyance had by now reached the bridge, and Father McLuchly saw the horse's hooves slide out from under him as he tried to keep his footing on the icy surface. In a panic, the animal fell heavily between the shafts, spinning the small gig out of control. He watched, horrified, as Laura's body hurtled from the seat out on the ground, where she landed in a twisted heap and lay motionless. He picked up the skirts of his cassock and, calling her name, began to run up to the road as fast as his legs could carry him.

CHAPTER ELEVEN

'CAN WE talk in the hall?' Dr Benning whispered to Michael Norton across the big bed where Laura lay heavily sedated. The physician was an imposing man, plump and sedate, who still wore his checked muffler round his throat, as he had not had time to remove it after they had arrived back at Olney with the patient. He kept a large linen handkerchief over his mouth when he spoke, as he was suffering from the first of the many head colds he habitually caught during the raw winter months.

The two men walked quietly from the room, leaving Maria standing at the bedside. She did not even touch the hand that lay so lifeless on the coverlet for fear of rousing her mistress. She still did not know how the accident had happened earlier in the day, but felt herself to blame for it. If I had only been with her, she thought in despair. But why had her *niña* run from the house to hitch up the trap all by herself, then ride crazily off in the direction of Wyckham? What had happened? Maria only knew that when she had brought in the breakfast tray she herself had laid earlier that morning, her mistress's bed was unslept in. She had knocked at Lord Skelton's door, but received no answer. She had not known then that Mr Norton was back from London, shut up in his room, or she would have tried to get some information from him. Instead, she had returned to the kitchen, the tray untouched. Meredith had not noticed; only Cook made mention of the breakfast, cold now, on the tray.

'If you'd bothered to ask me first,' she had told Maria curtly, 'I'd've told you not to bother with fixin' any breakfast for the lady. She took off, she did, early this mornin'. Went flyin' out of here—hitched up the rig by herself, she did—then went off up the lane like the divil was after her!'

'Why didn't you stop her?' Maria had cried.

'Me? I got enough to do here in the kitchen without mindin' everybody else's business!'

So Maria had learned little from Cook. Later, when Lord Skelton finally awoke, she had heard angry words between him and his secretary on the landing. She had understood nothing of what was said, but a few moments later Lord Skelton had stormed from the house in a rage. It was not long afterwards that Maria heard the carriage drive off at breakneck speed, and it had not returned until just before dark. The doctor's coach had followed close behind, with Laura lying semi-conscious against the cushions. Once his wife was put to bed and sedated, Lord Skelton had closed himself in the library with a decanter of brandy, and Norton had given orders that his employer was not to be disturbed.

Maria heard the voice of Dr Benning just outside the open hall door. She crept quietly over to where she could hear better, for she could no longer endure waiting for news of her mistress's condition. 'It was a bad accident,' the doctor was saying, 'but thank God no bones were broken. She is, however, a very sick young lady. I've given her sedatives, and she should sleep now. I haven't yet told her husband that she lost the baby.'

Maria's hand went over her mouth to stifle a cry.

'He didn't know of Lady Skelton's pregnancy,' the secretary murmured. 'And he is *not* to be told of it, is that understood?'

'Well,' the doctor went on, his voice muffled behind his handkerchief, 'she's young. There will be other children. I'll want someone with her at all times, of course. Now, I should like to speak to Lord Skelton, if you please.'

'He's indisposed,' Norton said. 'Let me talk to him. He's distraught, as I'm sure you understand.'

Maria heard the doctor and the secretary go downstairs, then the sound of Dr Benning's carriage as it headed down the lane into the black night. She came slowly back to stand again beside the bed. The big room was cold, despite the low fire that whispered on the hearth. The heavy portières at the windows had been closed against the chill of the evening, and a light rain murmured against the glass. If I could only say a magic word, Maria thought desperately, and we could be plucked back to Galveston where my mistress would soon be well again. Not for the first time she longed to be back on the island, where the bright sun warmed everything it touched and a soft breeze blew in off sparkling water. Here, in this damp English countryside, she felt as though a leaden pot had been turned upside down over her head, with the air trapped in it still and heavy.

She went to the fireplace and put another log on the fire. Then, working the bellows, she watched it spring to life. As she straightened, her eye was caught by a glint of silver on the mantelpiece. She saw that it was her mistress's silver cross. Surprised to find it there, she slipped it into the pocket of her apron, meaning to put it away later. She walked back to the bed and looked down at Laura, whose beautiful face was deathly white in the soft candlelight. Dear God, she thought, I shall never forgive myself if anything happens to my *niña*!

She pulled a chair close beside the bed, sat down and took out her rosary, prepared to begin her night-long vigil. But she could not concentrate on her beads, for she remembered other nights—at Crosswinds, where she had watched the fever rage through the young girl while she lay poised between life and death. Maria had felt guilty then for not stopping her mistress from running out into the storm. Why—*Why* had she not been more sensitive to the girl's distress then? And now? What made her do such a foolhardy thing today? There were no answers. Maria shut her eyes, conscious of angry voices below her in the library, where Lord Skelton and his secretary seemed to be having another argument. Slowly, as the worn beads of her rosary slipped through her fingers and the comforting prayers to the Holy Mother pushed all else from her mind, her body began to relax, and in just a few moments, she had drifted off to sleep.

She was suddenly jarred awake by a sharp sound of breaking glass which came from the library downstairs. Jumping up, she put her rosary into her pocket and crept out on to the landing. She moved quickly to the head of the stairs, peering down into the darkness. No lighted candle had been left in the hall, she noticed, but below her a narrow ribbon of light showed at the bottom of the partly open library door. She heard Lord Skelton's voice, raised in anger.

'Don't lie to me! I know you made her sign some sort of note! Get it!'

'She was hysterical when she saw the priest this morning, Edgar! You said so yourself. She was ranting. There's no note, Edgar. Why would I have her sign . . .'

'Where is it! Get it, or so help me God . . .'

'Edgar, please!'—Maria cringed at the panic in the young man's voice. 'Listen to me! All I ever wanted was to stay here with you, for things to be as they used to before she came . . .'

'Get it!'

'Put down that poker, Edgar! No—*No!*'

A series of heavy blows followed quickly, and Maria put her hands over her ears. As she held them there, she slowly became aware that all noise from the library had stopped. Frozen with terror, she still crouched in the darkness, afraid to move. Only when she heard someone coming towards the half-open door did she slip quickly back into the deep shadows and stand, praying that she would not be seen.

The library door swung wide, and Skelton lunged out into the hall, his figure looming large in the shaft of light that shot across the floor. He moved unsteadily past her, his breathing heavy, and crossed to the door of the servants' wing. He opened it, and she heard his footsteps fading as he disappeared into the black corridor. Still she dared not move, nor did she make an effort to look into the library. She knew too well what she would see there. She waited for what seemed an eternity before she again heard the sound of footsteps—this time coming towards her. In a moment she saw the shifting light of a candle flickering nervously along the ceiling of the narrow corridor. It was Meredith, the light playing eerily on the butler's dour face. Skelton followed close behind. As the two men entered the front hall, Skelton spoke.

'Just do as I say. Ask no questions.'

They passed not five feet in front of her, then disappeared into the library and shut the door. Still she did not move, for the boards of the hall and the stairs were old, and creaked underfoot. It was not until she heard the outside door of the library open and the sound of something heavy being dragged out into the night that she was at last able to make her way to the stairs and run quickly up to Laura's bedchamber. When she had closed the door, she went across and blew out the candle at the side of the bed, then took her place again in the chair, trembling with an unearthly cold. She took out her rosary and clutched it to her breast.

She was suddenly conscious of a sound from the garden—a grating sound, like a shovel digging into the frozen earth. Once again, her hands moved over the beads: 'Hail Mary, Mother of God.' The rhythmic noise continued, and she tried to close her ears to it. 'Blessed art thou . . .' But it was no use. The memory of that other night, so many years ago, began to flood in on her. She had thought it so deeply buried that it would never come back to haunt her, but it was back now, persistent, terrifying. On that night, too, she had sat in a darkened bedchamber at Crosswinds, keeping vigil at the bedside where Amanda Trevor lay, her cold, beautiful face no more serene in death than it had been in life. Then, too, she had heard the sound of digging in the back yard and had found it impossible to concentrate on the familiar prayers. She had tried to pray instead for the soul of the woman's dead baby as it was laid to rest in unhallowed ground, and even then the prayer had stuck in her throat. She had looked over at the tiny infant sleeping in the cradle next to her, who had been substituted for the dead child. She remembered the tear-stained face of the young mother who had, just an hour before, sat across from her at the table in the kitchen of Crosswinds.

'Oh, Maria, look after her,' the girl had pleaded. 'We have been good friends, you and I, and I trust you to take care of her as if she were your own!' She had reached into the folds of her cloak and had drawn out a crude silver cross. 'Keep this for her,' she had implored. 'I want her always to have it with her. And . . . try to understand. It is because I love my child so much that I must do this. He can give her everything, and I have only this cross to give her.' Maria had promised. But later, when she heard the sound of Señor Trevor's shovel turning the dry Texas earth under the Judas tree, she had shuddered with horror at what she had been a party to.

And now, tonight . . . Oh, she thought wildly, what can I do? 'I trust you to take care of her,' her mistress's mother had said. Maria, gripped with a new fear she had never known, stared wide-eyed into the darkness. 'Hail Mary, full of grace, pray for us sinners now and in the hour of death,' she whispered.

Finally Maria must have fallen asleep from sheer exhaustion, for she was woken by a heavy hand on her shoulder. Instantly wide awake, she looked up to see a woman, a stranger, scowling down at her. She jumped to her feet. The curtains had been drawn back to reveal a pale dawn, and the sullen face before her studied her curiously.

'There has been a change in the household,' she said coldly. Her steel-grey hair was drawn severely back from a stony face, and she ran flat eyes over the maid. 'I have been brought here to tend the invalid, and you will be working from now on with Cook in the kitchen.'

It took Maria a moment to comprehend her words. 'But, I don't understand, Señora!'

'My name is Mrs Emory,' the woman went on. 'I am Mr Meredith's sister. Now, be off with you!'

'My mistress will be waking soon, and she needs me!'

Mrs Emory shook her head. 'I just told you—things have changed here. Lord Skelton's secretary was called away suddenly last night, and my orders are to . . .'

'But I have always been the one to tend to my *niña*!' Maria cried.

'No more. Now, go downstairs. If you make any attempt to come into this sick-room, I shall have you dismissed.'

'No, no!' she whispered urgently. 'You would not do this . . . You can't!' She put a hand on Mrs Emory's arm, but the woman pulled it away.

'You are Mexican, I'm told. Didn't they teach you in Mexico to obey orders?' She grasped Maria's arm and led her forcefully to the door. 'Now, get out of here and stay out!' She pushed Maria into the hall, slammed the door and turned the key in the lock.

Maria's first thought, now that she knew she was to be kept away from the sick-room, was to seek help from someone, anyone, to let her take her rightful place at her mistress's bedside. And perhaps, God willing, she might find someone to rescue her *niña* from the forces of evil in this plagued house. She knew she must look outside the immediate household, for Lord Skelton, the butler and Cook each seemed to play a part in the conspiracy against her. Father McLuchly came to Olney several times during those first two weeks to see the invalid, but each time was turned away at the door.

'Surely,' Maria had heard him protest to the surly butler, 'you cannot deny Lady Skelton the sacraments of her church!'

'I have my orders,' Meredith had told him, and shut the door in his face.

Maria even tried to speak to the young coachman, whose duty it was to tend the fires in the big house. But Nettles could offer no help. 'If I'm seen talkin' to you, missus,' he told her, 'I'll be dismissed.'

There was never a chance to speak to Dr Benning, for on his frequent visits the butler never left the doctor's side. Meredith escorted him upstairs, then, after he had seen his patient, took him downstairs again and out to his gig. But at last, at the beginning of the third week, Maria saw an opportunity to talk to the good doctor. Dr Benning came down the stairs alone, and she waited, wide-eyed, at the foot of the steps.

'Ah, you are Maria, aren't you? She keeps asking for you. Why aren't you upstairs with Lady Skelton, instead of that ministering dragon, Mrs Emory?'

'They keep me away,' Maria whispered. 'I am not even allowed into my mistress's room, and I must see her. I must!'

'Well, now,' he buffed at his nose with a large handkerchief, 'it is not for me to interfere in the domestic arrangements of my patient's household when there is someone adequately equipped to care for her. But I worry about Lady Skelton. By now she should be regaining her strength. The loss of the baby has affected her deeply.'

'Please,' Maria begged, 'you must help me!'

'I have received word just this morning that my services are no longer required, since the lady is physically recovered. From now on, it is up to Lady Skelton to . . .' At that very moment Meredith appeared with Dr Benning's cloak and hat, and dismissed her with a dark scowl.

Maria's days were busy, for the butler found much for her to do, with the dusting, mopping, windows to be cleaned, rugs to be beaten, and the silver to polish. There was now a second room that she was not allowed into: the secretary's room, which was kept locked at all times. It was from Cook that Maria learned of Lord Skelton's curious behaviour, during these weeks when she stayed as far away from him as she could.

'He don't go up to London no more,' Cook told her. 'He just sits in the liberry there, with his bottle of whisky, and drinks the hours away like he's got somethin' on his mind, you could say.'

Yes, Maria thought, Lord Skelton has indeed got something on his mind—Mr Norton's murder!

The day before Christmas Eve dawned crisp and cold. Not surprisingly, nothing special had been done to prepare for the holiday except for the large goose that hung at one corner of the kitchen yard. Maria went about her work mechanically during the morning hours, polishing the panelling on the landing, as always alert for a chance to slip into her mistress's room. But Mrs Emory was no less vigilant about keeping the door locked whenever she left it, even for a moment. It was nearly time to go downstairs to help Cook to prepare lunch, when Maria went into the small bedroom to fetch a clean duster from the cupboard there. Laura's trunk, she saw with dismay, had been thrown open, and a few of her beautiful gowns had been pulled from their wrappings and lay scattered across the floor.

Who could have done this, she thought angrily, as she

picked them up one by one, and laid them carefully on the top of the trunk. What possible reason would anyone have to do such a vicious thing? She lifted the last of the lustrous gowns and held it to her, remembering when her mistress had worn it to one of the gala parties she had attended in Galveston. Maria closed her eyes and could see again the radiant beauty of her *niña* as she had looked that night—the laughter in her eyes, the lift of her head. She buried her face in the sweet-smelling lace at the neck of the lilac silk. She recalled how she had tried to close the intricate fastening at the back of the neck, as there had been a problem with the top hook. She held the gown away now, and saw that the fastening still was loose. The hand-embroidered label that Madame Georges sewed into each of her gowns had also become detached at one end, and must be sewn back before the hook could be secured. Perhaps, Maria thought, close to tears, since I can do nothing else to help my *niña*, I can at least repair this gown for her. She gathered up the shimmering yards of silk, then turned and made her way to her own room at the opposite end of the big house, planning to work on it later in the day.

But it was near midnight before the maid was able to begin stitching the silk gown. It had been a long day, and a busy one, for she had been kept occupied making Christmas pies all afternoon. There was no question but that most of them would disappear from the kitchen to find themselves in Cook's own larder at home. Still, it is none of my affair, she told herself sternly as she set about to snip the dressmaker's label from the neckband. She worked by the light of a single candle, and her eyes ached from the strain, for they were no longer as strong as they used to be. She could not dispel the utter helplessness of her situation. Imagine, she thought dismally, I can only sit here doing this small thing for my *niña*, and pray for her. She had despaired for days of ever getting word to someone who could assist her. Dr

Benning no longer visited Olney, and Father McLuchly, though persistent, was still kept away. If she could only find a way to speak to the priest, to tell him of the plight of her mistress, but how? She had not even been allowed to attend Mass these many weeks, for Meredith had told her that the carriage and driver were no longer available to her.

If she could only write, she might get word to Father McLuchly through Nettles, the coachman, for despite the young man's refusal to help her, there was a spark of kindness in him, and he was after all, the grandson of the priest's housekeeper. Truly, she thought, I am every bit as imprisoned as my mistress!

She laid the detached label down on her knee, smoothing the heavy satin gently with her fingers, remembering with what pride Madame Georges had always sewn her identifying label with her name and address into the back seam of her fine gowns. Maria leaned over to her small chest of drawers to find the proper silk to secure the hook, and when she opened the drawer, her eyes fell on Laura's silver cross. She had found it in the pocket of her dress on the night of the accident, and had laid it there for safe-keeping. She pushed it gently aside, searching for the thread, and as she did, the label fell to the floor. She picked it up and, suddenly—it was as though the Holy Mother herself had spoken aloud to her in the silence—an idea came to her!

She felt her cheeks burn with the thought of it! 'It might . . . It *might* work,' she whispered aloud. She did not sleep that night, but spent the hours until dawn going over and over the best way to carry out her desperate plan.

The next morning, Christmas Eve, Maria found Meredith seated at the table in the big kitchen, having his breakfast. She dropped into a stiff chair opposite him. He did not look over at her, but continued sipping his tea. 'Señor Meredith,' she said quietly, 'I find I have deep need of the sacraments of my church tomorrow on this, the most sacred day of our Saviour's birth.' She watched him closely. 'Since it is Christmas, may I ask someone to take me to St Jude's for Mass?'

'No.' The butler's face was impassive. 'You are not to leave this house. Besides, Mr Nettles has the day off.'

Maria waited a moment before continuing. 'I am an ignorant peasant woman, señor. My religion is the most important thing in my life.'

Meredith looked over at her, and frowned. 'I have my orders,' he told her sternly.

'Of course I understand,' Maria agreed, 'and I respect your loyalty to Lord Skelton. But my loyalty is to my God. Do you not see that I am deeply concerned for my soul, Señor Meredith? What harm might there be?' Her voice dropped to a whisper. 'I do not ask to make my confession, but only to attend a service there.'

'No,' Meredith said again, although she could see that his resolve was weakening.

'I will speak to no one, I promise you,' she persisted. 'I will sit at the back of the church and will say not a word to a living soul, on my honour. You may perhaps like to come with me?'

Meredith looked at her with disdain. 'I would not enter a Papist church!'

Maria nodded. 'I know how you feel, Señor. But pity me! I am alone in a strange land. Where else can I go for comfort, if not to my own church?'

At last he seemed to relent. 'Well,' he said finally, 'we shall see.'

Sure enough, on Christmas morning Maria received word from Cook that the butler himself was bringing the carriage round for her. 'Be at the back door, Mr Meredith says, and don't keep him waitin'!'

An hour later, Maria edged into a narrow pew at the

rear of St Jude's. As she knelt, she pulled her rosary from her small reticule and bowed her head. Meredith had accompanied her as far as the door.

'Do as you said you would do,' he cautioned her. 'Speak to no one. I will be just inside the door, watching you.'

'You cannot know how much this means to me,' she said gratefully.

'Go,' he told her. 'We'll leave the minute the service is over.'

She knelt now in the little church, only half listening to the mystical Latin words from Father McLuchly's lips. The service seemed interminable. She could almost feel the butler's eyes boring into her back. The building was damp, and the pungent aroma of pine boughs and incense was so heavy in the air that Maria felt quite ill. When at last the service was over, she stayed in the pew, kneeling, until most of the rest had left. Father McLuchly stood at the open doorway greeting the worshippers, and she went hesitantly up to him.

He welcomed her warmly, with hearty wishes for a blessed Christmas season, and asked for news of her mistress. 'I hope Lady Skelton is feeling better?' he said. 'We have been deeply concerned for her health.'

Maria could only nod. She had promised Meredith she would not speak. The priest took her hand, and a look of surprise flashed briefly across his face as he felt something pressed into his palm. Maria did not even meet his eyes. She dared not look at him, for Meredith would surely think that a message might be relayed in that way.

She felt Father McLuchly's big hand close over the small package she had put there. Then, in the most casual way, he put that same hand into the pocket of his cassock and drew out a handkerchief with which he mopped at his nose. 'I'm glad you could come.' He smiled down at her. 'Please extend my best wishes to Lady Skelton, and tell her that she is in my prayers.'

Maria moved out into the cold, bright sunlight and, with Meredith at her side, walked quickly to the carriage. She remained silent during the trip back to Olney, her eyes fixed on the butler's broad back as he drove. To herself, she prayed, Oh, God, please make the good priest understand!

Father McLuchly pushed his chair back from the table, groaning as he frowned across at Mrs Wetherill. 'You've done it again,' he told her. 'It's your fault that I'm getting too big for all my clothes, and I hope you're properly ashamed of yourself!' He turned to the housekeeper's grandson, who had shyly consented to have his first of two Christmas dinners with them. 'Eugene Nettles,' he warned, 'I hope your mother won't make you sit down to such a repast later today! These women of ours, nothing makes them happier than to stuff their menfolk as full as they stuff the goose! No,' he read the message in Mrs Wetherill's quizzical smile, 'no more plum pudding! Now, waste no more of your Christmas Day keeping a solitary priest company, but get on over to your family, the both of you!' He stood up and stretched luxuriously. 'I'll just take a short nap, and pray I don't explode in my sleep.'

'You should get some exercise instead!' Mrs Wetherill scolded as she and her grandson cleared the table. 'You shouldn't lie down and let . . .'

'Aha!' The priest wagged a finger at her, then turned to Nettles. 'See how she treats me, Eugene? She's a shrew, she is, and there's no place in heaven for the likes of her! Still——' he moved heavily from the room, his hands across his ample stomach '—it was a fine woollen muffler she made for me for Christmas, so I'll keep her here only until she knits me mittens to match.'

He went into his study, where, he noticed, young Nettles had brought in extra firewood for him so that he need not go outside later to fetch some. Eugene was a thoughtful lad, quiet as a stick, but with a ready smile. Father McLuchly pulled his chair up to the fire and sank gratefully into it, lulled by the sound of amiable voices from the kitchen. It had been a busy morning at St Jude's, with a long service. The afternoon stretched before him, quiet and peaceful. He would be glad to have the presbytery to himself and be as lazy as he liked, with no one to fuss over him, or remind him that this was the day he had promised to see to the kitchen pump, or the tread of the stairs that needed a nail.

His eyes were heavy and slowly closed, despite his intention to remain alert until Mrs Wetherill left with her grandson to join her family at her daughter's cottage in Wyckham. Before he realised it, he had dropped off to sleep, his feet propped on the fireplace fender, his hands clasped across his chest. He had no idea how long it was before he heard quiet voices behind him, then felt the rug spread gently over his lap.

Mrs Wetherill's voice whispered a warning. 'Walk on yer toes,' she said. 'We mustn't wake him, Eugene. D'ye like my decorations in here—the holly, the bits of fir branches?'

'T'was you, was it, that done it all?'

'You think he'd bother? Somebody's got to take care of him.'

The voices receded. It was Eugene's whispered words the priest heard from the hall. 'Can you believe that *naught*'s been done at Olney? Not so much as a sprig of mistletoe, Gran!'

'Sh! Close the door, and see you do it quietly.'

At the young coachman's mention of Olney, Father McLuchly's eyes snapped open. He suddenly remembered the small packet Lady Skelton's maid had pressed into his hand that very morning. Annoyed that his own curiosity as to the contents of the package had surely spoiled his chances of continuing his nap, he threw the rug aside and pulled himself to his feet. He dug down into the pocket of his cassock and pulled out the small rectangular package, then took it over to his desk, where the light was better, before he began carefully to open it. The square of linen was folded over and over as though what was inside was some sort of precious relic. As he laid back the last fold, he saw a simple silver cross, crudely made and heavily tarnished.

He picked it up, turned it over in his hand and was surprised to see that a message had been roughly scratched on the back of it. 'Defend, Oh Lord, this child,' he read. He had no idea why Lady Skelton's maid had handed it to him. Could it possibly be a gift? Perhaps she meant him to bless it and return it to her? He picked up the small wad of cotton that lay under it, and something dropped out on to his desk. He leaned closer to examine what appeared to be some sort of label, the kind fancy couturiers often sewed into the seams of their garments. It was of heavy grey satin, and the finely embroidered stitching read: 'Madame Georges, The Strand, Galveston, Texas.'

For a moment he thought it might have slipped in by accident, and was about to put it aside when he recalled how urgently the packet had been tucked into his hand, and the way the maid's eyes had not met his. She had been furtive, *frightened*, as she had handed it to him. He had felt then that it might have been because of the presence of Olney's surly butler, who had stood out in the vestibule throughout the entire service, his hooded eyes watching every move she made. What did it mean? What did she want him to do with it?

He searched further, and finding nothing more, walked over to the window and peered out at the bleak woodland that hemmed in the presbytery. A light snow had begun to fall: small flakes touching the frozen ground that turned it slowly into a gentle blanket of white. Finally, after many minutes of pondering all sorts of alternatives and wishing that there were an answer to everything, he went back to his desk and sank into his chair. He pulled out a sheet of notepaper from the drawer. Then, dipping his pen into the inkstand, and with more than a little hesitation, he wrote across the top of it, 'My dear Madame Georges . . .'

CHAPTER TWELVE

A SHARP KNOCK on Madame Georges's door startled her. In her apartment at the back, she looked up from her sewing, surprised, for she had expected no more customers at this late hour. It was after nine o'clock, and black night had long since drawn its curtain over the town of Galveston. She quickly laid aside the taffeta gown she had been working on, and, picking up a candle, made her way to the front of the shop. 'Who is it, please?' she called out.

'I got a letter here for you, missus.' The voice was rough, yet amiable enough, so she slid back the bolt and opened the door.

A stranger stood there, holding a greasy hat in one hand. He nodded politely when he saw her, and held out a soiled envelope. 'This come over with us,' he said. 'We've just this night got in from Liverpool, and the captain sent me over with it for you, missus.'

Madame Georges hesitantly took the missive. 'Thank you,' she told the man. She reached into the money-pouch at her belt. 'Please accept this.' She handed him a few coins. 'Kindly convey my gratitude to your captain.'

'Thank you, missus.' He pocketed the money, then turned and disappeared quickly down the dark, silent street.

Madame Georges took the letter back into her sitting-room and set the candle at her side as she scanned the envelope. The handwriting was not familiar. She sat down at her sewing-table, and when she tore it open, a heavy object fell out. She picked it up and held it close to the candle. Her eyes widened, and she let out a cry when she saw the silver cross glowing dully in the soft light. She studied it for a moment, then laid it down quickly while she took out the sheets of paper and began to read.

My dear Madame Georges,
I have only this morning come into possession of this cross. It was slipped into my hand by the maid of Lady Skelton of Olney, Wyckham. With it was a dressmaker's label, which I must surmise was yours and came from one of the lady's gowns. I can only guess that the woman meant me to send it to you, although she said nothing to me. Nor could she, for she was being carefully watched. I trust you may be able to attach some significance to this. Let me say only that Lady Skelton has been very ill following an accident. I have been several times to her home and have not been allowed to see her, told only that she was indisposed. On my first visit to Olney, Lady Skelton appeared to be most unhappy, and I assumed that she was merely homesick. Looking back now, I know her to have been deeply troubled, a fact borne out by her extraordinary outburst later here in my study. At that time she begged me to help her to escape from her life at Olney. I only wish I had known then of her true fears, and not believed Lord Skelton's explanation that his wife was mentally unstable. The blame is mine for not reading the situation there correctly. For I believe her to be held at Olney against her will, and in desperate need of family and friends. I can do no more than forward to you this urgent plea, for so it appears to be.
    Faithfully in God,
    Fr Dennis McLuchly,
    St Jude's Parish, Wyckham, England

As soon as Madame Georges finished the priest's letter, she was on her feet. Without a moment's hesitation she slipped the cross and the letter into her pocket, snatched up her shawl and snuffed out the candle. She ran to the front of the shop and let herself out on to the Strand. Hurrying through the darkness, she did not stop until she reached the front gate of Lucas Trevor's house at the end of the sea wall. She ran up the steps and pounded loudly at the heavy door of Crosswinds.

In a moment the door opened slowly, and a small woman, her thin face framed by a starched cap, stared out at her in the flickering light of a candle. 'Please,' Madame Georges was able to say with what little breath was left in her, 'I must see Monsieur Trevor. I bring an urgent message to him, Madame. I must insist that you let me in.'

The woman blocked her way. 'He is very ill,' she said curtly. 'He sees no one. Especially not strangers.'

'I am not a stranger, Madame. I used to work here as a seamstress many years ago. Please, you must let me see him. I have news of his daughter.'

The woman hesitated, then grudgingly she moved aside. 'Come in, then,' she said. 'But wait downstairs. I'll have to see . . .'

Madame Georges pushed past her into the dark hall.

'Stop!' the housekeeper called angrily. 'You have no right to burst in like this . . .'

But Madame Georges was already half-way up the stairs. On the dark landing, she felt her way along the familiar corridor until she stopped outside the door she knew to be the entrance to the master bedroom. She knocked softly only once, then opened the door and let herself in.

Lucas Trevor lay propped up against a mountain of pillows, his face gaunt and grey in the light of a candle at his bedside. At first he seemed unaware of her presence, his eyes fixed on the soft circle of light on the ceiling above him. But as she came closer and he heard the rustle of her skirts, he turned towards the shadows where she stood. Madame Georges stared at him, shocked at the physical deterioration of his once strong body.

'Who's that?' he called out, his voice only an echo of what it had once been.

'It is Thérèse, Monsieur. Thérèse Georges.'

He made an effort to pull himself higher on the pillows. She went to his side, but when she tried to help him, he waved her away. 'What are you doing here? What do you want?'

'I have news of Laura,' she said quietly. 'I am going to England to see her. I want only one thing from you, and that is to release me from my vow.'

'Never!' His answer was instant. 'You swore an oath . . .'

'I have just received word from a priest there that Laura is in trouble, and I can no longer keep quiet.'

'Trouble? What sort of trouble?' For the first time he looked directly at her.

'I don't know,' Madame Georges told him. 'But she needs me now, and she must be told the truth. I intend to tell her at last that— that I am her mother.'

'No!' A fit of coughing racked him, and she was quick to pour a tumbler of water from the jug beside the bed and hold it to his lips. But he pushed it away. 'No,' he said again. 'Laura must never know.'

Madame Georges straightened up and drew a deep breath. 'I have stood by all these years,' she told him evenly, 'and watched what you have made of her life. You, who promised to love and cherish her, to give her all the advantages I could not. You must have known what Edgar Skelton was. How could you have let her marry such a man? I myself know him to be . . .'

'What has he done to her? He promised me . . .' He

shifted his wasted body as if to throw off the coverlet. 'Why do you tell me this? Can't you see I'm dying?'

Madame Georges leaned closer. 'If you were well, would you go to her? I doubt it very much, for I don't think you ever loved her at all!'

'Don't!' Trevor groaned, and turned from her. 'One day,' he whispered, 'you will understand.'

'I shall never understand,' she told him. 'I have read unhappiness in Laura's face so often. I wanted to come to you many times to beg you to let me tell her who I am. But I trusted you to love her enough to do what was best for her!'

'Stop!' The old man held up a hand.

'You have betrayed my trust,' she went on. 'You made a promise to me, and you broke it. Why should I not be free to do the same? If you do not release me from my vow to remain silent, I swear to you that I will tell Laura—with or without your consent.'

He said nothing, only stared straight ahead with vacant eyes. His chest heaved suddenly, then the breath left his lungs. At last he spoke. 'Tell her, then,' he said. 'Go to her. Tell her.' He closed his eyes and waved her away. 'Now leave me alone to die.'

The dressmaker should have felt pity for this dying man, but instead she felt only anger and betrayal. She moved quickly away to leave the room, but at the door she stopped and turned back. 'She could have brought you a world of love and happiness,' she said, 'and you threw it all away.' She said no more, but let herself out on to the dark landing and never looked back.

When Madame Georges returned to her shop, it was after ten o'clock. She had passed through dark, nearly deserted streets on the way back from Crosswinds, walking quickly, her eyes straight ahead. She still shook with the anger that had swept through her at her confrontation with Lucas Trevor. Grateful as she was to be able at last to tell Laura the truth, she would never forgive him for what he had done to her child.

After she got ready for bed she blew out the candle, climbed into her narrow cot and lay staring up at the ceiling, trying to formulate plans for the next day. There was much to do in preparation for her absence. She must first find out when the first available sailing was scheduled. She must plan what to pack—but how long would she be gone? Would one trunk be enough? And the shop—there were shelves to be emptied, fabrics to be stored away, then, then . . .

But it was no use. Her mind kept going back to where it all began, to the frightened fifteen-year-old girl she was when the Quakers brought her here. The Friends had literally saved her life. They had found her wandering, dazed, through the streets of Marigot just two days after the devastating fire that had destroyed her father's sugar-plantation on the Caribbean island of St Martin. She had lost everything—both parents and her beloved younger brother—and had willingly come with them to Galveston, grateful for their concern, their compassion. They had found employment for her as a seamstress at Crosswinds, and in time the wounds of her disastrous loss began to heal.

There was little happiness in the big house on the Strand, but in her room on the third floor the young French girl was far removed from the constant bickering and arguing that took place below. The master of Crosswinds, too, seemed to find solace there, as he would sit across the sewing-room from her some afternoons and encourage her to talk, to practice her English with him. Had it not been for him and the young Mexican maid, Maria, she would have been friendless. But during her two years at Crosswinds, Thérèse had seen the slow erosion of Trevor's buoyant spirit in a marriage that emasculated him, and her heart went out to him. Then, that last night when he had come to her room, desolate and lonely, she had not been able to turn him away, for she had grown to love him.

She closed her eyes in the darkness. Oh yes, I loved him, she thought bitterly. And it was because she loved him that she had packed her few belongings and left Crosswinds the very next day, for she knew that she could never again refuse him anything he asked. After she left, only Maria knew that the young seamstress had gone to work in the scullery at the Pelican Inn, and it was Maria who had first learned from her of the child she carried. Sworn to secrecy, the maid told no one either of Thérèse's whereabouts or of her condition.

But on one of the maid's frequent visits late at night to Thérèse's tiny room at the Pelican, Trevor followed her, and found out about the pregnancy. It was then that he began sending her money through Maria, which was always returned. It was the Mexican woman who had helped to bring Thérèse's baby into the world. Then, just three days afterwards, Maria had come to her in a state of shock. 'The Señor . . .' She had stood in Thérèse's dark little hall bedroom, her face wet with tears. 'He has lost both the Señora and the child tonight! Within one hour, both of them were taken from him! He begs you, Señorita, he begs you to come to him tonight.'

Thérèse remembered how right it had seemed, those many years ago, to relinquish her child that night to Lucas Trevor. Her eyes filled with tears at the painful memory, but as she looked about her at the cosy apartment, dimly lighted now by the low fire on the hearth, she was grateful that she had been able to make a full life here. It was thanks again to the Quakers, who had, through some sort of special fund, bought this shop for her so that she might earn a livelihood. She owed them so much, and only years later was she able to repay them in part for their kindnesses. When she had learned that they sought help in their abolitionist activities—more specifically that they needed someone to arrange overland transport of their freed Africans, she had wholeheartedly volunteered to help. It was through her work with them that she had met the young Abolitionist Sloan Benedict. Oh, she thought, I shall miss him so much, and our work together!

In the darkness, she once more tried to turn her mind to the coming day and all the preparations that had to be made. She must write notes to all her customers to tell them that she had been called away suddenly; she must arrange with . . .

But as she remembered the urgency of the priest's letter, those things seemed so unimportant. The only thing that mattered was her daughter's safety. 'Oh Lord,' she whispered, 'don't let me be too late!'

At a little before nine o'clock on the following morning, Madame Georges set out to walk the seven blocks to the bank, where she went straight to the man who had always handled her affairs. She settled herself across from him at his desk, and her manner was direct. 'I should like to withdraw some money from my account, Mr Tolson, if you please.'

She mentioned a large amount in cash, and the banker looked at her in surprise. 'You are going on a buying trip, then? It has been four years, I think, since your last visit to Paris. Will you stay long?'

'I'm not certain how long I shall be away.' She saw no reason to tell him that her destination was not Paris this time. Mr Tolson's usually cheerful face looked drained and ashen. 'Is something wrong?' she asked him. 'Do you feel ill?'

He took off his spectacles and polished them with a handkerchief. 'It is a sad day for us here,' he told her. 'We have only an hour ago received word that our bank president, Lucas Trevor, passed away shortly after dawn this morning. He had been ill, but we hoped . . . Well, he had been failing for some time. Still . . .'

Madame Georges's heart plunged. '*Mon Dieu*,' she whispered.

The man cleared his throat. 'He will indeed be sorely missed. Now,' he said, trying to assume a more businesslike air, 'we have the unfortunate duty to inform his family: his sister, Mrs John Messersmith in New Orleans, and his daughter in England, both of whom I believe you are acquainted with, Madame.'

'Yes.' The dressmaker spoke confidentially to him. 'Mr Tolson, I am going to England this time, not Paris. Perhaps I may convey to Mr Trevor's daughter the sad news of her father's death?'

He smiled thinly at her. 'That's kind of you, but we have our own channels of communication. If you were a member of Lady Skelton's family, then, of course, it would be different. But thank you for offering, all the same. Now, if you will excuse me, I'll see to your request.' He left her, and was back in only a few minutes. 'That's very odd,' he said, sitting down again and holding in one hand a thin brown envelope. 'Mr Hersch, one of our vice-presidents here, was named as executor of Mr Trevor's estate some years ago. When he heard just now that you were here at my desk, Madame Georges, he said there was something for you among Mr Trevor's effects. Here . . .' He held out the envelope. 'It was evidently meant to go to you in the event of his death.' He looked quizzically at her. 'I can't think why,' he added absently. Then, instantly, he regained his former impersonal air. 'And here is the money you asked for.'

Madame Georges picked up the tight packet of notes and fastened it securely into the pouch at her belt. She, too, was curious about the contents of the envelope, but took it from him with no change of expression. She thanked Mr Tolson, and now that her business was completed, she took her leave of him.

Once out on the street, she headed towards the busy

quays at the end of the Strand. She was pleased to be able to secure a passage in the *Mermaid*, a little packet that would leave at first light next morning for Liverpool. She made arrangements for her trunk to be picked up that afternoon, then started the long walk home. She had not gone far when she saw a man coming towards her with the easy rolling gait of someone long accustomed to the motion of the sea. She recognised Cayo Aristo at once, and was again struck by his one white unseeing eye. As he neared her, his face broke into a toothless grin. When he came abreast, he mumbled in Spanish, 'The *Liberty* is in . . .' and would have walked on, but she turned and put a hand on his arm to stop him.

He shook it off, motioning to a covered arcade further up the street where they could talk. She followed him, and they stood together in the shadows. He did not look at her, but kept glancing out at the street. 'This is dangerous, Señora,' he whispered. 'I think I am being watched.'

'Is Sloan Benedict aboard, Cayo?'

'I don't know,' he said. 'No one has yet come ashore.'

'If you see him,' Madame Georges said, 'please tell him that I leave Galveston tomorrow. Say goodbye to him for me.'

But Cayo Aristo had already moved away into the bright sunlight, and by the time she got back to the street, he was no longer in sight. When at last she reached the sanctuary of her shop, Madame Georges bolted the door behind her and went quickly to her small apartment. She stirred up the fire, added more wood, and set the kettle to boil. All the while, her eyes scarcely left the thin brown envelope Mr Tolson had given her, which she had laid on the chimneypiece. For a moment she considered dropping it into the fire unopened, for she wanted nothing from Lucas Trevor but what she had secured the night before, his release from her vow of silence. Still, her curiosity was aroused, no less than the banker's. But what could Trevor possibly have left for her? She had never accepted anything from him, and she would not now. But what a final humiliation, she thought, if he has left me a small legacy in an attempt to atone for his disastrous mismanagement of our daughter's life!

When she could no longer contain her curiosity, she picked up the envelope and took it over to her cot in the recessed area at the back of the small room. Before she sat down, she pulled back the curtains behind her to let in more of the morning light, and opened the window a crack to let in some air, as the room was stuffy. She sat down and slowly opened the envelope to look inside. The contents appeared to be only a thin sheaf of mismatched papers, some full-sized, some mere yellowed scraps. She pulled them out slowly, puzzled that a man as neat as Trevor would leave behind such a jumble of seemingly unimportant bits of paper. Each piece bore a sample of his script. Some were smudged and others barely legible, with words run together and candle-wax splattered across them.

She scanned the top one impatiently. The words, crookedly spaced on the heavy foolscap, leaped out at her. 'Last night, I committed the unspeakable crime. I murdered my wife.' Madame Georges froze in disbelief as she studied the barely decipherable words, which she read several times over before she went further.

> I have locked myself in my room, for how can I face a living soul with the knowledge of what I have done? The world must know only that my wife Amanda died last night giving birth to our girl-child, not that she died at my hands . .

The writing broke off to continue further down the page.

It was Victor duFlon's will that did it. I have always known of Amanda's greed, but I was to find out last night the destructive extent of my own! After her father's death only two weeks ago, I was as anxious as she to see written proof that Victor duFlon's fortune was at last hers —*ours*! 'Read Father's will aloud to me,' she said, for despite her long hours of difficult labour and the sleeping infant beside her, the promise of this new wealth excited and revived her. She had broken her father's heart many times with her excessive immorality, as she could not break mine—for I had never truly loved her. I'd been flattered that Amanda duFlon, twenty years my junior and the most sought-after heiress in New Orleans, had noticed me at all. But love her? No. I was blinded by her beauty—and she was beautiful, as an icicle is beautiful. And she was rich, as I one day wanted to be. I read her father's will to her as she asked me to. When I got to the words: 'I leave nothing to my daughter Amanda, but direct that my entire fortune go to Amanda's *issue*', I was as shocked as she was that her father had exacted his final revenge on her by cutting her—his only heir—out of his will. She went wild with rage . . .

Madame Georges turned the paper over with trembling hands.

. . . I have seen evidence before of my wife's madness, but I was not prepared for this. I ran into the next room to get a sedative, hoping to calm her, but when I got back . . . I shall see it as long as I live. Amanda was holding a pillow over the baby's face. 'If I don't get my father's money,' she screamed at me, 'I'll make sure that nobody does!' It was too late; I could not help the child. I

went crazy. I put my hands around her neck, and
squeezed . . .

There was nothing more written on the page. She
stared at it for a moment, her eyes wide with horror,
unable to believe all that she had read. Then she put it
down and picked up the next piece of paper.

Here the handwriting was more controlled.

> The fourth day here in my room, alone. Maria is
> walking up and down outside my balcony door,
> cradling the baby. Thérèse's baby and mine! Yes,
> add this to my list of sins, you scribes of darkness!
> For murder was not my only crime that night. As
> I looked down at the dead child, I realised that
> with the death of Amanda's only issue, I myself
> would never see a cent of Victor duFlon's money;
> for although it would have come to our child, I, as
> the baby's legal guardian, would have had access
> to and control of it. Even then, with my wife's
> blood still on my hands, it was the money I
> thought of! Maria had brought me word only
> three days before that Thérèse Georges had been
> safely delivered of our child. Suddenly I saw what
> I must do. I destroyed Victor duFlon's will, and
> then sent Maria out into the night to fetch
> Thérèse. When the two came back, Thérèse with
> the baby in her arms, I . . .

The writing broke off, and she went quickly to the next
page. The ink was different here, and the writing better
spaced.

> My sister Ernesta came today. It is part of my
> punishment that I must listen to her weep over
> my wife's untimely death in childbirth, extol
> Amanda's saintly beauty, and lavish me with
> well-intentioned sympathy for my tragic loss! I
> have sent Thérèse money, which she refuses to

accept. When I think how she sat across from me at the kitchen table that night and slowly, slowly, I saw her believing me, trusting me as I sobbed, broken with my grief. 'I have lost a wife and child tonight! For the love of God, give our daughter to me,' I told her, 'and I will see that she has everything you cannot give her.' I played my part well, for she . . . Oh, God!

The entry stopped. Madame Georges's fingers tightened on the paper. She threw it down, then stood up and went to the fireplace to pour herself a cup of tea. Her hands shook so badly that she spilled most of the pot on the hob. She began again to pinch out the proper amount of loose tea, but gave up. She left it on the hearth and walked back to the notes, dreading what she would read there, but compelled to continue. She sat down again and picked up the next sheet. As with the others, there was no date. It began clumsily, the words ran together.

. . . this lie—I must live it out. Everyone believes me! Even Maria, who alone was with me in the house that night, suspects nothing. I have managed, through the Quakers, to buy a small piece of property on the Strand for Thérèse, where she can go into business for herself. She will never know who her unknown benefactor is and I pray that, in this small way, I may somehow atone for my deception.

Madame Georges read this entry over again, appalled at the new disclosure. It was a moment before she could go. Written below, in the same erratic hand, were the words:

I saw Laura this afternoon digging out under the Judas tree in the back yard! God, suppose it were discovered! I buried Amanda's child deep, but who's to say that one day it may not be found? I pray I may never again scream at Laura as I did today. She shrank from me, terrified, and ran. Am I slowly losing my mind? I see shadows everywhere in this house. It is full of circling ghosts, waiting to drive me over the ledge. There is a Catholic mission school in west Texas. I'll send Laura there. I want her . . .

The words continued on the next page:

far away from the mincing little idiots at Miss Porch's school, who already can speak of little but boys. They play a kissing game at their parties, Ernesta informs me. She thinks it's cute! I must get Laura away from this!

Another change of ink in the next entry.

Each time she comes home to Crosswinds, each year that passes, I see a change in her. She will be beautiful, it's already clear. I see the way boys look at her on the Strand. She'll be tall. She will break men's hearts. Unless . . .

The next page yielded far more decisive writing, and was more orderly than those that had preceded it.

I have arranged with Father Jiminez to keep Laura at Santa Clara after graduation. She has shown a marked talent with the nursing nuns in the hospital there, and enjoys the work. The priest agrees with me that she might enter the convent when she is ready. Then—then no man will kiss her, or hold her. She will be pure, chaste . . . Wait! It is not only that, for I still cannot put the *money* out of my mind . . . Victor duFlon's fortune. In just four years Laura would get it all. But if she were to take the vows of chastity, obedience and *poverty*! Aha, I know myself very well. Make note of that, you chroniclers at Satan's gate. I know myself as well as you do!

On another page:

> Laura has come back to Crosswinds to stay! I hear her step on the stairs, and I look up to see Thérèse standing there, smiling down at me! *Her* eyes, the eyes I loved. I dream at night that my hands move across the familiar silk of Thérèse's body, over the beloved places, and I wake . . . dear God, it's Laura in my dreams. The two of them inseparable now! Yesterday I went up to the old sewing-room on the third floor and sat where I always sat when I visited the little French seamstress there, long before I knew what she would come to mean to me. I saw again the shaft of late afternoon sunlight coming through the dormer, turning her cheek to gold, playing with the tips of her lashes . . . I watched her beautiful hands, so sure, so deft as she sewed Amanda's clothes. I heard again the soft, infinitely gentle throb of her voice . . . I remembered that night I touched her, held her, and she melted against me in my arms. It was right. It was the only right thing I ever did, loving Thérèse. Yet, when I came downstairs again and saw Laura sitting on the edge of the fountain in the courtyard, the sun on her, and she looked over at me with Thérèse's eyes, I ran. I could not . . . I cannot . . .

The writing stopped, and the words blurred in front of Madame Georges's eyes, and she felt as if a hot knife had been plunged into her heart. Slowly she turned to the final page.

> It has always been Victor duFlon's money. This, I thought, was what kept me going. Then tell me, wise Fates who have watched my agony over the

years, why I so eagerly parted with it last night? His name is Edgar Skelton. I offered him Laura. 'Take her away to England as your bride,' I said, 'and in a little over a year you will be well rewarded, for she will come into her inheritance!' Like *that*, I gave up my lifelong dream of riches. Surprised, you scribes? But how can you know the agonies of a mortal soul? Have you ever lusted after your own daughter, whose very nearness set you afire? Have you wakened in the dead of night, cold with fear that another man's hands will know her? Now do you see why I gave my beautiful Laura to Skelton, a man I know will never kiss her, will never touch her . . .

Scrawled crookedly below were the words:

Today Laura left me. I watched her sail away with Skelton, out of my life. May God have mercy on my soul!

There were no more notes. Madame Georges stared down at the scraps of paper that lay before her, the wretched confessions of a soul in torment. Her mind reeled from Lucas Trevor's words. She could only offer up a silent prayer for him now, obsessed man that he had been.

But, oh, *Laura*! What it had done to Laura, this love of his! And Edgar Skelton, whose perverted tastes would ensure that Laura remained chaste! Knowing this—*because* of this—Lucas had given their beautiful Laura to such a man. She put the scraps of paper back into the envelope, got up and laid it on the chimneypiece. I must put this aside, she told herself; I dare not take time now to reread it. Nor did she need to. Every word was etched on her memory in burning acid.

She set about quickly to attend to the many tasks that faced her. She had much to do, and little time to accomplish it. She was thankful for the hours of daylight left. She must keep her mind on practical things and her hands busy, for the sake of her own sanity.

CHAPTER THIRTEEN

THE MOON climbed slowly over the flat Texas mainland, brightening as it rose, and a few puffs of cloud clung to it as if to escort it on its journey across the night sky. The silver path of its light clearly etched the dark figure of a solitary oarsman as he strained to speed his small boat the last half-mile to shore. Once he had pulled away from the *Liberty* that night for the last time, Sloan Benedict's heart was heavy. It had been an emotional farewell. Most of the men had been with him on the frigate since the beginning.

'We've a record to be proud of,' he had told them quietly. 'There are over three hundred negroes who can thank you for their freedom.'

The men had already been told, when their captain came aboard in Charleston, that this was to be his final trip with them, and they had listened attentively to him earlier, crowded into his cramped little cabin. As he spoke, his eyes ran over each familiar, serious face. He would miss these fine men who risked their lives so they could restore freedom to others.

He had said nothing to them of his fears for the future of the perilous operation. He did not have to. They knew as well as he did that they had come too close to failure on their last foray, just three nights before off the coast of the Bahamas. Besides, it was up to Mr Merritt now, who would be taking over. Only this morning, Benedict's first mate had sat across from him in his cabin, leaning close, his voice quiet. 'We must expect that every ship of the Monarch Lines that tries to smuggle blacks over here from now on will double her watches,' he had said to Benedict, 'now that they knew our raids will continue despite your supposed death.'

Benedict had nodded. 'It's a hell of a time for me to leave it in your charge, Mr Merritt.'

'No, sir,' Merritt had argued. 'If you'll pardon me for saying this, sir——' his dark eyes traced the path of light from the overhead lantern as it swung in a long ellipse on the green baize table-top '—I think it's a good time. I watched you on this last raid, Captain. It was as if you didn't cared whether you lived or died. You've got to admit,' he hesitantly added, 'that taking on that seaman in hand-to-hand fighting was foolhardy. The man could have recognised you. You're taking unnecessary chances, sir. You're in a dangerous mood, Captain, if you don't mind my saying so.'

Benedict had been forced to acknowledge the truth in his first mate's words. 'Still,' he had said, 'are you sure you want to continue with this, knowing the added risks?'

'Sir, as long as there's black ivory being smuggled in, I don't see how I can help but continue!'

Benedict had smiled at Merritt's words, so like his own to his father. 'Very well then, I'll need a boat tonight to get me across to the island. I want to thank our two stalwart confederates there for their help in the past. Then I'll ship out from Galveston to Charleston, and home. Just because I'm going home, Mr Merritt, don't think I won't be waiting for news of your activities.'

'You'll get it, sir. We'll keep you posted.' A silent crew had watched from the deck tonight as Benedict's boat was lowered into the water, and the young Abolitionist took his place at the oars for the crossing to Galveston.

At last he felt the prow of the boat nudge the sandy beach. He leapt out and pulled it behind him up into wind-flattened grasses, where it would remain well hidden. Then he turned and made his way across the darkly-glowing sands towards the small hovel where Cayo Aristo lived. It was a sturdy little shack, despite being put together crudely, consisting mainly of crosshatch patches nailed up haphazardly to keep out the elements. Many of the slats had been torn loose by winds and rain and never put back in place. It was a bleak and dreary outpost, with the strong smell of fish everywhere.

Benedict pulled his cloak round him and approached quietly. He peered in at the single paneless window, where only a tattered rag hung limply to guard against the weather. A small lamp burned inside, and through a slit in the grimy cloth he could see that the room was empty. He listened for a moment, but the only sound was the whisper of a light breeze through the tufts of tall grasses, the murmur of a rising tide against the shore, and the stamp of a horse's hooves from a small lean-to behind the shack. He crept stealthily to the door and put his ear to it. Nothing moved inside. Slowly he lifted the latch, and the door swung wide on its rusted hinges to reveal the dimly-lighted room he had come to know so well. How many hours he had sat here with the fisherman, planning new signals for Cayo to flash to the *Liberty* when the coast was clear and it was safe to head to a cove on the mainland!

He stepped quickly over the threshold and looked about. The single straw-filled pallet in one corner left little room for what few necessities the man had accumulated over the years. The makeshift bed was a jumble of greasy coverlets and shabby garments, and Benedict recalled the night he had lain there after he had been shot in the alley behind Crosswinds, in agony from his chest wound. He had listened, half-conscious, as Cayo had tethered his horse, then brought his fishing-boat closer for the trip back to the waiting *Liberty*. The small room was, as always, cluttered with all manner of fishing gear—nets, baskets, boat-hooks, gaffs, coils of sturdy rope—most of it hanging from nails or strewn carelessly across the floor.

He picked up the soot-smoked lantern, turned down the wick and was about to blow it out before leaving the dreary shack, but he became conscious of a sound not unlike the low moan of the breeze, only this was closer at hand. He walked further into the room and saw, sprawled in a tangle of rags at the foot of the pallet, the twisted figure of the Mexican.

Benedict turned up the light, thinking that once again Cayo had been felled by dipping heavily into his ready store of whisky. But when he turned the fisherman over, he cried aloud, 'Cayo! My God!' He had been stabbed over and over again, and his bare chest was covered with blood. His eyelids fluttered, and he lifted one hand, so there was life in him still. Benedict knelt beside him. 'Cayo, who the hell did this to you?'

It was a moment before Cayo's one good eye stared blankly up at him, his dark face glistening with sweat. 'Two men—Englishmen,' he whispered hoarsely in Spanish. 'Someone . . . recognised you. They . . . know you are still alive.'

Benedict swore softly and leaned closer. 'How long ago were they here?'

'Minutes . . . They left only minutes ago, Captain. They tried to make me talk.'

'Save your strength. I'll go for a doctor.'

'But,' Cayo went on weakly, 'I told them . . . nothing. Nothing.'

'Now, hold on,' Benedict told him. 'Say nothing more,' but the fisherman closed his eyes, and a shudder ran through his body. He turned his head away, breathed one last tortured breath and lay still. Cayo Aristo was dead.

When he saw it was too late to do anything for him, Benedict picked up the lifeless body and laid him gently on the pallet. 'Rest in peace, *amigo*,' he whispered. So

Merritt was right, he thought, as he covered the body with a blanket. He *had* been recognised on their last raid, and they knew he was alive. Thérèse, he thought! They would certainly go to her next, knowing her to have been his only other contact on the island!

He quickly blew out the lantern and ran outside and back to the shed where Cayo kept his horse. He did not stop to saddle the big mare; just turned her loose, threw a leg over her back, grabbed the halter-rope and set out on a fast gallop towards the town.

Not ten minutes later he found the streets of Galveston nearly empty as he made his way along the dark alley that paralleled the Strand. He pulled the mare up just a block from the dressmaker's shop, dismounted and tied her to a hitching-post. He went the rest of the way on foot, and when he got to the corner of Thérèse's little building, he saw that the high window that faced the alley was partly open. He leaned close and put an ear to the crack. It was Thérèse's voice he heard, and he recognised the bantering tone she so often used with him.

'But I've heard that British seamen are notoriously superstitious, Monsieur. Perhaps it was only Sloan Benedict's *ghost* walking the decks? You tell me the helmsman was knocked unconscious, so who is to say that he did not only imagine that he recognised his assailant?'

A man's voice now, young and very angry. An Englishman, judging by his accent. 'Stop playing games,' he shouted. 'We know very well he's alive! There are only two people on this island who helped Benedict—you and the fisherman. You say you're not working for him any more, so how the devil do you explain that meeting of yours today on the Strand with Cayo Aristo?'

'Is it unusual for two old friends to exchange greetings in a public street?'

'You were seen going to the bank today and drawing out a large sum of money. You then booked passage on a ship leaving Galveston tomorrow. Why? What does that Abolitionist plan now?'

'It is not unusual for a couturière whose customers demand the latest in Parisian styles and fabrics to take regular buying trips . . .'

'Enough of this!' The Englishman's voice was shrill. 'You may be sure, Madame, that this man here at my side knows how to extract information quite effectively. You are no longer dealing with that bumbling boob, Skelton, who was supposed to have ended this piracy. My father is Thomas Ripp, owner of the line those renegades prey on!'

Benedict strained to hear Madame's words, which were spoken quietly now. 'Why would the esteemed Mr Ripp send his son all the way over here to catch a ghost?' Despite the irony in her voice, Benedict detected the first note of fear in it.

'I tell you, Monsieur, I know nothing!'

'Those were the last words that greasy Mexican said before we killed him,' Ripp cried. 'Now, Gridley, show her we mean business!'

'Take your hands off me!' Thérèse said. There were sounds of a scuffle inside.

Benedict lost no time in rounding the corner to the doorway, and with one kick he smashed it open and stood on the threshold, hands on hips, his figure outlined against the pale lamplight behind him. 'Are you fellows looking for me?' he said.

'Benedict!' Instantly, in the glow of a lantern on the table, Benedict saw one of the men pull a knife and leap towards him. But before he could strike, Benedict hit him full in the face, and he staggered back against the wall as the knife clattered to the floor.

'Gridley, you fool!' Ripp yelled, lunging towards Benedict. 'Get that knife! Finish him off!'

'Not so fast, my friend!' Benedict caught the Englishman and held him. 'You'd like to kill me with the same weapon you used on Cayo, wouldn't you, you bastard?' He wrenched Ripp's arm, and the young man cried out in pain.

'Sloan! Behind you!' Thérèse suddenly cried.

Benedict, his hand still holding the Englishman's arm, turned to see the seaman behind him, the dagger upraised to plunge into his back. Quick as a cat, he hurled Ripp away from him, where he slammed against the wall and lay there senseless. As he swung to hit the seaman, he heard a loud explosion behind, and the man's dark face lit up in a burst of red light as Benedict's fist hit him squarely on the jaw and he dropped like a stone. Suddenly the entire back room blazed with an angry crimson glow. Benedict watched, stunned, as flames spilled from the table on to the floor in writhing sheets, and caught the alcove curtains, which instantly erupted in a blinding flash. He threw one arm up to shield his face from the blistering heat, and saw Thérèse standing at the doorway into the shop. 'Get out now!' he yelled, over the roaring inferno.

Already the fire had reached the rough-hewn beams of the low ceiling, feeding ravenously on the dry timber. He looked back and saw that the bodies of the two men were separated from him by a wall of fire. He ran to the dressmaker, who stood, frozen, her eyes wide, watching the furious flames devour the room. 'My God, come on!' he yelled, taking her arm.

'No, wait! There's something . . .' She broke away from him, ran to the fireplace and grabbed an envelope from the mantelpiece.

'Come, for the love of heaven, Thérèse!' Benedict cried. She quickly ran to his side, but at the doorway looked back just once, then hurled the envelope into the flames. 'Now,' she told him, 'I'm ready!'

He took her hand and together they ran into the shop.

Already the curtain that hung across the open doorway had caught fire, and the room glowed with a brilliant light. Benedict slipped back the bolt of the front door, and the wind caught it and blew it wide. At the sudden rush of air, the flames burst into the shop, wrapped round the counters and leaped up the walls.

Once they were safely out in the street, he made a dash towards the rear of the building, hoping to be able to reach the two men inside and drag them out to safety. But flames belched from the open door, lighting up the narrow alley in a blaze of orange. He felt Thérèse's hand on his arm, pulling him away. Already they could hear the fire marshal's horn echoing from further up the street, and the rumble of hose-carts along the cobbled paving.

'Come,' she said.

'My God!' Benedict shielded his eyes from the heat. 'Everything you have in the world—gone!'

'Come with me,' she insisted, 'to my cabin on the ship. We'll talk there. We can do nothing, Sloan. It's too late.'

He saw that there was indeed no hope for the doomed building or the two men inside, and fell into step beside her as she headed down the alley. He stopped every few yards to throw a despairing glance at the reddening sky over the shop. Everywhere doors were opening as curious townspeople began to throng the streets.

'Don't look back,' Thérèse said, her eyes straight ahead, her steps quickening. In just a few minutes they had reached the dock. There was an eerie stillness along the deserted wharves, where black hulks of ships loomed like ghostly giants in the darkness, and an occasional lantern set out on a piling lighted the way. The silence was broken only by the sound of straining ropes as the ships rolled gently against a rising tide, and water lapped softly against the bulkheads below. But it was impossible to shut out the fire-bells, far off now, but setting up a hollow echo down the dark streets of the town.

At last Thérèse stopped beside one of the transocean packets moored at the dock. 'Here we are,' she said quietly. 'Stay down in the shadows, *mon ami*, and when you see your chance to slip aboard unseen, follow me.'

She left him, to walk resolutely up the gangway. He could hear the few words she exchanged with the young seaman standing watch on deck.

'I am booked for the dawn sailing,' she told him, 'but I wish to spend the night on board as the early hour is most inconvenient. Now, if you will help me to find my accommodation, please?'

'I got to keep to me post, lady,' the young man told her, and began to explain the route she must follow to her cabin.

'But I shall surely lose my way!' she protested. 'If you take me there, I will make it worth your efforts, Monsieur.'

'Well, come along then,' Benedict heard the young seaman say grudgingly, and he waited only a second before he himself leaped up the gangway after them. He followed at a safe distance, and once below deck, took care to duck when he saw them enter the cabin Thérèse had booked. At last he heard the seaman go by him, rattling loose coins in his pocket. When he had gone, Benedict crept up the corridor and into the cabin, closing the door softly.

Thérèse was already seated at a table, a lantern in front of her. He fell into the chair opposite, and for a moment they only looked at each other, both too exhausted, too overwhelmed by what they had been through, to say anything.

Finally, lulled by the gentle motion of the ship and the comforting amber glow of the lantern between them, the dressmaker spoke first. 'Thank God you came,' she whispered. 'What a miracle that you came ashore! How did you know that they would come to me tonight?'

'Cayo told me. They killed him.'

Thérèse put a hand to her mouth. 'I didn't want to believe them.' She was silent for a moment. 'It has been so many months since I saw you last, *mon ami*.'

'A long time,' he agreed. 'But, Thérèse, this is the second fire you've been through, with everything you had destroyed.'

She shook her head. 'It was not like the last one, for I lost only a shop. Last time, *mon cher*, I lost my entire family, don't forget.'

His eyes held hers. 'How did this fire start? What *happened*?'

Thérèse tried to smile. 'You do not recognise a diversionary tactic when you see one? Ah, you were the one who taught me of such things. When I saw that they meant to kill you, I threw the lantern into a big pile of flammable fabric I'd been measuring before I stored it away. When those two men came in, I'd moved it to one side of my table.'

'But why?' Benedict leaned forward, his face smudged with ashes from the fire, and his shirt smelling of the acrid smoke that had engulfed them in the apartment. 'I could have handled those two men!' As he said it, he smiled wryly. 'Of course, there might have been a little difficulty, with a knife in my back! But now, Thérèse,' he placed both his hands palm up on the table between them, 'what will you do? You've lost everything.'

She put her hands in his, and his fingers closed over them. 'I can always rebuild,' she said. 'But what of you? You have been spared once again, but how long do you think you can . . .'

'Wait!' He cut in. 'I'd already made up my mind not to continue, but instead to return to South Carolina after this final raid. It's a good thing, too, for I'm no longer of use to the operation. I—I had to have it pointed out to me that I'm a . . . a hothead, Merritt called me.'

'So you are,' she agreed. 'But that's one reason for

your success! You have always taken chances where other men would not.'

'No, it's different now, Thérèse. I counted the costs before, and if they were too great, I altered the plan. But now, Merritt was right. I'd never have been recognised on that last boarding if I'd used my head instead of my fists—an action that nearly lost me two of my best men. And managed to kill Cayo Aristo, and very nearly killed you!' He stroked her hands gently. 'I guess the only thing I'm good for now is planting cotton!'

She smiled across at him. 'Oh, come now,' she scolded him lightly.

'But it's true! Besides, it may be the end of our work in the Caribbean. Two men died in that fire tonight. It will soon enough be apparent that young Ripp was one of them, when his absence is noted. I have a feeling that his father will find the cost of smuggling in black ivory too dear, now that he has lost a son.' He smiled wearily. 'Who knows, it may be thought that the second man who died was me. Then I'd be free to walk down the Strand in daylight, with no need for a disguise. Oh——' he jumped to his feet '—if only she . . .' He stopped, and began to pace the cramped cabin. 'That's my problem! Why can't I get her out of my mind? She's married, she's half a world away from me!'

Madame Georges wanted to comfort him, knowing full well that it was Laura he spoke of. She had noted, sitting here, a new sense of uncertainty and sadness in the young man. He had always been so sure of himself before. She sat very still, watching his tall figure as he walked back and forth.

Suddenly he stopped and came back again to sit opposite her. 'At least let me help *you*, Thérèse? I owe you so much. I can get this situation here straightened out for you while you're gone. Give me the name of the man who handles your affairs.'

'It isn't necessary, Sloan. He'll know what to do.' But

when she read the earnest entreaty in his eyes, she consented. 'Very well, then.' She opened her reticule. 'Let me write a note for you to take to Mr Tolson.' As she pulled out her small note-pad with its gold pencil attached, something fell from the bag on to the floor.

Benedict leaned over to pick it up. 'What's this?' he cried. He straightened, and held it next to the lantern, staring numbly at it. 'It is! By God, Thérèse, it's Laura's cross. Where did you get this?'

'Please, Sloan . . .'

'How did you get this?' he persisted. 'There's something you're not telling me!'

She got to her feet and slowly walked across the cabin to the small porthole and stood with her back to him. 'I didn't want to say anything to you, *cher ami*, for I don't see how . . .' She stopped. 'But perhaps you should know about it, after all. In my bag, there on the table, is a letter from a priest in England. Take it out, and read it.'

She steeled herself for what she knew would come, and heard him mutter angrily to himself as he read it. 'My God, I don't believe this!' he said. In a moment he came to her side and turned her round to face him. 'You would have let me leave here tonight and said *nothing* about this? You're going to England, aren't you? Not Paris!'

Madame Georges nodded unhappily. 'I so wanted to tell you,' she began.

But he cut her off. He was so angry that he had trouble finding words. 'But how . . . Why . . . How could you keep this from me, Thérèse? Don't you think . . . Don't you *know* that if Laura is in danger . . . How do you expect me . . .'

'Wait!' She stopped him. 'You have yourself admitted to being a hothead. What good would it have done you to know of this? Laura is Edgar Skelton's wife, Sloan.

I can only go there to see if there's anything I can do—nothing else!'

'Why you? Why wasn't this letter sent to Laura's father, or to that crazy aunt of hers? Why did the priest send it to *you*?'

'I am her mother!' Madame Georges said too quickly, without thinking. When she saw the instant effect of her words, she was sorry she had not prepared Benedict for this. 'There is so much you don't know, Sloan. Laura is Lucas Trevor's and my daughter. Now come and sit down.'

But he did not move. 'I don't believe you!'

'It's true,' she told him, meeting his stare directly.

Benedict moved angrily away from her. 'God almighty!' he cried. 'Why didn't you tell me?'

'I couldn't. Lucas Trevor released me only last night from my vow of silence, just hours before he died.'

Benedict groaned aloud. 'Does anyone else know of this?'

'Only Maria. Laura still does not know.'

'I can't believe,' he said finally, 'that you and Trevor . . .'

Madame Georges went back to her chair and sat down. 'Sloan,' she said quietly, 'I owe you no explanation, but I want you to understand all the same. In the two years I worked at Crosswinds as Amanda Trevor's seamstress, I did everything in my power to keep it from happening. He was a married man. I was only seventeen, and he was a gentle man, a loving man. In many ways you are like him, Sloan. I watched him suffer in a loveless, degrading marriage, and I couldn't help myself. I fell hopelessly, helplessly, in love with his strength, his many kindnesses. You, of all people, *mon ami*, should understand, I think.'

Benedict came back to the table. 'I know too well,' he told her quietly. 'You don't have to say anything more.'

They sat there in silence, and once again heard the

sound of the ship's timbers straining against the pull of the tide, and the rattle of chains far below on the dock. Slowly he lifted his head to look at her, and she saw that his strong face was set now in a new determination.

'I'm going with you,' he said. 'I'll go to the captain and arrange for a cabin. But first,' he got to his feet, 'there is something I must do. There are still several hours before we sail. I must see to Cayo's burial. I left his horse close by, in the alley.'

'Oh, be careful, *mon ami*, and hurry back!' Madame Georges's eyes filled with tears. 'If you only knew . . .' she began. 'Oh, Sloan, I didn't dare hope that you might come to England with me!'

He looked down at her, his fine green eyes glowing in the soft light of the lantern. 'Oh, Thérèse,' he said, 'how could I do otherwise, when my heart has been there all along?'

CHAPTER FOURTEEN

BY EARLY evening a heavy rain had settled in over the valley outside Wyckham. Father McLuchly stood with his back to the blazing logs in the fireplace of his study. He heard Mrs Wetherill's quick tap at his study door. 'Supper, is it?' he called out.

At her answer, he walked reluctantly from the warmth of his fire to the cold dining-room across the narrow hall, his spirits heavy. It was almost two months since the morning Lady Skelton's maid had pressed the small package into his hand, and he had still received no word from the woman to whom he wrote in Galveston. Perhaps, he thought, as he sat down at the table, he had been correct to think that the maid merely wanted him to bless the silver cross, and, when she could, she would return to claim it. But she had not been back.

He had again, just this morning, made the trip to Lord Skelton's home and again had been denied entry. 'Look here,' he had told the sullen butler angrily, 'I demand to see her. You have no right . . .'

A voice had come from somewhere inside the big house, a voice thick and blurred with whisky, 'Shut him out, goddamit! Meredith, be quick!'

It was an impossible situation. Father McLuchly could do little now for Lady Skelton but pray, and continue his efforts to see her.

As was usually the case, Mrs Wetherill's supper proved to be rich and abundant. The priest loosened his cassock before he settled again in front of the study fire. Too often given to falling asleep after one of her heavy meals, he kept a small handbell on the arm of his chair.

After a short period of sleep, his elbow would usually nudge the bell and knock it to the floor with a loud clang. If that did not wake him—and sometimes it did not—Mrs Wetherill did. She had sharp ears, and would come running in from the kitchen to see what he wanted. Once awoken by her bustling concern, he would then find himself sufficiently refreshed to go over to his desk for a few hours of work.

Tonight, however, with the steady patter of soft rain drumming on the windows, he slept soundly and never heard the bell fall. He might have continued sleeping there until Mrs Wetherill called him in the morning, but at a little after one o'clock he woke with a start at a sharp rapping on his front door. He jumped up and struggled to extricate himself from the warm rug his housekeeper had wrapped snugly round his legs, and hurried into the dark hall. A single candle burned on the table. The knocking continued, louder now, and he went to the front of the house, his mind still groggy from his deep sleep.

'Just a minute—I'm coming,' he called out, and threw open the door.

Two strangers stood there, a man and a woman, huddled together under the protective eaves of the porch. 'Father McLuchly?' the man asked.

'I am, I am,' he acknowledged.

'Please forgive the late hour, but it is of the utmost urgency!'

'Come in, and get out of the weather!' The priest stood aside as they crossed the threshold. Once they were inside, he took their wet cloaks. 'I suspect you'll be looking for warmth on such a night,' he said. 'Come in to the fire.'

At that moment, Mrs Wetherill's head, done up in a pink night cap, peered down at them from the head of the stairs. 'What is it, Father?' she called.

'A pot of tea would be greatly appreciated, my good

woman,' he said. 'Will you be kind enough to bring us some?'

'Certainly,' she called down to him with only a hint of archness in her voice, for she could never altogether approve of the odd hours he kept. Father McLuchly thanked her, then turned to hang the strangers' cloaks on a peg in the hall.

The man spoke behind him. 'Thank God we've found you! We've come a long way, and we want to get straight to the business we came for.'

'In time, in time,' the priest assured him. 'But first come into my study. I'll throw some wood on the fire and we'll have you both thawed out in no time at all.' He led the way and proceeded to bring the smouldering embers to life. When he had put on more wood, he straightened up to see that neither of his visitors had moved from the doorway. 'Come in,' he urged again impatiently, 'and sit down.' He pulled two chairs close to the fire.

'We haven't time,' the man said.

'Nonsense,' Father McLuchly told him, gathering up the rug he'd had thrown down in his haste to answer the door. 'Madam, if you would sit here.' As the woman came forward, the priest saw that she was simply but becomingly gowned in grey wool. She was tall and slenderly built, and her hair, as she untied the ribbons of her bonnet and uncovered it, was a lustrous black. *Handsome* was the first word that came to his mind to describe her, but there was no hint of severity in her mien. When she spoke, her voice was pleasant, and the priest detected a charming French accent.

'We must introduce ourselves, Father,' she said, as she sat down. 'I am Thérèse Georges from Galveston, Texas, and this——' she indicated the young man who paced the floor behind her '—is my impatient young friend, Sloan Benedict.'

At the mention of her name, the priest went over and grasped her hand. 'Madame Georges! Of course—

it was you to whom I sent Lady Skelton's silver cross!'

She nodded, and from under the collar of her gown she pulled out the cross that hung round her neck.

The priest recognised it at once. 'You are a friend of Lady Skelton, then?'

Her companion came instantly to stand behind Madame Georges's chair. 'She is Lady Skelton's mother,' he said.

'Oh?' The priest drew back, surprised. 'Well, I must have misunderstood. I had thought . . . But never mind. You cannot know how glad I am that you're here. Lady Skelton needs . . .'

'How is she?' the man cut in. Even now, in the warmth of the fire, he remained tense and wary. 'You mentioned in your letter to Madame Georges that Laura was in an accident.'

'I have no way of knowing,' the priest told him, 'since I have not been able to see her.' He studied the stranger. He was a fine-looking lad, Father McLuchly thought. He reminded the priest of his own younger brother, Eamon, who had died in a fight for the love of a lass. This man, with his flashing green eyes and an impetuous urgency in his bearing, appeared to be quite capable of such a foolish passion. A sudden thought came to him. Lady Skelton, here in this very room, had spoken of her love for another man, a pirate. But could this be he? The priest was puzzled. 'Perhaps you will be kind enough, Mr Benedict, to explain the nature of your own relationship with Lady Skelton?'

'I love her,' he said simply.

Father McLuchly nodded. It was Eamon all over again.

Benedict fastened the priest with eyes that burned in the firelight. 'See here, Father, I've kept the carriage that brought us here, and the driver is waiting outside. Please tell me how to get to Skelton's house. I mean to go there at once and take Laura out of that cursed place!'

'Whoa, whoa!' Father McLuchly said. 'It's one o'clock in the morning. Besides, since I myself have been denied entry at Olney these many weeks, I rather think you would receive the same treatment. And were you to get past the front door, what would you do then? You can't break into another man's home, sir, and spirit his wife away! Sit down, Mr Benedict, I insist.'

'But there's no time to lose,' he cried. 'You yourself said in your letter that there's been an accident—that she was ill, that she's being held there by Skelton against her will!'

'I also said, Mr Benedict, that my analysis of the situation at Olney was based on scanty evidence. Come now, we must take time to discuss this before we do anything. Surely you can see . . .'

'I know the kind of man he is,' Benedict said. 'A man who bartered in human flesh, who will do anything for money—including holding his own wife prisoner so that he can claim her inheritance!'

'That is a most serious charge, my young friend. Are you sure of this?'

Madame Georges spoke at last. 'Sloan, please?' She frowned at her companion, then turned to the priest. 'What he says is true, Father. You have no idea what kind of a man we're dealing with. No, I must go alone. Surely they cannot keep her own mother away!'

'No, Thérèse,' Benedict insisted. 'I'm the one to go. God knows what I'll find there!'

'No one is to go,' the priest said firmly. 'Not until we put together what information we have, after which we can make plans. Perhaps first I should tell you of my brief visit to Olney, and of Lady Skelton's extraordinary behaviour when she came here the morning of the accident.' He told them all he knew and was relieved to see Mrs Wetherill at last standing in the doorway. 'Now, then,' he said as he helped her to arrange the cups on his desk, 'we'll have some tea. Sit down, Mr Benedict, and I'm warning you . . .'

'Warning me?'

The priest nodded. 'Yes. You are much too impulsive. Remember, we want no harm to come to Lady Skelton.'

Mrs Wetherill dropped a cup from the tray, which shattered at her feet. 'Oh, Father,' she stammered as she knelt to retrieve the bits of china, 'I'm sorry. It was just . . .'

'I know,' the priest consoled her as both he and Benedict stooped to help her. 'It's the late hour, my dear.' But there was something in her manner that made him probe further. 'Or was it the mention just now of Lady Skelton?'

'I'll go and get another cup,' the housekeeper said quickly, not looking at him.

The priest turned to Madame Georges. 'Mrs Wetherill's grandson drives for Lord Skelton. He has been Olney's coachman for a year. Eugene Nettles knows more of the situation there than I.'

Mrs Wetherill, now that all the pieces of crockery were collected, started to leave the room, but stopped at the priest's words and drew herself up indignantly. 'My grandson is no gossip, Father! He don't say nothing to me about the people where he works. He's a good boy.'

'Good boy he is indeed,' agreed Father McLuchly, 'and I'm certain he's never been guilty of telling a lie—not even a small lie—any more than his grandmother has.'

'No, Father. Oh, no!'

'Good. Then give us the truth now and continue in the company of earthly saints. Has Eugene ever mentioned Lady Skelton at all, or her condition?'

'Well, he has seen her, of course.' She held herself very straight and looked at a spot on the opposite wall.

'And?' the priest nudged her.

'Well, that's all, Father. Of course he's seen her. He *used* to, anyway.'

'What do you mean, *used* to?' Benedict asked abruptly. When the housekeeper did not answer him, his manner softened. 'Please,' he said quietly, 'tell us anything you know of what's happening over there. This lady,' he indicated Madame Georges, 'has come over five thousand miles to hear news of her daughter.'

Mrs Wetherill melted visibly. She looked down at the dressmaker. 'Ah, then,' she said, 'that's different, isn't it? You're the lady's mother. Well, there's peculiar things going on over there. Eugene seldom drives the coach now, except for errands. Mostly he does odd jobs about the place, like seeing to the firewood. He used to bring the wood upstairs for Lady Skelton's fireplace.'

'*Used* to?' This time it was Father McLuchly who echoed her words.

Mrs Wetherill nodded. 'No more, he don't. Not after the time . . . Well, the nurse don't let anybody into her room, you see, and Lady Skelton never leaves it. It's said in the village that the lady is daft, begging your pardon, missus, but Eugene says she's as sane as you or me. The last time he was let into the lady's bedchamber, she come at him, quiet-like, and said, "Help me, please, they're holding me here. My life is in danger!" She couldn't say no more, for that nurse come up and pulled the lady away.'

'There!' Benedict cried. 'What more evidence do we need? We're wasting time here. Can't you see? Isn't it obvious?'

'Enough!' Father McLuchly said. 'I'll say it once more, Mr Benedict, *patience*. Now, Mrs Wetherill,' he turned towards his housekeeper, 'go on. What happened then?'

'Well,' she continued, 'Eugene never got to see her again after that. Lord Skelton, now, he used to go up to London pretty regular, but not lately he hasn't. He stays in the house too, since his secretary left. That's all I know, Father,' she added, a little out of breath. Then, as if only at that moment recalling a new bit of information, she went on, 'I said that peculiar things go on over there, like the morning Eugene was called into the liberry to set the books back. Every book was off the shelf, Father, tossed helter-skelter across the floor like somebody had been searching for something.'

'H'm,' said Father McLuchly. 'Well, thank you, Mrs Wetherill. If you remember anything else, anything at all, be sure to tell us. Now, if you please, will you bring us another cup?'

The housekeeper was almost through the door when she turned back. 'It may be nothing, Father. It's about Lord Skelton's secretary.'

'Yes?'

'His room's kept locked since he left. Only last week Eugene was told to clean the fireplace in Mr Norton's room. The butler let him in and stood outside the door while Eugene took up the ashes. Never did he see such a mess, Eugene says. Clothes all over the place and everything scattered on the floor, bureau drawers pulled out, all manner of things thrown about as if a wild man had been in there!'

'Are you saying that the secretary left Olney and took nothing with him?' Benedict asked.

'He did, sir. And there's something else. In the secretary's room he found something, Eugene did, while he cleaned out the hearth. It was stuck up under the chimneypiece, and Eugene says he must have shaken it loose. He's a right careful lad, and thorough. Remember, Father, how he spent one entire day cleaning out . . .'

'What did he find, Mrs Wetherill?' asked Father McLuchly impatiently.

'A note, Father, all folded up. It's got the date on it, sir. And it was the very next day—which Eugene remembers because it was his birthday—when the butler told my grandson that Mr Norton had packed up and left Olney. But nobody saw him leave. Eugene wasn't never ordered to bring round the carriage, either, and it ain't as though Mr Norton would walk all the way to Wyckham, is it, the house being so set apart and lonely?'

'Well, what did the note say, Mrs Wetherill?' the priest asked.

'I didn't read it, of course, but my grandson gave it to me. It's a fine piece of letter paper, heavy, kind of creamy-like. I've been using it as a bookmark in my Bible.' She added that for Father McLuchly's benefit, for she said it with a sanctimonious lift of her chin. 'I'll go and fetch it, then I'll get an extra cup. And it wouldn't hurt at all if I brought in my cinnamon cake, d'you think? Looks to me it'll be a long night ahead, and you'll all be needing nourishment.'

She left them, and the three waited, tense and silent, listening to her tread as she climbed the stairs. Benedict paced the floor, Madame Georges stared into the fire, and Father McLuchly sat tapping one foot on the floor. As she began to descend, the priest sprang to his feet and was at the door waiting for her when she appeared. 'Well done,' he said as he took the folded note. Already he had turned and brought the note close to the lighted candle, with Benedict beside him, and the dressmaker—who had risen at the housekeeper's return—on his other side.

'H'm,' Father McLuchly said, 'this seems to be some sort of a promissory note, made out to—Michael Norton. Norton! Aha! This is the note, then, that Lady Skelton spoke of! It's dated the same day she was here, when her husband burst in. The same morning as the accident. Then she was not hallucinating at all! Why didn't I see?'

Each in turn took the note and studied it, and it was Benedict who finally spoke. 'But why would Laura promise to pay Edgar Skelton's secretary? I don't understand.' He scanned the paper again. '"*On receipt of her legacy*", it says. What legacy?'

Madame Georges turned abruptly away, and it was a moment before she spoke, her voice barely audible over the whisper of the fire.

'It was always the money,' she said. 'It has ruined every life it touched. Amanda Trevor's greed, Lucas's, Edgar Skelton's, Michael Norton's.' They waited, straining to hear her words. 'Gentlemen,' she said quietly, 'I must tell you what I know about Laura's legacy. It is a long and bitter story. I can tell you only a part of it, for the rest is mine to keep locked in my heart. But . . . that part may be enough to get us past Olney's front door. To Laura.'

CHAPTER FIFTEEN

MRS EMORY's firm footsteps echoed in the hall at Olney, and her sensible shoes took each step dead centre as she began to climb the stairs to her patient's room. She held herself so rigidly that not even the cup of tea on Lady Skelton's breakfast tray vibrated in the slightest. After many weeks of dismal rain and mists, early morning sunshine streamed through the casement windows on the landing, but Mrs Emory did not notice. Instead, she took a moment to scrutinise the dark panelling as she passed, studying the solemn portraits that hung above it, looking for signs of dust. But everything gleamed in the broad bands of gold light that washed the walls, and she could find no evidence of neglect.

She was constantly alert for signs of carelessness, hoping to find a valid reason to dismiss Lady Skelton's maid. She could hardly dismiss her for her maddening habit of appearing out of the shadows on the upstairs landing as if she had been lurking there, waiting for a chance to slip into the sick-room. Maria did her work conscientiously and showed a marked willingness to take on any new task that fell to her. Still, Mrs Emory remained vigilant.

Perhaps, the nurse thought sourly, she herself was the only person who sought to maintain order in this disrupted household. Her brother Meredith was more sullen than ever of late, and moved about the house like an old man; bent, his eyes hooded, seeming to come alive only when that priest knocked on the door and had to be refused entry. And Cook! Well, if it were up to Mrs Emory, the woman would be sent packing. She was gross, vulgar—and a thief! And her cooking! The nurse lowered her eyes disdainfully to the greasy mound of scrambled eggs and kippers on Lady Skelton's tray. As always before, the food would be returned to the kitchen later, hardly touched, and Cook would have a few terse words to say about the mistress of the house: 'She's an uppity one, she is, her and her fancy ways!'

As she reached her patient's room, Mrs Emory noticed that the door to Lord Skelton's room was open just a crack. Instantly she suspected the Mexican woman of hiding there, waiting. She set the tray down on the table outside the sick-room, walked softly over, and gave the door a quick push to open it all the way. But there was no bustle of black skirts, no stammered excuses—no brown face appeared. There was no one in the shadows, after all. She peered in to see that the heavy portières at the windows were still closed, the oversize bed with its dark brocade curtains was still turned down from the night before in preparation for its occupant, and Lord Skelton's night garments were still laid out in a neat pile at the foot of his bed.

So Lord Skelton had not come to bed the night before! Meredith had not mentioned it to her over their morning cup of tea; yet that was not unusual. Her brother was steadfastly loyal to his employer, and it would not be the first time he had tried to conceal the truth of Lord Skelton's frequent bouts of drunkenness from her. Twice before, in the early morning, she had looked into the library to see Skelton slumped low in a chair at the side of a spent fire, an empty decanter of brandy at his side. It was always Meredith who tended him after one of these nights, and never afterwards mentioned it to anyone. But, as he had told her when she had first arrived at Olney, 'Lady Skelton's care is your only responsibility. See to it, and leave all the rest to me.'

She had offered no argument. It was enough of a task keeping the Mexican woman out of the sick-room and ministering to the invalid. She went across the landing, found the proper key on the ring at her waist, opened the door, picked up the tray and let herself quietly into the darkened chamber. She was instantly struck with a sense that something was wrong. The room was not as dark as she had been ordered to keep it. She had been told never to open the portières that covered the casement windows. But now she saw a narrow shaft of sunlight falling across the floor and the figure of Lady Skelton standing at the window, looking out at the garden below.

'What's this?' Mrs Emory cried, placing the tray on the table beside the bed and going quickly to where Laura stood. 'You are in no condition to be out of bed, my lady! You are too weak. Come, now,' she put a firm hand on the girl's elbow and led her back to the bed, 'come back to bed and behave yourself,' she told her patient crossly. 'I have brought your breakfast.' None too gently, she helped her into bed, then arranged the pillows behind her. 'If you do as I say, you'll be well in no time.'

'But I am not sick!' Laura cried. Her eyes were huge, dark and feverishly bright. 'I want to open the curtains. I need fresh air and sunshine!'

There was a defiance in her patient's manner lately that Mrs Emory did not like to see. But she had nursed stubborn invalids before, and knew how to deal with them. 'Listen to me,' she said. 'You're talking nonsense. We only want to get you well. You must obey orders.'

'But whose orders?' Laura asked. 'Dr Benning hasn't been to see me in weeks!'

'And you haven't been taking your medicine, have you?'

Laura indicated the empty glass beside her bed. 'It's gone, isn't it?'

That was it, Mrs Emory decided. The girl had somehow managed to get rid of the daily dose of laudanum her husband had ordered, and had only pretended to drink it. How long, she wondered, had this been going on? She set the tray down on the bed. 'I'll go and get your medicine, and just stay with you while you drink it down, my lady. It's a restorative, you know.'

'It's not!' Laura said angrily. 'I won't take it any more. It puts me to sleep.'

'Sleep restores, my lady.'

But she shook her head. 'I won't take it any more, I tell you!'

The nurse smiled. 'Lord Skelton is only thinking of you. He wants you well.'

'He wants me dead!'

The nurse was by now accustomed to such outbursts. 'Now, we don't want to get excited, do we, and say things we don't mean?'

Laura threw back her covers and would have jumped from the bed, had not Mrs Emory restrained her. 'Now perhaps you see why you need your medicine, Lady Skelton!' The nurse was a powerful woman, and had no touble in pushing her back against the pillows and settling the tray on her lap. 'You heed what I say,' she said. 'You don't want me to send for Meredith to tie you down with those linen straps again, do you, dear?'

As Mrs Emory prepared the mixture of medicine, keeping an eye on Laura to make certain she did not again try to leave her bed, she was unable to suppress a question in her own mind. Why was Lord Skelton determined to continue this daily dose for his wife? The nurse had seen patients caught in the nightmare of reliance on strong opiates before, and it was not a pretty sight. Laura, physically recovered from the accident that took the life of her baby, needed only to do as she asked, to get out into the sunshine so that her strength and her appetite would be restored. But Lord Skelton had made it clear that his wife's illness was not of the body, but of the mind. Mrs Emory knew nothing about mental illness. But how tragic if this beautiful girl were indeed deranged! Sometimes she had watched the sleeping invalid, her black hair fanned out across the pillow, her dark lashes thick against the pale cheeks, one hand tucked under her cheek like a child. Often, in her sleep, she would sigh or cry out in the darkness as if some secret sadness held her in its grip and shut her away in an unhappy dream world.

However, it was not for Mrs Emory to question her employer's orders. Still, when she measured out the proper dose of laudanum, she poured some of it back into the bottle. She went back to Laura's bed and held the glass to her lips. 'Drink it all down, my lady,' she said, 'and then you can have your nice breakfast, there's a lamb.'

Downstairs, at that very moment, Meredith heard carriage-wheels on the gravel at the front of the house, his ears sharply attuned by now to even the slightest sound at Olney that might present a difficult situation. He had thus far this morning managed to drink only half of his eye-opening cup of tea, and stiffened warily at the prospect of an unwanted visitor so early in the day. His employer was stretched out asleep in the library, and he himself needed more of the stimulant to prepare himself for the unpleasant duty of getting him up to his room.

The butler moved quickly, and was through the service pantry and into the dining-room in record time. It will be that prying priest again, he thought darkly. Father McLuchly was a pest, showing up at any time of day or night—and all to save Lady Skelton's soul by hearing her confession or administering the sacraments or some such Papist nonsense! But as he passed the windows, he noticed that it was not the priest's small gig that stood on the drive but an enclosed carriage. He went through to the hall and had the front door open before the visitor could even reach for the bell-pull.

The man who stood on the steps was a stranger. He

was of advanced age, tall, his shoulders stooped, his gloved hands clutching a dog-eared portfolio to his chest. His dusty black coat, cut high across the front with tails at the back and a standing velvet collar, was quite out of style, as was his bulky black stock. Not only that, but he wore old-fashioned knee-breeches that were too tight. His lean face, framed with grey side-whiskers, showed strain and weariness. He removed his high-crowned hat with its narrow curling brim, to reveal overlong grey hair parted precisely in the middle.

He squinted at the butler through thick wire-framed spectacles. 'My good man,' he addressed Meredith in an apologetic voice. 'If it would not be too much trouble, I should like to see Lady Skelton, if you please.'

'I'm sorry,' Meredith told him pleasantly enough, for the gentleman's manner was hesitant and shy, 'but Lady Skelton is indisposed.'

'Oh dear! I have somewhat distressing news for her. It's of the utmost importance that I see her.'

'She sees no one,' the butler said brusquely. 'Now, if you will leave, please.'

'I must say . . . what an inconvenience!' the stranger said. 'For, you see, I have come all the way from Galveston, Texas, on a most delicate mission.'

'Galveston?' Another voice spoke behind the butler. 'I'll handle this, Meredith.' The door opened wider, and a pale face looked out with bloodshot eyes at the visitor. 'Did you say Galveston?'

'I did indeed, sir,' the stranger said respectfully.

'Anything that concerns my wife is also my concern. I am her husband, Lord Skelton. Who are you?'

'Ezra Comstock, if you please, sir, of the Independent Bank of Galveston, of which Lady Skelton's father, the late Lucas Trevor, was president.'

'The *late* Lucas Trevor?' Now at last the door swung all the way open.

'Indeed. And that is the unhappy purpose of my visit,

sir, to inform Lady Skelton of her father's demise just four weeks ago.'

'You came all the way over here to tell her that?' Skelton asked incredulously.

'Well, there is something else, sir. I have papers here having to do with a legacy, of which the late Mr Trevor was trustee.'

'Her legacy? Come in, come in.' Skelton stood aside to let the banker in, then turned to his butler. 'That will be all, Meredith. I'll take care of this.'

'Are you sure, my lord?'

'Yes, quite sure.'

As the butler left them, Ezra Comstock entered the hall timidly, and ran his near-sighted eyes over the spacious entry. 'My soul, this is a grand mansion, sir,' he said, obviously impressed.

Skelton ran his hand through his rumpled hair. 'We'll go into the library, Comstock.' Once the two men were alone, and the library door closed behind them, he said, 'Let me see those papers.'

Mr Comstock, stiffly ill at ease, fumbled with his hat in one hand and the portfolio in the other, seeming uncertain what to do with either. Skelton reached out for the portfolio, but the banker handed him his hat instead. 'I thank you, sir,' he said. 'But, as I told your manservant, I must see Lady Skelton in person.' The banker stopped as if he had for the moment forgotten his mission. Then, slowly, he began to remove a glove by pulling at the tips of the fingers, as he scanned the book-lined walls. His eyes lit up behind the thick lenses of his spectacles as he wandered over to the crowded shelves and ran one finger lightly along the spines of a row of finely-bound volumes. 'Beautiful bindings,' he muttered appreciatively. 'Why, upon my word, this looks like a first edition!'

Skelton protested behind him, 'Suppose we get to all that later, Mr Comstock. Say what you have to say, leave the necessary documents with me and I'll see that my wife gets them immediately.'

'You must forgive me, sir,' Comstock said apologetically, 'but I am an incurable bibliophile.' He pulled at his side-whiskers thoughtfully. 'I'd wager that my small cubicle at the Galveston bank is about one-eighth of the size of this handsome room.'

'Come on, man!' Skelton snapped, his pale eyes riveted on the portfolio, which the banker was now clutching against his chest with both hands.

'Forgive me,' Comstock said again. 'I suspect that I am only seeking to delay the unhappy time when I must divulge my communication to Lady Skelton. For it is your wife I must see, sir, if you please.'

'Good God, do you think I'm incapable of relaying the information to her that her father's dead?'

Comstock frowned. 'There's more, sire.'

'Devil take you, man, we've already established that there's more. Just hand it over to me!'

'You don't understand, Lord Skelton. The contents of Victor duFlon's testament will come as a shock to Lady Skelton, if I'm not mistaken, and I must be the one to . . .'

'Let's get *on* with this, Comstock!'

'I can understand your impatience, sir, so I shall—as you say—get on with it.' He smiled. 'But I really must see Lady Skelton, for it is my unhappy duty to inform her that she has no legal claim whatever to the estate of her late grandfather, Victor duFlon.'

It was a full moment before Skelton, his mouth gone slack, could speak. Then, his eyes wide with shock, he managed to say, 'What's that? What did you say?'

'Simply that Victor duFlon left his entire estate to any issue born of his daughter, Amanda duFlon Trevor—and Amanda Trevor died childless. Laura Trevor—er, Lady Skelton—was not her own child, you see, as was universally supposed. She was, instead, the result of—of an amorous dalliance, one might almost say.'

Skelton's face flamed. When he could summon breath to speak, his voice was thin, high in his throat. 'But . . . wait! She *was* his daughter! He acknowledged her as his daughter! Of *course* she was his daughter!'

'*His* daughter, yes, sir.' Comstock nodded. 'But she was not Amanda Trevor's issue. *Issue*, sir. That is the word Victor duFlon specifically stressed in his will, which was found in Mr Trevor's effects after his death. It's all here,' he patted his portfolio affectionately, 'I have the original will here.'

'Let me see that!' Skelton sprang at him, but he turned quickly away.

'Lord Skelton,' he said quietly. 'I urge your restraint, if you please.'

Before he could spring again, Skelton stopped dead, and a new expression crossed his face. '*Original*, you say? Are you the only one who knows of this? Are there any copies of that will?'

Comstock shook his head. 'None, sir. There is no copy. That is why I must ask you to . . .'

'Give me that!' This time, with a sudden lurch, Skelton managed to dislodge the portfolio from Comstock's arms. But before he could get a firm grip, it fell to the floor, scattering its contents. Skelton dropped to his hands and knees and began to search frantically through the papers. 'Wait! Why! These are . . . There's nothing here but a bunch of religious pamphlets!' he roared. 'You lied!'

Comstock watched him, a bemused smile on his face. 'Only about having Victor duFlon's will in that portfolio, Lord Skelton,' he said mildly. 'That document was destroyed many years ago. And while it's true—that part about his leaving everything to Amanda Trevor's issue—Lady Skelton will indeed become heir to it, for there's no proof that she is not exactly what Lucas

Trevor wanted the world to believe she was—his daughter.'

Skelton jumped to his feet. 'Why, you deceitful old buzzard! What kind of a game are you playing?' He was shaking from head to foot, and his face darkened to an alarming shade of crimson. 'By God, I killed that fool Norton for this money, and I'll kill again!'

He sprang once more—this time at Comstock's throat —but the banker, with surprising strength, pushed him away. 'Easy does it, Skelton,' he said. 'Yes, too bad about Norton, but he was an ineffectual lad—and a poor shot, too. He never even managed to kill off that Abolitionist for you in Galveston, did he?'

Skelton froze. Every drop of blood seemed to leave his face as he stared at the banker with vacant eyes. 'Who—Who are you?' he was finally able to say.

Comstock bestowed a benevolent smile on the stricken man. 'You may well ask,' he said as he reached up, took off his spectacles, grabbed a handful of grey hair and slowly stripped off his wig. 'Actually,' he went on, enjoying Skelton's widening stare, 'you have given us sufficient evidence to see you hanged, old chap. However,' he pulled off his side whiskers, 'that is not why I am here.'

A cry of dismay burst from Skelton's lips. 'My God! It's you! It can't be!'

Sloan Benedict stood revealed at last, his green eyes narrowed with hatred as he looked at the dishevelled figure opposite. 'There's no way out for you now, Skelton. You are guilty of many things for which you cannot be tried . . .' He moved to the door. 'But at least we've got you for murder!'

Skelton, wild-eyed, drew back as Benedict threw open the door. 'Constable,' he said to one of the two men crouched outside, listening, 'this is your man.'

'We heard it all, sir. You'd best see to the lady.'

Benedict ran into the hall and started up the stairs two at a time.

'Oh no, you don't!' Skelton screamed. He made a dash to the fireplace, pulled down the heavy sword from over the chimneypiece and began waving it crazily as he came towards the men who stood in the open doorway. Both men made an attempt to grab him as he burst into the hall with his weapon, but before they had a chance to stop him, Skelton was already stumbling up the stairs like a wild man, shouting obscenities.

Benedict had reached the landing and turned to see Skelton coming after him, slashing the air with his sword. Suddenly one of Skelton's feet missed a step, and he reached out frantically for something to hold on to. But already he had begun to fall as the weight of the sword pulled him down; slowly at first, then faster, his body striking the banister, then lurching away towards the opposite wall. Still he held tight to the sword until it flipped from his grasp and began to plunge beside him down the stairs. For a split second the hilt lodged between the carved railings and, as Benedict watched, horrified, the blade caught his falling body and impaled it. The echo of Edgar Skelton's scream resounded the length and breadth of the big house.

The scream woke Mrs Emory from a light nap she had been enjoying in the darkened sick-room. It was an unearthly scream, unlike anything she had ever heard. She looked over at Laura's bed, thinking at first that it might have been the girl crying out again in her drugged sleep, but her patient lay quietly, undisturbed. Jumping up from her chair, she fumbled among the keys at her waist. She had the door open in an instant, but drew back as she saw a stranger standing there. His tall figure was brightly illuminated by the sunlight from the landing below. 'You cannot come in here,' she began.

'It's all over,' he told her. 'Get down there and see to

your employer. He's gravely wounded.' Benedict moved aside as she quickly pushed past him and started down the stairs. He hesitated a moment before he entered the room, again assailed by the fear that had plagued him during the long crossing from Galveston. Suppose Laura, in all these months, thinking him to be dead, had banished him from her mind, forgotten him completely?

As his eyes became accustomed to the darkness of the bedchamber, the outline of the big four-poster bed took shape before him. Overcome with the realisation that at last his Laura was only a few steps away, he could wait no longer, but crossed the room quickly to stand at the side of the bed. He looked down at her sleeping face. Even in the half-light he could see that she was deathly pale.

'Laura,' he whispered hoarsely, 'what have they done to you?' He took her in his arms and held her against his chest. She moaned softly and turned her face up to his, her eyes closed. He kissed her gently on the forehead. 'Laura,' he said. 'My love, my love!'

Suddenly she stiffened in his arms. 'No!' she cried.

'It's all right,' he told her quietly. 'You're safe now. I'll never let you go.'

'No!' she cried again, trying to push him away. 'No, for the love of God, no!' She began to beat at his chest with her fists, then flung herself away from him and buried her face in the pillow.

Benedict stood there, helpless, cursing himself for doing exactly what Thérèse Georges had warned him against. 'Go slowly, *mon vieux*,' she had told him as he left her with Father McLuchly in the gig at the foot of the lane where they would wait for a signal from the constable. 'She believes you are dead,' Thérèse had said. 'Do nothing to shock her.'

He was conscious suddenly that a figure stood at the door. He looked up, and recognised at once Laura's

Mexican maid, whom he had seen only once in the courtyard at Crosswinds.

'*Niña!*' the maid cried, peering into the darkness.

'Is it you, Maria?' Laura sobbed as she looked over at the door. 'Thank God! Oh, wake me, wake me. Don't let me dream of him again!'

The maid came instantly to the side of the bed. 'It is all right, *niña*. They have come for you. Lord Skelton is dead.' She stopped, only now aware that someone stood across from her. She looked over at Benedict and searched his face, puzzled. Then, as though suddenly aware of who he was, she smiled at him, then lowered her eyes to Laura's face. 'And *he* is here, *niña*, the one you have called for in your dreams these many months.'

Benedict's heart leaped. So Laura loved him still!

'Oh, stop!' Laura cried. 'How can you do this to me, Maria? He is dead. I saw him die. But, in this dream, I felt his arms round me, I heard the beat of his heart—he was so *real*!'

'It's true, *niña*, he is alive!' Maria walked quickly over to the window and drew back the heavy curtains. Instantly the room was flooded with golden light. Without a word, her dark face wet with tears, she left them together and closed the door.

Laura sat up, fully awake, and shielded her eyes from the brightness. Benedict took her hand, and slowly she turned her head towards him. He said nothing, wanting her at last to believe what her eyes told her: that he was no dream, that he was indeed real.

But she pulled her hand away. 'No . . . no,' she whispered.

Benedict reached into his pocket and pulled out the silver cross. He laid it gently in the palm of her hand. 'One other time,' he told her quietly, 'I brought this back to you. Do you remember that night, Laura?'

She said nothing, but her fingers closed over its familiar contours. Her eyes, still on his, softened as she reached up to touch his face. Her hand was cold against his cheek, and he longed to cover it with his own, to warm it and hold it there. But he still waited.

Suddenly, with a cry, she dropped the cross and threw herself into his arms. He held her to him, cradling her head against his chest.

'Oh, Laura, Laura.' He whispered her name, only her name, over and over again.

EPILOGUE

A WARMING South Carolina sun had already burned away early morning mists as Sloan Benedict guided his big stallion the last few hundred yards to the house. As always now, on returning from checking work in the fields, he felt his spirits soar. In these few months he had known happiness unlike anything he could possibly have imagined. For one thing, his abiding love for Westerly had changed and deepened. He hugged his heart in secret pride at the beauty that lay around him this morning, as though he himself had wrought the luxuriant plantings of vibrant pink azaleas, waxy magnolia trees heavy with creamy blossoms, and bridal-white sprays of spiraea arching gracefully over gentle slopes of velvet lawn.

For another thing, his senses seemed to have sharpened acutely, filling him with a keen awareness of new sights and sounds that had gone relatively unnoticed before. The hum of night insects, the liquid trill of a thrush deep in the woods—even the raucous warning cry of a crow as it wheeled overhead filled him with an almost holy awe. There was not a minute of the day or night that did not exert its magic on him, as if he stood always at the very centre of an enchanted fairy ring and was constantly being taken unawares by sensations unfamiliar to him. Even . . . He laughed now as he pondered this almost childlike sense of discovery, even *food* tasted better, like exotic offerings of loving and benevolent gods!

At the thought of food, he had a sudden vision of hot cakes fresh from the oven; of strawberries, new-picked, still sun-warmed and bursting with sweet juices, and he realised all at once how ravenously hungry he was. He had left for the fields before daylight to check on preparations for the job ahead, to turn under three fields of clover to enrich the soil for a later planting of cotton. He had found all in readiness there, mule-teams hitched, the men ready to begin, as Preston Ames had assured him he would.

'So, you see, there weren't no call for you to quit your warm bed so early after all, Mr Benedict,' the foreman had told him, indicating with a leer that if Ames had a beautiful young bride at home, he surely would be in no hurry to leave her.

Even Ames's sly innuendo failed to dampen Benedict's buoyant spirits as he reached the side porch of the big house. He slipped easily from his horse and made his way into the cool dining-room, where Maria was laying the table for breakfast. She looked up at his entrance and smiled a greeting, pointing at the same time to the cinnamon cake she always set out for him on the sideboard after one of his early trips to the fields.

'All asleep still?' he asked her quietly. 'Has my lady come downstairs, yet, Maria?'

'She and the Señora have been out in the garden this half-hour, cutting lilacs for your father's breakfast tray.'

Benedict shook his head, and laughed. 'You have all spoiled him utterly, and how he loves it! But he will miss Thérèse Georges's company, I know. We all will. But she's an independent lady, Maria, and will be happy only when her new shop opens.'

'*Sí*,' Maria agreed. 'Besides, Charleston is not very far away.'

At that moment they heard light laughter through the open doors on to the veranda. Their eyes met for an instant, and each smiled. It was Maria who spoke first of the thought they shared. 'The song of the nightingale is no more beautiful than the sound of my *niña*'s laughter, Señor. I had once thought never to hear it again.'

Benedict went to her and put a hand gently on her shoulder. 'It is thanks to you, Maria,' he told her, 'that we hear it now.' Then he turned and went out on to the wide porch and stood watching as the two women strolled up the sun-dappled lane beneath towering elms only now coming into full leaf. Their heads were close together as they walked arm in arm, through shifting patterns of soft leaf-filtered light. Benedict's heart swelled in his breast until he thought it would burst.

At last Laura looked up and saw him standing there, watching their approach. With a word to Thérèse, she handed her flowers to her, then picked up her skirts and ran quickly to the steps and on to the veranda, where she faced him. She had kept a single spray of lavender lilac which, with a smile, she held out to him.

'For my love,' she said, out of breath, her blue eyes sparkling in the morning sun. When he reached out to take it, she would not let it go. 'You must take my hand, too,' she teased.

He took it and brought it to his lips, burying his nose in the sweet-smelling blossom as he cradled her hand in his, smiling down at her. 'And what were you two ladies conspiring about so early in the morning?'

'My last conspiracy,' Laura laughed. 'And it worked, my dearest. A letter arrived from Father Jiminez in this morning's post. He's full of plans for the new hospital at Santa Clara. There's to be a new school, oh, think of it, Sloan. There's money enough to fulfil all his dreams!'

'H'm. I should think so! He could probably buy half of Texas with all the duFlon money. Has he guessed who his mysterious benefactress is yet?'

Laura peered up at him in mock dismay. 'But how could he? Wasn't it you who once told me how singularly adept I am at play-acting?'

Benedict put one finger to his chin and pretended to ponder her remark. 'If I recall correctly,' he said, 'you were never really very good at it, my girl. I saw through you from the start.' He added softly, 'I also loved you from the start. Remember?'

Laura nodded. 'Oh, yes, I remember.'

Without a word, the pirate pulled his lady to him and held her there as if he would never let her go. And, in truth, it would always be in the circle of her pirate's arms that Laura would know that she was home at last—to stay.

Conscience, scandal and desire.

A dynamic story of a woman whose integrity, both personal and professional, is compromised by the intrigue that surrounds her.

Against a background of corrupt Chinese government officials, the CIA and a high powered international art scandal, Lindsay Danner becomes the perfect pawn in a deadly game. Only ex-CIA hit man Catlin can ensure she succeeds... and lives.

Together they find a love which will unite them and overcome the impossible odds they face.

Available May. Price £3.50

W RLDWIDE

Available from Boots, Martins, John Menzies, W.H. Smith, Woolworths and other paperback stockists.